# MURDER AT BEAULIEU ABBEY

# MURDER AT BEAULIEU ABBEY

## Cassandra Clark

SEVERN
HOUSE

First world edition published in Great Britain and the USA in 2021
by Severn House, an imprint of Canongate Books Ltd,
14 High Street, Edinburgh EH1 1TE.

Trade paperback edition first published in Great Britain and the USA in 2021
by Severn House, an imprint of Canongate Books Ltd.

severnhouse.com

*British Library Cataloguing-in-Publication Data*
A CIP catalogue record for this title is available from the British Library.

ISBN-13: 978-0-7278-9089-4 (cased)
ISBN-13: 978-1-78029-775-0 (trade paper)
ISBN-13: 978-1-4483-0513-1 (e-book)

*All Severn House titles are printed on acid-free paper.*

Typeset by Palimpsest Book Production Ltd.,
Falkirk, Stirlingshire, Scotland.
Printed and bound in Great Britain by
TJ Books Limited, Padstow, Cornwall.

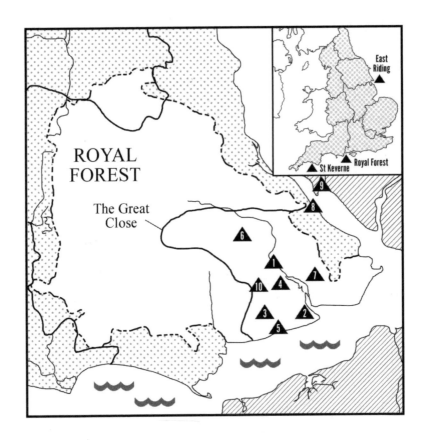

## THE GREAT CLOSE

1. Beaulieu Abbey
2. The haven
3. St. Leonard's
4. Beaufre
5. The bergerie
6. The mounds
7. Otterwood
8. Hythe
9. Hampton
10. Marsh

# ONE

The Prioress stepped out of the shadows near her private altar and took a pace forward into the light. Her white robe shone like pearl.

She observed the expression of the nun who had just entered with some wariness, like someone expecting opposition. She spoke first. 'You are aware, dear Hildegard, that the Papal Schism is ripping our Order apart?'

Hildegard made a brief obeisance. 'Of course, my lady. I would have to be blind and deaf not to know it.'

'And you are aware, then, my dear, that we must appear to be neutral in the battle between the two popes until they can resolve their dispute and pick just one of them to wear the triple crown?'

'I am.'

'Good. Our survival here at our little priory at Swyne depends on it. I believe I can trust you to show much diplomacy when I send you down to Beaulieu Abbey.'

'*Beaulieu?*' Hildegard stared in astonishment at this bolt. Her protest arose at once. 'But it's far down on the south coast, my lady, miles from anywhere, heavily defended against pirates and in the middle of a royal forest with no nunnery that I've ever heard of and just wild folk, plundering venison and fighting the French privateers and smuggling . . . and what all,' she finished lamely when she saw that her Prioress was indifferent to these reasonable objections.

'We both know where it is, and what you say is quite true by all accounts.' The Prioress offered one of her warmest smiles. 'But listen, my dear. They are closer to France than we nuns up here in our corner of the East Riding. We should not judge them. Yorkshire is far from the quarrels of the anti-pope Clement with our Pope Boniface. The monks of Beaulieu, though sequestered in the vastness of the Royal Forest, bear the brunt of the papal dispute. They are being driven to extremes. I fear they are being forced into the French camp by those who bear ill will towards this realm of ours.'

'How might that be?'

'Their dear old and much-beloved abbot, William Herring, died last June. The monks elected a new abbot but then a faction, urged on by the false pope, so-called Clement, from his power base in Avignon, refused to accept him.'

'Is there a good reason for rejecting him?'

'None whatsoever. He is a perfectly good choice. Except for the fact that he favours the legally elected successor to Pope Urban in Rome—'

'The new pope, Boniface?'

'Correct.'

'And, forgive me, my lady, this must mean our English Chapter support him, as is right?'

'Indeed.'

'So' – cautiously Hildegard fixed her glance on the weather-beaten face of her superior – 'what is this to do with me – directly, I mean?'

'You are to go to Beaulieu and report back on how things stand. Are they secretly planning to break rank? We want no foreign influence in our English abbeys. King Richard will not want an enemy within the realm until his peace treaty with the French is ratified.'

'That seems fair enough.'

'So it is. But not everyone sees it that way. With a French pope ruling the roost it would mean the appointment of the abbots in all our houses throughout England and Wales would go to Frenchmen. The taxes on our labour would fill French coffers and not our own where they are most urgently needed. If an abbot is chosen by our opponents it cannot fail to be to our detriment. So it was and, sad to say, so it will be for time to come unless we can solve the problem of two claimants to the papal crown of Rome.'

Hildegard searched for another argument against the Prioress's decision to send her back to the south. It seemed like only five minutes since she had been in the New Forest at Netley Abbey.

'Surely,' she began, 'the monks at Beaulieu will object to a nun appearing in their domain without explanation or excuse? They'll guess I've come to spy out their allegiance.'

'You will have an explanation and an excuse.'

Already prepared to argue, Hildegard waited to hear it with a sinking heart.

'You will be there for the purpose of meeting the little heiress Sir William de Hutton has procured for one of his sons.'

'Heiress?'

'You will escort her back by sea to Ravenser, where she will be met by her future mother-in-law, Lady Avice.'

'Why can Avice not go down there herself?' Hildegard objected forcefully.

'She considers it unseemly to show such eagerness. The boy is nine and perfectly acceptable. But you know Avice.' The Prioress gave Hildegard a complicit glance.

Hildegard smiled faintly. 'Mostly by reputation, my lady.'

'Enough for anyone!' When the Prioress smiled as she did now her face softened into countless wrinkles and for a moment she looked surprisingly girlish. 'We must not be uncharitable,' she reproved, 'but it crossed my mind that Sir William may be of the same opinion as are we about his wife, for the good reason that he is now, himself, away from home and in the port they call Hampton. His excuse is that he's conducting some business related to the export of his wool clip. He will be a guest at the abbey when you arrive because, I am told, he insists on providing the armed escort on the second part of this child's journey up to Holderness.'

'Why does he wish for a nun to escort her?'

'Because until she is of age she will live here at Swyne, close to his manor.'

'I see.' She could also see that her case was lost. 'How old is this heiress, my lady?' She paused. 'I expect you know.'

'Naturally I do. She is said to be about twelve. An only child. The attraction for William is, of course, her dowry. She is expected to bring part of it with her from her father's court near St Keverne in Cornwall. Hence the escort.'

'I see.'

'I know you do. That's why I chose you to take on this little task.'

Hildegard sighed. 'I thought I might have some time to devote to my nuns.' She sighed again, more hopelessly. 'I've got a few ideas for bringing in more wealth so we can take in extra pupils – after we've extended the school-house and . . .' She trailed off, sensing that it was useless to object. Her voice dropped. 'It seems I'm always being sent hither and yon.'

'It's your own fault.'

'How so?'

'You're clever, capable and if I may say so, surprisingly good in a fight. The latter is not a quality many of the nuns here at Swyne can claim. I expect it's to do with those two Jerusalem monks who escort you around. They've no doubt shown you a few tricks of the trade.'

'Egbert and Gregory?' Hildegard brightened. 'Are they to escort me?'

'More. You'll set sail with not only those two reprobates,' she smiled fondly, 'but with the abbot himself.' The Prioress gave Hildegard a triumphant smile. 'Now I know you will not turn my request down.'

On hearing that Hubert de Courcy would be on the voyage Hildegard at once dropped her glance and fought a blush as she gave a ferocious examination of the tiles at her feet. When she looked up again she was composed enough to say, 'You read my mind, my lady. No one can help admiring Abbot de Courcy unless they're made of stone. It will be a privilege and an honour to be escorted by him – and by the two monks militant, of course.'

The Prioress laughed out loud. 'Well said! I have to add, though, that he will leave you at Hampton to take ship for Calais. From there duty will send him on to Cîteaux for a meeting of the French chapter to discuss this burning issue of the rightful pope. But worry not. Those two monks will accompany you all the way to Beaulieu and escort you and the child back here.'

'When do we leave, my lady?'

'Shortly. You will be informed.'

The Prioress organized things with her usual efficiency. Not many days later Hildegard rode out from the Abbey of Meaux with the three Cistercians to the haven at Ravenser on the Humber estuary where their ship, a well-founded merchant cog, was already at anchor. As soon as they boarded, the ship set sail and with a following wind made swift passage down the east coast towards the Narrow Sea.

Only Egbert suffered. As they rounded North Foreland into the Channel he continued to be seasick as always and was forced to hang over the side with a face as green as a leek, heaving up his insides without shame or let. He only became himself when they eventually docked at Hampton a week later and he could set foot on dry land.

Hubert, Abbot de Courcy, left them there to pick up a ship to France as arranged. With a slow, lingering glance and prayers for Hildegard to be blessed by the saints in all her endeavours he reluctantly took his leave. Each of his monks was given a hearty thump on the back in farewell. With a last dark-eyed look at Hildegard the abbot was conducted by his servants to the ship where, standing in the stern as the lines were cast off, he held her glance until the tide took him far out of sight down Hampton Water towards the open sea.

'He'll be sailing past Netley Abbey in a while,' Edgar remarked as they watched the ship become a small speck in the dancing waters. 'I wonder if it'll bring back memories?'

He referred to a time when the abbot had broken his leg in a fight with a gang of robbers in the woods last time they were down here. The group from Meaux had carried him for refuge to the nearest Cistercian monastery. This was Netley Abbey, a daughter house of Beaulieu Abbey.

The boys, as the Prioress referred to the two monks, seemed pleased to be free of the strictures of abbey life again. Years guarding pilgrims on the road to Jerusalem had nurtured their wanderlust.

At Hampton they efficiently hustled Hildegard across the quay at the busy port to where a smaller, single-masted ship was ready to take them on the tide to the mouth of the Beaulieu River.

Gregory was impatient to arrive. 'Soon we'll be at journey's end. Then we'll see how this Beaulieu measures up to Meaux, if it does!'

It was as he said. As soon as the merchant cog reached the shelter of the island at the mouth of the river a small, two-man boat appeared alongside to take them off. They found themselves sitting among a stack of purchases from Hampton being sculled upriver by a couple of brawny lay-brothers while the river wound serpent-like between banks bristling with dense woodland. At last the high stone walls of Beaulieu appeared.

Egbert punched Gregory on the arm. 'The royal abbey at last! We'll probably be so comfortable here we won't want to leave.'

They crossed a quay to the outer gatehouse built over a sluice and moments later the porter showed them into the inner close.

Ahead appeared the imposing inner gatehouse with guest lodgings and other buildings attached. Stables ran down one side of the lane within and the Domus, the two-storey building for the lay-brothers, gave an idea of the impressive number of labourers employed here.

'This is what I expected from a royal abbey,' Gregory admitted. 'Our Cistercian houses are often austere to say the least. At least that's what people say.'

'It's according to St Bernard's Rule,' murmured Egbert in mild reproof.

'I confess I feel I always have enough for my needs,' Gregory hastened to add.

The porter's assistant conducted them to the guest lodge where Hildegard would stay and before going on into the abbey precinct Gregory said, 'We'll let you know if there's any news of the betrothal party.'

Hildegard saw them enter the precinct where visitors and most especially women were not allowed then turned to the guest master to ask after Sir William before she was conducted inside.

'He has arrived, domina. But he's out with his men. He took hawks and hounds so I expect he'll be hunting until the light goes.'

Hildegard could not tell from his bland expression whether Sir William met with his approval or not. At Castle Hutton he was regarded by Lord Roger de Hutton's vassals as the Devil incarnate. It would be akin to a miracle if he created a better impression here.

As for his enforced pilgrimage to Jerusalem a few years ago with his wife, Roger de Hutton's strait-laced stepsister Avice, their penance for a trick they played against Roger, it had wrought no obvious improvement to his character. She was not looking forward to having to deal with him and hoped he would make life pleasant for their little charge.

'Journey's end!' Hildegard dropped off her travel bag in her allotted corner of the dormitory with a sigh of relief. Soon the bell for Vespers would begin to toll, the ritual here the same as in every Cistercian abbey everywhere. It brought a sense of order and security and a feeling of contentment but now, guessing that she had time to take a quick look round, she left the guest quarters and strolled back towards the outer gate and out onto the quay.

On all sides the Royal Forest pressed in, wild and dark, as far as the eye could see. With the weather typical of February at its greyest and grimmest and the imminent threat of rain, it was a sinister scene.

The tide that had carried them here was ebbing fast. The black waters ran in a swiftly flowing channel midstream with slimy brown mudflats near both banks. A short wooden bridge linked the opposite side with a line of rough-built huts where a few people in secular clothing were coming and going. Noticing that they wore no head coverings and were generally barefoot she guessed they were sanctuarymen.

The abbey was famous for two things. Its founding by King John in atonement for one of his many sins, and its provision of lifelong sanctuary to any felon who was able to find a way through the Forest without being arrested by the sheriff's men before reaching the Great Close.

The folk over the river sounded cheerful enough – as well they might now they lived in safety, she thought. She even noticed one or two women among them, *femmes soles*, perhaps, or widows fallen foul of the money-lenders, or maybe young women of ill-repute unable or unwilling to bribe the Watch.

The peaceful scene made her wonder about their guilt or whether they were the victims of someone with more privilege and power than themselves.

It was unlikely she would meet any of them. Once the little Cornish heiress from St Keverne had been handed over by her escort they would join the ship Sir William had engaged to convey her back up north. Hildegard couldn't help wondering how the child would take to life in a priory. Swyne was a remote place in the Holderness marshes and the nuns, though kindly, were driven by feelings of reverence to God which did not allow for much frivolity.

To be hoped she enjoys making silk and singing in a choir, thought Hildegard, momentarily overwhelmed by the sorry prospect awaiting the girl. It would be an advantage if she liked her future husband. At least the marriage would not be celebrated for some time. Sir William's second son, Hugo, was no more than nine. The girl would have to spend so long at Swyne she would probably begin to think of it as home – another possible wrench for her when she had to leave.

Poor children, she thought, nothing but pawns in the dynastic ambitions of their fathers! It was sorrowful but it was the way of the world. All she could do was to make sure her journey to her new home was as pleasant as possible.

She turned back and quickened her pace towards the gatehouse.

It wasn't every day she joined a betrothal party. She was looking forward to meeting the child. Elowen, a pretty Cornish name, the lady of St Keverne. The betrothal would be an event of much rejoicing.

The quayside was now almost empty. A few coracles lay upended on the bank and the boat that brought them up had been hauled out of the water alongside them.

She was pulling up her hood to go back inside when a lone horseman emerged at a gallop from between the trees on the other side of the river. Just then the bell announced the evening Office and she began to hurry.

It so turned out that the horseman had been making for the abbey with a message. It was all over the guest lodge when

Hildegard came out of Vespers: the ship from Cornwall had arrived!

The guest master announced the fact to everyone in the hall. 'The ship will enter the estuary and anchor in the haven with other large merchant cogs. From there the betrothal party will be brought up in the small boats as you yourselves were. There's no need for anyone to come ashore until they reach the quay.'

He added, 'Hospitality is offered for three days as is our duty. After that I imagine the Cornish party will return home and you and the little lady Elowen will sail north.'

He turned out to be kinder than his earlier reserve suggested, instructing his servants to prepare the tower chamber for their Cornish guest and to make sure the furs on her bed were properly aired.

'And for you, domina, a jug of wine after Compline, perhaps?'

She sent one of the pages to search out Gregory and Egbert.

'Let them know I would like to be at the haven to greet her when Lady Elowen arrives.'

She sent another page with a similar message for Sir William whenever he might return from hawking. He would be sure to want to join them.

# TWO

As mist still transformed the trees into gossamer the three monastics set off on foot late that morning. Sir William had acknowledged Hildegard's message by saying he would make his own arrangements.

To their astonishment they discovered that this meant nothing. He had already gone out earlier with his falconer and informed the porter that he would not return until sundown.

'Is this how he marks the arrival of his son's betrothed?' Hildegard asked in amazement.

Egbert was also somewhat scathing. 'What? Give up a day's hunting for the inconvenience of greeting a future daughter-in-law? Fie, Hildegard!'

Gregory added, 'We'll be there to welcome her. The porter says it's an hour's walk, assuming we don't get lost in the woods!'

'No chance of that!' Egbert countered. 'Not after our years in Outremer!'

'These lay-brothers know the way. Keep up or we'll be left behind!' Hildegard increased her pace. She felt sorry that they had little in the way of gifts except for what the servants guiding them through the woods brought to mark their welcome.

'Did you meet Sir William or merely send a message?' Gregory asked Hildegard as they walked along.

'I was told he was too tired after hunting to meet me yesterday. He dined in his chamber. Have you seen him yet?'

'We've been too busy with Church matters to leave the precinct.'

'I hope you'll be able to see which way the wind is blowing over this dispute between Rome and Avignon,' she remarked, having already let them know of her Prioress's wishes.

'Strong for Avignon—' said Gregory.

'And another faction equally strong for Rome,' added Egbert. 'If I were a dicing man, which, of course, I'm not, I would be hard pressed to bet on one side or the other being victor.'

Without further conversation they made good time, striding out with their usual vigour, and when they reached the haven they eventually saw the cog ghosting past the low-lying islands at its mouth. Along this part of the shore were nothing but sand-banks, shifting and treacherous, piled up by the strange double tides that swept the coastline in this part of the world. Several long, flat islands, little more than drifts of sand bound by marram grass swarmed with screeching seabirds at the mouth of the river.

While they waited for the tide a group of river men assembled a flotilla of small boats to row the guests up to the abbey wharf. Egbert strode down the bank to have a word with them.

'Where's this place they're sailing from?' one of the lads making himself busy asked him.

'St Keverne,' he replied. 'It's a place in Cornwall. I've never been there myself.'

'We have our herring-fishing trade and some of yon monks to organize everything from down there,' one of the older river men told him.

The young lad who had questioned Egbert shrugged. 'I wasn't allowed on the boats until this Martinmas past.'

'They're good lads,' replied the older man. 'Good seamen. They bring up the herring and we cure it or salt it at Pennington then sell it on when the monks have taken what they want for their own needs.'

The lad looked more interested in their present cargo. 'And this damozel on board?'

'Above your station, don't fancy yourself! She's the daughter of an earl.' He turned to Egbert again. 'This Sir William from up near you, does he have much land?'

'Enough, somewhat similar to this,' Egbert told him. 'Estuary holdings, often inundated by the sea. It's been a continual fight in recent years to keep his crops and his animals safe.'

'Not a good match for the little 'un, then?'

Egbert looked bemused. 'What do you think, Hildegard?' he asked as she joined them.

'We must not make judgement about things of which we know nothing!'

Everyone smiled. It seemed to be common knowledge that Sir William was to be approached with caution.

Gregory came down to join them. 'I wonder how many servants she's bringing with her?'

Nobody knew. They waited impatiently for the cog to come up while they speculated. The lines must have already been thrown off because she was making way towards them already.

It was a wide-bellied wooden ship with a high forepeak to accommodate cargo and now, as the tide lifted beneath her, they saw garlands made of strips of coloured cloth fastened in the shrouds with a few pennants to make it look like a betrothal ship. From the height of the main mast the earl's silken pennant was unfurled and rippled in the breeze.

The sound of a hurdy-gurdy playing a jig floated across the water. A few musicians were evidently onboard and in reply the three abbey minstrels standing on the shore took up the refrain with pipes and drums while the lay-brothers added their loud choir voices.

After an age when the ship seemed to be locked by wind and tide she gathered way again as the tide flooded in with greater force, bringing her as close as she could come. Eventually their patience was rewarded when the anchor went over the side, the sail clattered onto the foredeck, and from those onboard came several rousing cheers, echoed by the men ashore.

Suddenly everything was festive. People smiled at each other. The ones on board waved and cheered again.

A coracle was pushed by several willing hands into the water to carry over flagons of wine to show goodwill.

'Now they'll transfer to the shallow-draught boats to catch the tide up to the abbey,' murmured Gregory as the rest of the river-craft set off. 'Are we ready to go on board?'

'Which one is Elowen?' Hildegard asked, peering at the crowd lining the ship's rail as they waited to get into the boats. She held in her hands a welcoming coronet of myrtle, all she could find along the way.

By now the coracle had reached the ship and as they watched a conversation seemed to follow between the abbey man on the oars and the boatswain of the cog. It ended with one of the travellers climbing over the side and beginning the descent into the coracle by means of a rope ladder.

The smaller boat swayed alarmingly as a woman of some years took her seat. A second figure in blue started the short descent after her. Both had their hoods up.

To everyone's surprise instead of setting off upriver towards the abbey the boat started to head for shore.

Hildegard frowned.

One of the larger rowing boats had already reached the cog in preparation for the transfer of passengers and they watched as one of the oarsmen grabbed a spar as soon as it reached the cog and looked up, evidently to listen to instructions from someone onboard.

'Servants?' assessed Egbert. 'Is she sending them ashore?' He looked puzzled.

'The older woman in the coracle must be the governess.'

Hildegard peered across the water as the two passengers were rowed towards them.

Egbert nodded. 'She'll tell us what's what. And three maids by the look of them, about to climb down into . . . No, they're holding back, scared of a rope-ladder by the look of it! Come on, silly geese! Get a move on! The day's half gone! This tide won't last forever.'

'Is there an armed escort onboard?' Gregory narrowed his eyes. 'I can see what look like several men-at-arms. They're letting everybody else off first for some reason.'

'Here she comes!' Hildegard went down to the water's edge.

'Is she only twelve, do you say?' Gregory joined her.

The coracle beached on the strip of sand at the bottom of the bank just as the second vessel bumped ashore. People started to step over the sides. One or two slipped. Laughing, others gripped their companions by the arms to hold them steady.

'Those pages could show more deference to their lady.' Egbert came down to see if he could lend a hand. 'Now the maids at last.'

'There, the coracle seems to be staying here while the rowing boat goes back for the rest of them.' Gregory glanced down river towards the saltings.

'What's the matter, Greg?' Hildegard asked.

He shook his head. 'It's nothing . . .' He turned back. 'You'd think the armed men would have come ashore first. It seems a little odd.' He scanned the woods then shrugged. 'Come, let's find out what they intend by coming ashore here.'

After clutching the sides of the coracle on the way across, the woman they took to be a governess had climbed out and was standing shakily by the edge of the water gazing round. One by one the others came ashore. Most of them seemed a little dazed to be standing on dry land at last. One or two started to climb towards the path. The tide was already seeping closer as the rest of them scrambled stiff-legged up the bank.

One of the pages had nearly reached the top but when he glanced back to see how the older woman and her lady were doing he went back down again. The page took a pace or two then changed his mind. The older woman, having stepped gingerly towards him, stopped to wait for the little heiress to rearrange her trailing cloak.

A vessel full of maids, giggling and shrieking and dipping their fingers in the water, came to ground with a bump and they all shrieked again.

One of the girls called to the lanky indecisive page to give them a hand and her companion stood up unexpectedly and the boat tilted and more shrieks followed. Laughing, he loped back to the waterside.

At the same moment the pounding of horses' hooves was heard as several horsemen came galloping from out of the woods. Everyone on the foreshore turned to look.

The little lady Elowen in her blue velvet cloak was almost halfway up the bank by now. In her arms was a small casket.

Before even Gregory or Egbert could move the horsemen slowed as one of them rode right up to her and snatched the casket from her grasp.

A second horseman scooped up the girl herself and threw her, kicking and screaming, across his saddle before urging the beast back to a gallop and disappearing after his accomplices into the trees.

It all happened so quickly. Barely five seconds from start to finish passed. Everyone was transfixed.

Hildegard's first thought was that it was Sir William, playing a trick with a typically extravagant gesture, but there was no sign of the men's allegiance and she had no idea who they were.

While everyone was still gaping, Gregory and Egbert started to sprint in pursuit up the bank but it was futile. By the time they reached the stand of trees at the top the horsemen had disappeared into the undergrowth and soon even the sound of their mounts crashing between the trees faded to nothing.

It left chaos on the foreshore. All attention had been on the horsemen. Now, from frozen shock everything became movement and noise. Another boat, halfway across, bumped onto the shore and several servants leaped out. Back on board the cog the men-at-arms, having watched helplessly, were yelling to the boatmen to fetch them off.

'It will do no good to come ashore. Without horses they'll

never catch up with them.' Egbert punched one fist into his palm in helpless dismay. 'Who the hell were they?'

Gregory looked furious. 'To abduct her before our eyes! Dolts! Sotwits! What complacent fools we are!'

# THREE

In moments he and Egbert were striding down to the foreshore and helping push off a few coracles to send out to the cog.

Gregory was shouting, 'Tell the oarsmen to take the St Keverne men-at-arms to the abbey stables as fast as they can. Egbert and I will follow in another boat. We need horses. Hurry!'

In what seemed like only moments a boat reached the shore with a cage of hounds in it. A kennelman and his assistant jumped out and hauled the cage and its cargo onto dry land. Egbert helped them.

'Are we following on foot?' the kennelman asked.

'I reckon so, if you will?'

The kennelman unhasped the cage door and nodded.

Egbert grabbed one of the abbey men by the arm. 'Where does that lane lead?' he demanded, pointing after the horsemen.

'Straight to St Leonard's, a few miles up.'

'What's there?'

'It's the Great Barn where we keep produce for export and store our own goods to send to the granges.'

'And after that?'

'Nothing but woodland as far as the great boundary wall. There's a postern on the way to a hamlet called Lymington and nothing much else than the Royal Forest.'

As he went to stare after the horsemen a lay-brother followed his glance.

'Don't worry, brother, the gatekeeper won't open up without a docket and the wall is ten feet high or more with a ditch all round. We might lose them here in the woodland but it won't be for long. They're trapped within the Great Close!'

'Come,' Egbert invited. 'Let's go. How far is it?'

'A handful of miles.'

The kennelman let out his hounds, a lymer and a brace or two of scenting dogs, all obviously delighted to be on land again. They circled and sniffed the air and then looked to the kennelman for instructions. He showed them the fresh prints of the horses and, noses to the ground, they set off with wild eagerness. The kennelman and his assistant followed at a run while Egbert gathered an eager group of lay-brothers to join them.

Hildegard went down to the waterside. Most of the boats were filling up again with the little travelling household of Lady Elowen and were preparing to be taken up to the abbey but she was in time to place a hand on the arm of the woman in grey who had come ashore first.

'Mistress, may I ask why you left the ship to land here?'

'We thought this was where we were supposed to alight.' She avoided Hildegard's glance. 'Who would tell us otherwise, sister?'

'The shipman would know where his guests were making for,' she observed. 'The abbey receives many visitors. We were waiting on the shore only to greet you and accompany you upriver. Tell me something else. Did you have any hint of an abduction?'

The woman was unable to answer. Suddenly on the point of fainting, she clung on to a couple of maids, breathing heavily and shaking her head. 'Did you girls hear of anything?' she managed to gasp.

The maids shook their heads.

One of them began to sob. 'Will they harm her? What will they do to her?'

'She'll be safe enough,' Hildegard assured her. 'It'll be a ransom they want. Do you have any idea who they were?'

The woman in grey was beside herself and appeared incapable of giving a plain answer. Hildegard glanced round. Surely there had been three maids in the boat? Now there were two. 'Where's the other maid?'

The two girls glanced quickly at each other then stared at the nun from under their brows without replying. Hildegard tightened her lips. 'Better tell me what you know before you get into trouble. Where is she?' she demanded more sharply.

'We don't know nothing, sister, honest. What would we know?'

The girl who spoke nudged her companion with one elbow and stared defiantly into Hildegard's face. 'There's only us.'

'You must think we're blind fools.'

'She ran off,' blubbed the first maid in a rush. 'Tell her. We don't know where she's gone. It's not our fault.'

Hildegard turned on her heel and went back to the top of the bank where Egbert was about to set off after the hounds.

'What's up?' he demanded when he noticed her expression.

'Those lying little maids must know something. How many maids did you count making the crossing just now?'

'Three?'

'And how many do you see now?'

He glanced down the bank. 'So where's the third?'

'Exactly.'

The rivermen were as dazed as everybody else. Some of the boats conveying the visitors were frail craft and now weighed heavily. They took some pushing off from the bank.

Their captain climbed back up the slope. 'What shall we do, domina? Shall we take the rest up to the abbey while we've still got them?'

'Yes, without delay. Brother Gregory will organize a search party as soon as they have horses.' She gestured towards the lane Egbert had taken with the kennelmen. 'Is there any reason for them to head that way?'

'Not that I know of.'

'What's there?'

'The Great Barn of St Leonard, the chapel, the grange.'

'Plenty of men around?'

'Not at present. It being Lent, the lay-brothers are called to worship at the abbey and the grange is empty enough. They won't want to proclaim their presence with an heiress and her dowry unless they're looking for trouble.'

'And further on?'

He repeated what Egbert had been told about the wall, adding, 'After that nothing but Forest – and Forest folk.'

He seemed shocked that armed men were roaming about abbey lands.

As he went off to see the last of the guests into the boats Hildegard's glance swept the riverbank.

Someone else was missing. It was the page who had laughingly held out his hand to conduct one of the maids ashore. Was it the missing maid? She had no idea. There was no time for speculation now.

Gregory, gripping the side of one of the coracles as it took to the water, shouted, 'Hurry, Hildegard!'

She called down, 'I want to have a look round here. I'll catch up with you later.' She watched as the riverman pushed the boat into the current.

One boatman remained. The first of the travellers from St Keverne were rounding a curve in the river and by now Egbert had disappeared up the track with the others.

It was heavily silent without the men's shouts of panic.

She called down to the remaining riverman. 'Will you take me back in a while? I need to have a look at something first.'

He nodded and climbed up the bank towards her with a heavy tread. He was a burly, unsmiling fellow and stopped a pace or two in front of her, looking her up and down. 'Just me and you then, domina?'

'So it is.'

'What do you want me to do?' He raised both brows.

'Stay by the boat. I won't be long. Don't leave without me.'

His mouth quivered in an ironic smile. 'As you request, my lady. Don't forget the tide.' Before he turned to leave he thought to ask, 'This heiress, so-called. Wealthy beyond our wildest dreams?'

'Why do you ask?'

'It's only what some of that Sir William's lads were a-boasting of last night in the lay-brothers' refectory where we all sup together.'

'Was Sir William with you?'

The boatman showed broken teeth as he opened his mouth to jeer. 'Dines with the abbot's stand-in, don't he? Too good for us!'

'Fret not. I doubt whether he's too good for anybody.'

Chuckling with a certain malice the boatman made off down

the bank and she watched for a moment as he began to pull his coracle higher up the slope as the tide swelled within the confines of the river's course.

She climbed up to the path where it divided three ways and ignoring the lane that led to St Leonard's took the one to the coast in the opposite direction from the abbey.

She wondered how much time she had before she was stranded by the tide. It would be impossible to scull a frail craft like a coracle against the full power of the ebb and she didn't relish walking back through the woods to the abbey with armed men on the loose. She quickened her pace.

After all the recent activity the woods were uncannily quiet. They seemed to be waiting on an indrawn breath for something else to happen. She stood at the top of the bank for a moment to listen, ears sharpened to every nuance of sound, birdsong, the wind brushing the tops of the winter grasses, a little sigh through the high branches of the stripped oaks.

Beyond the nearest copse was a sense of unending space. The sound of distances enclosed the river landing. Was that possible? The sound of distance? There was nothing else. Her own breathing, frail, scarcely audible, close. Nothing more.

She glanced back at the boatman lower down. He was sitting on the ground beside his coracle, gazing at the water as it rippled past.

So that was the rumour, she thought as she set off, eyes sharp for any clue as she walked along. Riches beyond an ordinary man's wildest dreams? And where had the rumour started? . . . This knowledge that there was something worth purloining down by the haven?

At St Keverne? Surely it would be common knowledge there. Celebrations at the castle. Acceptance of a welcome alliance between North and South. Why come all the way here merely to purloin a casket that could have been more easily stolen at home? Why take the girl?

On board the merchant cog? A ship full of St Keverne folk? And others? Strangers coming up from Cornwall to trade? No doubt a whisper would reach them. A reason for the voyage. Curiosity about the casket the girl carried?

Is that how the rumour came to roost here in this wood in the middle of nowhere – if you deemed towns somewhere?

Someone had thought it was worth the risk of defying the law of the land.

The monks had their own rules. They cared for nothing of material value. Their yearnings were set on more ephemeral riches.

The conversi? Those nameless lay-brothers who did the farm work, the husbandry, made all the implements of use, in rope, iron, wood, were forbidden to read, write or marry, monks in all but name, allowed only to assist the tonsured brothers in their privileged ascent to heaven?

But again, how would they know or care of the worth of what the girl brought with her?

Dowry, a powerful word that could mean escape from earthly sorrow. It could buy freedom, comfort, and a sweet and respected old age. Would it matter to devout men such as the lay-brothers mostly were?

In the hierarchy of the world a dowry could mean an end to oblivion. A name remembered. The price of a marble monument to one's eternal glory.

Anybody could be tempted.

By now she was walking between the trees along the path near the sea. She bent to peer at something visible in the mud.

Footprints.

Not horse's hooves but those of a human being on two feet. Not Egbert's big boot prints, going and coming, but smaller, soft-soled ones. A maid's prints?

Nearby, in and out of the grass, followed a slightly larger set, the toes digging into the soft mud like someone running to catch up.

They eventually stopped at a stretch of water, a small pond after heavy rainfall cutting right across the track and obliterating the prints with one sweep of a rain sprite's hand.

All else was salt-stunted bushes, coarse and thorn-rivetted, and further along the beginnings of the saltings again, marsh, rivulets, sea-grass, a treacherous network of shingle dunes gathered by the regular incursions of the waters in incessant, elemental battle.

Conscious of the changing tide and the need to return she

narrowed her eyes for a glimpse of horsemen or at least for two distant hurrying figures but nothing moved in the barren stretches of the saltings except for seabirds rising screaming from their nests and settling and rising again. And the clouds above, racing.

In all the barren landscape she saw no one hurrying along the top of the dykes to a secret destination. Doubtfully, she began to retrace her steps.

On the way she tried to make out a returning set of prints but failed. She could guarantee that once she crossed the flood cutting off the path she would find the prints again.

Had a boat, prearranged, already picked the pair up from some out-of-the-way landing on the beach in the company of the kidnapped heiress? But they could not have made such good time, nor surely, have decided on such a plan?

She checked the prints carefully again, aware that her desire to find a trail, to make sense of the nonsensical, could lure anybody into believing what was not. But they were clear once picked out from the morass and unlike the hoofprints they went in one direction. Away. Towards the sea.

She reached the haven. The light was already failing on this short February day.

At least the boatman was still waiting. He had not abandoned her as she feared he might. No sign or sound of Egbert and his followers, of course, because he would be well on the way to the Great Barn, the hounds circling and scenting, maybe, and urging the men to greater speed.

She slipped a little as she made her way down the bank to the water's edge. Her boots were covered in mud. To no avail.

The boatman lifted his head.

'It's on the turn. I thought you were never coming back. Get in quick.'

As they were leaving he commented, 'So you didn't find the runaways, then.' It was a statement. He seemed to know already that she would fail.

'Where might they make for, out there on the saltings?'

'Hell,' he replied.

'We must send someone to find them.'

'Down into hell? For a couple of no-good servants? It's them horsemen you should be after, them, the dowry and the girl.'

'I thought that on foot I might catch up with them and they might be able to tell me something about her kidnap.'

Sitting in the stern he sculled the craft into the strong current midriver and proceeded silently after that in the direction of Beaulieu.

# FOUR

The governess, if that's what she was, with her hair pulled back out of sight under a snood, and a voluminous cloak clutched tightly against the weather, was pacing on the quay when the boatman angled the craft against the side so Hildegard could alight.

'So you had no success, my lady?' She stretched out a hand from inside her cloak and held it out. 'Careful now.'

'My thanks, mistress.' Hildegard took her hand and stepped ashore. Once on the quay she looked the woman up and down. Her manner had changed. She looked calm and capable.

'And now, mistress, perhaps we might introduce ourselves. It appears we are allies in this matter.'

'I know who you are, domina. The porter told me. You are to take over my job and accompany our little angel to your priory where she will live until of age to marry.'

'I am she, but let's go to the guest house and share our knowledge about what has happened. We must find a swift solution to this mishap.'

'Mishap, you call it? I fear my lord will be more inclined to regard it as a catastrophe if we fail to find her.'

As they walked back towards the enclave Hildegard asked about Brother Gregory. 'Do you know if he found enough horses and men to track down these men?'

'Indeed. One group of monks were most helpful but they were at odds with another group. There was some argument about whether the horses should be taken by strangers until your brother drew on his authority and forced the issue.'

'That's like Gregory—!'

Despite her wary expression the woman allowed a smile to flicker across her face.

They reached the guest house and entered the refectory. It was empty at this time of day. They found seats on opposite sides of the big table and took each other's measure.

'To business, then! I am Mistress Goda, as I believe you already guess. I've been nursemaid to dear Elowen since she was a baby. I regard her with as much love as if she were my own child.'

'In that case it must be a wrench to let her come to us?'

'It is. We know little of this Sir William. I believe he met Earl Richard on pilgrimage in Outremer and some arrangement was hatched between them, neither at that time having children and probably unable to understand the nature of their pledge.'

'Men away from the familiar customs of home often bind themselves to more than they understand at the time,' she agreed. 'But tell me, how is the betrothal viewed in general?'

'As a good thing. In general,' she added.

'And more specifically?'

'I for one regret that she should be sent so far from home.'

'You must be desperate to get her back unharmed,' she observed, puzzled by the woman's lack of emotion despite her sentiments.

'Of course,' Mistress Goda agreed in the same practical tone. 'Who would not be anxious for the safety of their charge? We are consoled by the thought that a ransom will be demanded and, such is the Earl's wealth, I doubt not that it will be paid promptly and everything restored to its old way.'

'To be hoped so,' Hildegard agreed. 'But tell me about the two servants who absconded at the same time. Could they have known who their mistress's abductors were?'

Goda shook her head. 'How could they? We had scarcely set foot on dry land. My view is they took a chance when it presented itself. Both are known hotheads. I wash my hands of them. Let them go. Servants can be replaced.'

'I would sorrow for anyone caught out on the saltings, especially with night coming on and in ignorance of its dangers. We have similar country in Holderness at Meaux, low-lying marshland where the sea can be treacherous, inundating good farmland, bringing down barns, drowning stray cattle, cutting off one home from another.'

'In that case I'll find a man to send.' She half rose to her feet. 'Mayhap he will root them out in their sty of iniquity.'

Somewhat chilled by Mistress Goda's words which, she allowed, might hide more concern than she showed, Hildegard was prepared for a few last-minute questions about Sir William on a more personal level and, at pains to say nothing that would alarm the woman until Elowen was safely returned to them, she warned herself that Sir William's temper was not the issue. She followed Goda to the door.

'As for young Hugo,' she hastened to mention the little suitor, 'he's a most charming and lively fellow, like his elder brother. We fully expect him to grow into an excellent young man.'

'Is he more like his father or his mother?' Goda asked as she pushed at the door.

Hildegard wrinkled her brow. To speak honestly might alarm the nursemaid. She would not lie but nor could she avoid the issue of William's nature. 'His mother is a meticulous chatelaine,' she admitted.

'Not given to fun and frivolity then? And,' she moved briskly on, 'the castle?'

'A manor only, but large, moated, with extensive riverside land and several well-run granges – and much trade with Norway,' she finished somewhat lamely.

Goda showed no emotion. 'Well, so be it. We must find our chick first, of course. Let's hope your monks and our men bring back their trophy. We must leave it to the hunting party, mustn't we? Now I must check on the welfare of my servants. We will keep each other informed.'

After the governess left, Hildegard decided to go out. To sit and wait was impossible.

Finding her way to the stables she sought out the master. When she explained who she was and why she had an interest in what had happened he was affable and forthcoming. To her question about Sir William and whether he had been informed of this debacle he nodded with a lop-sided grimace.

'He got back early, raging about his wasted day. His falcon

refused to fly then they got lost up near the bogs somewhere. When he heard what had happened he raged about the insult to him. "How dare they!" That sort of thing. At the end of it nothing was damaged and no one harmed.' His smile was apologetic for this criticism, adding, 'We thought he took it quite well . . . considering. I have to say, without disrespect to you and your brother monks, domina, that we thought he might have shown more concern for the safety of his son's betrothed.'

Allowing that William was a bad-tempered, easily affronted devil Hildegard held her tongue. 'I'm glad to hear he was back early,' she replied diplomatically. 'Did he ride out after the others?'

'No, he said it was best to leave it to them.'

'I'm told that some of the monks objected to Brother Gregory requisitioning your horses?'

'They'd no right to object. We'd do the same for any guest. Now Abbot Herring is dead and buried they imagine Cîteaux and Avignon are protecting them, but mark my words, that schism is not ended yet and they may well find themselves on the wrong side. But there you are, monks are as battlesome as any men. It's too soon for anyone to be counting their chickens.'

'We have a similar problem at Meaux although our abbot is a young man still very much with us. Clement's men have decided they want him to step down so they can put their own choice in as abbot. Fortunately for us Abbot de Courcy is a man not used to stepping down for anybody – and certainly not for a French pope imposed on us against our will.'

'Ah, the times.' He shook his head.

'May I ask you, master, how confident you are that the abductors of the little lady Elowen will be apprehended?'

'Apprehended and brought to justice however long it takes. I'm confident that they won't have been able to get beyond the boundaries. Extensive though the abbey lands are, we have a formidable wall to protect those within. My men will winkle them out. Have no fear.' He gave a quick glance to left and right and beckoned her to bend her head the better to hear. 'You understand about our folk across the river?'

Hildegard widened her eyes to encourage him to explain.

'The sanctuarymen? Those felons and renegades? You know about them? On the run from the law? Cheating justice?'

'I have heard about them. What do you mean?'

'I mean they are not slow to see a chance for themselves, being as they are, men of sin. It's going round that the betrothed was carrying in her arms a casket brimming with gold. If you want the fiends that have stolen her away I'd look no further than over there.'

He gave a meaningful nod and turned to chivvy the stable lads but Hildegard detained him. 'Do you believe they could organize themselves to do such a terrible thing?'

'When every other stone has been turned over, then may you turn that one and spy what's under it.'

Hildegard hesitated. 'I would have asked a boon, master, but now I'm not so sure.'

'Ask on.'

Time later to question the sanctuary seekers if all else failed. 'I was going to ask whether you happened to have an old hobbler in your string that might take me to the grange where Brothers Gregory and Egbert and the rest of the men expect to waylay the kidnappers? I have a burning desire to follow them to witness how their luck is holding.'

'Dicing men, are they?' The old fellow chuckled. Obviously this met with his approval because he indicated to Hildegard to follow.

He led the way down the length of the stable block to a stall at the far end where a pretty little pony of not much more than twelve hands was peacefully nuzzling into a manger of hay.

'Suit you?'

'Very well indeed.'

He was already giving a shout to the nearest couple of lads to get the pony bridled up. 'She even knows the way to St Leonard's but don't let her stop at Beaufre or you'll never get her out till morning.'

As they returned to the yard he explained which path to take once she left the hamlet over the river, up the hill where from the top she might well be able to spot the group on the heath in the far distance as they left the woods.

'It's not a hard ride to the Great Barn at St Leonard's.' He grimaced. 'To be hoped you even meet them on the way back with the little lady safe and sound and her kidnappers roped up for their evil intentions.'

'If they in fact took her there. They could be hiding out anywhere within the enclosure,' she added cautiously.

Wondering if she should have waited to make sure Goda had sent a man out to look for the runaway servants, she mentioned the fact to the stabler and he assured her that he himself would send somebody at once.

'With the tide on the ebb I'll send a couple of our fellows down in time to watch the beaches for the runaways. It's no easy thing to cross the saltings,' he explained. 'It involves a lot of doubling back on yourself round the salt pans. Easy to get lost. I doubt they'll know that, not being local. Yon Cornish housekeeper mightn't understand the nature of the land round here neither. She won't realize how dangerous it can be. More sea than good earth, most of it—' He turned to shout down the yard, 'Where's that pony?'

The pony was ready and a tall, grinning, bean-shoot of a lad led her out into the yard. The horse master slapped her on the quarters saying, 'This is Bluebell. She'll take you to St Leonard's and back.' He turned to him. 'Allard? You go with our guest. And,' he admonished, 'do exactly as she asks you. Understand?'

'I do, master.'

'Then be off with you.'

As they left she heard him shouting for men to get down to the boats and take flares with them as night would be falling before they could get back upriver. In no time Hildegard and Allard were clipping out of the yard under the echoing arch of the gatehouse.

# FIVE

A llard led the way across the wooden bridge into the darkening lane.

Hildegard moved her pony up beside him. 'So, Allard, you may call me Hildegard, if you will. It's irksome to have a companion calling me "my lady" or "domina" at every turn. How far is this place we're heading for?'

He brushed a swatch of dark hair back inside his cap revealing sharp hazel eyes and crinkled them in a smile. 'The Great Barn at St Leonard's? Not far, my la– Hildegard, if you please. If we ride briskly we can arrive well before Vespers and may, if you plan it so, return to the abbey before the last Office. Depending what happens,' he added.

'At this time of year it'll be dark well before then.'

'No problem for us. It's a clear sky with a full moon tonight and our horses are creatures of habit. They like to bed down in their own straw once they know their duties are over for the day. They won't dawdle on the way home.'

'They sound sensible creatures.'

'The master would have it so.'

In friendly silence they rode as fast as they were able up a low hill high enough to afford a view over the undulations of the heath as far as the treeline on the horizon.

'Fear not. We'll not go so far,' he explained, noticing the direction of her glance. 'Beyond those trees they would eventually come to the boundary wall of the Great Close. They'll not easily get out. The distance to St Leonard's isn't so far, if that's where they decided to hide out. We'll be there soon enough and no doubt find them held in custody.' The prospect seemed to appeal to him because he began to press his pony more urgently onwards.

Once Allard saw that Hildegard was companionable despite being a nun he chatted about all sorts of matters to do with the running of the stables and how he hoped to be master himself one day.

'But not for years yet as I would wish no harm to the horse master you met and there are others before me, equally worthy. The master's bark is fearsome but he rarely bites. He thinks your monk, Brother Gregory, is a good sort. He's leading some of Guido's men. That's our Chief Forester. They'll show him many secret ways these strangers will not know.'

'Strangers?'

'The abductors?' He glanced at her. 'Strangers from Hampton, doubtless. How would anyone here conceive of such a grievous plot? To kidnap a child of twelve? Devils, they are. If our dear old abbot was still alive nothing like this would have happened.

'It's the times. A world turned upside down by schism and bad blood, as the master was telling you. I doubt whether any of the monks, schismatics though they be, would imagine anything like this to befall in the absence of our dear Abbot Herring.' He crossed himself.

'Your horse master suggested the sanctuarymen were to blame.'

'He has a special dislike of them. They cause problems within the Close with their drinking and set a bad example to the novices, which is why they're banished from the Inner Close. But he may be right. There it is. We shall see. Now, my lady – Hildegard,' he corrected with a faint blush, 'how is your pony? Is she to your liking?'

'She's most biddable, my gratitude for the honour of riding such a quiet beast.'

'Don't be taken in. She holds some strong opinions.' He gave Hildegard a shy smile. 'I can see she likes you.'

They followed the track until they reached a few well-built stone buildings looming out of the darkness. 'This is the Beaufre,' Allard explained. 'It's where we breed our cattle. The teams of oxen are here as well.'

He muttered something sharp to Hildegard's mount when the animal tossed her mane and rolled her eyes sidelong at the yard next to the ox-sheds but at his word she obediently relinquished her hopes for a rest and quickened her pace to keep up with him.

Soon they were hastening along a winding road between tall oaks. It seemed to go on forever but as night fell it brought them out at a three-way junction dominated by a high stone building.

'This is it,' Allard told her. He turned to her in surprise. 'It looks quiet.'

He quietly slid down from his mount and led it into the yard. When Hildegard followed she could just make out his expression in the moonlight.

'You look mystified, Allard. What's wrong?'

'There's usually a couple of well-armed fellows keeping an eye on things at this time of year.' He turned to her. 'They need to keep a watch in case thieves get over the walls into the Close.'

They reached the doors. They were more like the entrance to a church than to a store. From the outside it looked as if the entire building was planned on ecclesiastical lines, with a high-ridged roof up to twenty feet above their heads, the only difference being that there were no windows nor openings of any other kind except for small regular put holes high up, big enough to let in fresh air or something no bigger than a kestrel.

Still looking puzzled, Allard put his shoulder to the door almost as if he expected it to be locked but it swung open into the darker cavern of the interior.

'Anyone here? . . . Mark? . . . It's Allard. Are you here?' There was no answer. 'Mark? Godric?' he repeated more urgently.

He took a step into the darkness with Hildegard close behind when a rough sound somewhere in front of them brought them to a halt. It was like the growling of an animal. 'Mark?' Allard repeated with more urgency.

It came again. It was an animal in pain. Allard gripped Hildegard's sleeve. A surreptitious movement was detected from somewhere in the darkness. A human voice grated, 'Here . . .' and fell silent.

Allard edged towards the sound with his hands stretched in front of him like a blind man. 'Careful,' he advised Hildegard over his shoulder. 'The stores are stacked up in front of us. Don't dislodge them or we'll be buried alive.'

The heavy doors crashed-to behind them, cutting off what little light there was. She put one hand on his arm. 'Wait. Let me wedge the doors open to give us some light.'

She groped her way back and heaved open first one side and then the other.

Kicking a couple of stones against them she felt for the cresset on the wall, fumbled for tinder, lit it then turned to peer back into the barn.

It was enormous inside, with no dividing floors, and stretched straight up to the distant roof timbers. Her attention was drawn down to where that faint sound had come from. Allard was already leaning over something wedged like a discarded sack between some bales.

He was murmuring, 'Come on, let me lift you,' as she went over.

'Is it someone?' she whispered.

'It's Mark. He seems to be hurt.'

'Let me look.'

She handed the cresset to Allard then crouched down. A wide pool of blood had seeped from beneath the curled-up body of a man of about thirty. From a brief glance at his clothing he was one of the lay-brothers. 'The blood has congealed,' she observed to Allard. 'It must have happened a little while ago.'

Putting her mouth close to the man's ear she asked, 'Where are you hurt?'

'Arm—' He struggled to add something but his breathing, as shallow as a bird's, made the effort too much and she saw his eyes close.

'We've come to help,' she whispered. 'Can I shift you so I can see your wound?'

'My arm,' he repeated, not opening his eyes. 'Cut through. Feels like. Keep blood in.'

'He might mean by lying on his arm he's preventing further loss of blood,' she murmured to Allard. 'Go at once and get the reins from one of the ponies. Have you got a knife?'

'Of course.'

'Then cut off a length about two feet and bring it to me.'

Without wasting time asking questions Allard hooked the cresset into a wall bracket and hurried off to do as she asked.

The wounded man was drifting in and out of consciousness. When he opened his eyes for a moment to look up into her face she asked again what had happened.

'Some fellas . . . out of nowhere . . .' His eyes closed again. With a huge effort he forced some words to his lips but they were too faint to make out.

'Did you know them?' she whispered.

'Murdering devils,' he managed before sinking back in a faint.

Allard appeared with a length of leather, thicker than twine but no wider than his thumb. She took it. She explained: 'I can't see what has happened until we move him but it looks as if his wound might begin to bleed when the pressure is lifted. I'll make a tourniquet. Will you help me raise him to sitting?'

Allard went to one side and slid an arm underneath Mark's shoulders. 'Come on, fella, grit your teeth.'

'Now,' Hildegard instructed. They both heaved him upright so that he was resting with his back against the nearest bales.

Blood, released from the pressure, began to pump from a wound in his lower arm. In a trice she had the leather strap tied above his elbow and tightened it until she saw him wince. 'All right?'

He was not too far gone to understand what she was doing. 'More,' he urged. 'Mother of God, have mercy. More.' His head sagged forward as he muttered a desperate prayer.

'You've staunched the blood,' Allard observed after a moment. 'And look! Here's his knife. He must have tried to defend himself with it.' He picked up a blade, maybe fifteen inches long and two inches wide, that had been underneath him.

'We have to get help,' Hildegard muttered urgently. 'Is there an infirmarer at the abbey? Can you fetch him? I'll stay here.' She felt around in her leather scrip and found a needle and a length of coarse thread and began to stitch up the wound as best she could.

'I can't leave you in case those devils come back.'

'Why should they?' She glanced up. 'Didn't you call out to someone else?'

Allard straightened. Even in the gloom she could see his face blanche. He bent down and asked softly, 'Was young Godric with you, Mark old fella?'

Mark gave a small nod of his head but the effort cost him and he slumped back. Allard had a look further inside the Barn and when he returned he pointed between the bales where there was a narrow passage. 'There's blood. I'll have a proper look.' He groped between the bales to find a way through.

Hildegard spoke to Mark again, urging him to stay awake, asking him what had happened and eventually managing to elicit a slurred response to her question *how many*.

'Two in here. More outside. Left me for dead. The blood and that. In a rage of a hurry.'

'Did you hear where they were going?'

'Cursing us for being here. Something about a siege. Rode off into the Forest . . . somewhere to hole up. Heard the hooves. All gone. I thought I was gone . . . Bleeding . . . Couldn't stop it. Then men, hounds, went straight on at pace.'

While he was talking she finished stitching and took a tincture from her scrip to moisten his lips, watching him gradually coming back to himself, gaining strength, a tough young fellow, and when he lifted his head with eyes wide open to take some more of the tincture he gave a gasp of surprise. 'You a nun?'

'Do you mind?'

'You're a saving angel. Let me up.'

Just then Allard returned. 'I found him.' He made a stricken sound in his throat and stumbled towards them.

Hildegard rose to her feet. 'Rest awhile, Mark.' To Allard she said, 'Show me.'

He hesitated but such was Hildegard's insistence he obeyed, albeit reluctantly. 'You don't want to see. It was done the way you'd butcher an animal. A blade to the throat.' He began to sob and for a moment he leaned against the shoulder she offered.

Gathering strength from somewhere he pulled himself together and led her deeper into the barn with bales of produce towering on both sides of the passageway.

When he eventually stopped deep in the heart of the store it was almost too dim to see anything. As her eyes adjusted to the darkness she noticed a greater darkness of something lying on the ground. It was exactly as Allard had said. It was the body of a young man. A gash to the thin neck, the windpipe showing, more blood than seemed possible, his hands clutching at something no one could see. She felt sick.

No time for weakness, she admonished.

Allard had control of himself now but his face was set in a rictus of grief and horror.

'He would have felt nothing,' she told him.

He made the sign of the cross. 'St Leonard and all the saints bless him world without end.' Cuffing the back of one hand across his eyes he stood for a moment simply staring down at the body of his friend until a sound from Mark drew them back between the bales to his side.

He was still slumped where they had left him but was watching intently for them to reappear. 'They've done for him, haven't they?'

Allard crouched down beside him, grief weakening him again, and the wounded man lifted his undamaged hand and rested it on the crown of Allard's head. 'Bless him and bless you, young lad. He was a brave one. Now get on. Do what you have to do. Leave me. I'm all right. There'll be the carter up from Sowley in a while. Get on after them devils before dark sets in. Don't let them get away with it!'

After a few further questions about who was expected to turn up they found that he would be in luck of a sort. Help would be on its way in the shape of the carter due to pick up a broken shaft from a winch and take it down to the ironworks at a place called Sowley Pond.

'You'll see him on the way up here,' Mark told them. 'He'll take me on to Beaufre. Somebody there will know what to do.'

With no sign of any of the others who had set off in pursuit, they decided to make Mark as comfortable as they could, brought water from the well and, telling him they intended to track down the murdering gang, left him with assurances that they would let the carter know where he could be found if they passed him on the road.

'Leave the big doors open,' were his final words, weakly spoken, 'that way he'll know there's somebody within.'

'I don't like leaving him,' Hildegard remarked as they rode away. 'I've a mind to go back. We have no idea which way to ride nor what we'll do if we come across this gang, though find them we must before they manage to escape for good.'

Just the two of us, she thought, and maybe Egbert and the kennelmen. But where is Gregory? She said more in hope than conviction, 'Brother Gregory and his men will have caught up with them by now.'

'They murdered Godric in cold blood,' Allard muttered through clenched teeth. 'There would have been a fight.'

Not wishing to think of the outcome she said, 'I fear Mark has lost more blood than he realizes. He needs expert help.'

'We've done what we can. The carter will be there soon. He usually stays overnight and returns to the ironworks next morning with whatever has to be repaired. One or two men will be somewhere around. They'll help lift him onto the cart.'

Dissatisfied with the situation but aware that the youth knew more about the routine of the granges than she did she urged the borrowed pony, Bluebell, into a canter and Allard followed down a wide track that led into the woods.

Now, instead of pursuing kidnappers they were in pursuit of a gang of murderers too.

# SIX

The moon was little more than a hand span above the trees that lay along the perimeter of the Great Close when they emerged after leaving St Leonard's and its victims. Beyond the line of oaks, Allard reminded, was the outer wall, less high than the ten feet that bounded the abbey itself. It was enough to keep out casual poachers in this part of the Forest but not too high to prevent deer having innocent access into the killing grounds.

The three or four horsemen, strangers to the area as they probably were, would not know about the walls and how they would need to find a way out for their horses as well as their captive if they wished to make an escape.

'And they'll never have found a way along the twists and turns of the lanes,' Allard continued with forced optimism. 'I'm sure the abbey men will have managed to track them down.'

She knew he was trying to keep up his spirits by keeping up hers and encouraged him to talk. It had been a horrible shock to find the boy dead. The sight of his poor mutilated body would stay with them forever but now they had to get on to prevent further horrors.

As often happens the trees had been drained of light before anything else. Shadows cast by the moonlight filled the spaces under them. Now and then a shriek would rend the silence as a predator fell on its victim.

Eventually Hildegard slowed to a halt. 'We've already passed one fork in the road, Allard. How do we know we're now on the right one?'

He rubbed a hand over his face. 'We don't.' He hesitated before saying, 'The lane we passed leads to a grange called the bergerie where they deal with the wool clip. From there it curves back towards the river.'

In the shaft of moonlight splintered by the branches of the trees, his expression was both ashamed and desperate.

'Tell me, Allard, what else is it?'

'The truth is,' he replied with great reluctance, 'I'm afraid of what we might find if we ride down to the grange there.'

To Hildegard's consternation he began to heave with sobs and she realized he was probably not as old as she had first thought, for all his competence. *He's just a child*, she thought. Moved by his grief but with no idea what she could do to help she decided it would be best to get a clearer picture of what was likely to face them if they took that route. 'Are there many living down there?'

'A family, the head shepherd and his little twin daughters and his wife and her sister. If – if—' He could not get the words out. 'Those devils will stop at nothing, Hildegard,' he finished. 'We've seen that.' He need say no more.

She leaned across and placed a hand over the back of his own. 'You will not need to enter the grange if you'd rather not. I will think no less of you. At present you are not yourself. How can you be? You've had the most dreadful shock. I would not expect you to face more but it's best we know they're safe.'

'I'm nothing but a coward,' he muttered angrily. 'Say it! You must despise me.'

'Nothing could be further from my mind. I've had many years to become accustomed to death and the violence men wreak on each other. You're young, and I would guess, have scarcely ever left the precincts of the abbey. Other than a rabbit or two I doubt you've seen many dead creatures outside the butcher's yard, let alone a human being with a departed soul and deep ties to you and the people you love. I expect it will be something you will have to grapple with for some time to come . . . as we all do,' she added. 'But we must find out if she is being held there and if the shepherd and his family are safe.'

'The abbey doesn't prepare us for violence,' he muttered. 'It's always been a place of peace – at least it was, until this war of words flared up over the right of the French pope to rule us.'

'Go on.'

'The novices have a scuffle now and then but the worst is never more than a bloody nose.' He gripped Hildegard's arm fiercely. 'I can't run away but I daren't—!'

'I have faith in your courage.'

He gritted his teeth. 'So? We go down to the bergerie?'

'Will you?'

He struggled for no more than a moment. 'I will.'

The lane was well rutted with the passage of cartwheels and they approached the low-lying building at a sedate pace to save the legs of their ponies and out of wariness at what they might encounter.

A candle flickered between the shutters of a downstairs chamber and now and then a shadow passed, briefly visible beneath the low-hanging thatch. To herself Hildegard whispered, *so far so good.*

She had no wish to find another body nor anyone wounded past repair and it was not from cowardice but from a desire that all things should be well and all people in the true glory of the world should be at peace that made her reluctant to seek out more horror. The fate of Elowen held cause for hope that the abductors were not such fools that they would harm their prize but first there was this trial to face. It had to be done.

After a brief look round it was obvious there were no other horses here apart from a couple looking out of their shadowed stalls with an inquisitive interest in the arrival of strangers.

'I'll go ahead,' she told Allard firmly, swinging down from the pony.

She trod quietly across the yard towards the light. The door of the farmstead was a lop-sided piece of elm, rough-hewn but serviceable. It was all silvered by moonlight. With the utmost caution she stepped nearer and looked through a small window opening beside the door.

Nothing more alarming appeared than a couple of small girls in a cramped kitchen playing with a puppy.

Deciding to risk it she knocked on the door. At once it summoned a male voice demanding, 'Who's there?'

More boldly she answered, 'I'm a nun from the priory at Swyne in Holderness. I'm visiting the abbey. I seek the head shepherd.'

A wooden latch was heard to lift on the inside and a head poked through the gap as the door was slowly opened. She noted he kept his foot behind it. A child peered out about knee height but a hand gently pushed her to one side. 'Leave it, Amy, let me speak first.'

The occupant was holding a candle and opened the door wider to look her up and down. 'Are you alone, sister?'

'I'm accompanied by Allard, who—'

His face broke into a smile. 'Allard! Bring him in! Where is he?' He came out onto the step. 'Where are you hiding, you young devil?'

Allard, still a little shame-faced, emerged from the shadows. 'We have bad news, Chad. Are you safe yourselves?' He tried to peer inside as if expecting to see a felon with a knife against the shepherd's back.

He came right out into the yard, calling over his shoulder, 'Go back inside, Amy, this is grown-up business.'

That'll bring the child to eavesdrop, Hildegard thought, but Chad was ahead of her and went back to shut the door. 'So what is it? I can see by your faces things are not well. What's happened?'

'Are you sure you haven't seen any strangers riding through the woods?' Allard began.

'Not us. Off the beaten track. Seen no one. Who might they be?'

'We don't know. We only know what they've done.'

With heads bent close they told the shepherd what had happened since earlier that day, about the arrival of the folk from St Keverne, about the abduction of the heiress, about the men setting out from the abbey in pursuit led by a Cistercian monk, about the possibility that the future father-in-law of the betrothed with his mercenaries was also on the trail.

'Rumours of a huge dowry carried in a casket are already being inflated so that now it's grown to be the size of a king's ransom,' Hildegard told him, adding, 'but of more worth is the child's life.'

'And then,' broke in Allard, 'when we reached the Great Barn where we thought they might have been apprehended we found Mark and Godric—' and he completed the story.

By the time he finished his grief was apparent and the shepherd clasped him in a burly hug and shook him by the shoulders and rumpled his hair and hugged him again and again and said, 'He was a good lad, that one. A good lad. We will never forget him, Allard old son, we will never forget him.'

'And now,' added Allard, his face contorted, 'there's poor Mark with his arm hanging half off.'

'The carter won't be there this day. He's in bed with the ague.'

Hildegard made a decision. 'If everything is well here I'm going back to the Great Barn to see what I can do for him. It's clear we're not going to come across the search party tonight. Why don't you, Allard, ride back to the abbey to fetch the infirmarer and his apothecary to see if they can help?'

'Even better,' interrupted the shepherd, 'I'll come with you.'

'Won't your family need protecting?'

'Not with my sister's lad and a couple of his iron-foundry mates here. Fore-warned is fore-armed,' he said, turning to Allard. 'If young Godric and Mark had expected an attack even five armed men wouldn't have bested them. We'll set everything here to our advantage then put our noses to the trail like foxes. Come. Let's go!'

'Agreed, then?' asked Allard as Chad went back into the house, where they could hear him rousing his defences.

'Agreed.'

Chad went one better than they expected when he came outside, shrugging on a cloak, and saying, 'Her lads said take their fresh horses. The quicker we reach the abbey and get those healer fellas on the road the quicker we can hunt the wolves in the fold.'

Reassured by Chad's decisiveness they were soon back on the road and in short time saw the roof of the Great Barn silhouetted again the pale, moonlit sky.

'We'll go round by the side of the chapel, tether our mounts and come in at the back,' murmured Chad. 'Just in case they're paying a second visit.'

A narrow footpath wide enough for their horses to walk along one at a time led off the main track. The path petered out at a small chapel behind the Barn. It was intended for the many labourers who brought in produce from the other granges. They would stay overnight until they could oversee its loading onto river boats. Then it would be shipped round the headland to Hampton or exported overseas. Later the carters would return with stores brought from the ships for the abbey's use.

At this time of year, Lent, it was deserted.

The conversi would already have been summoned to worship in the abbey. Only a few field-workers would remain, as Allard explained.

They tethered the horses and walked back stealthily towards the Barn.

The doors were as they had left them earlier. Chad took out his tinder and lit another flare then, lifting it from the sconce, held it above his head and strode inside.

Hildegard followed him in time to see the tableau of the burly shepherd leaning down in the glow of light to peer into Mark's face. He was sleeping peacefully after the tincture she had given him.

Chad straightened. 'Is this his blood?' He glanced at the dark stain on the ground.

Hildegard nodded. 'We need to move him into the infirmary as soon as we can. I've stitched up the wound but it needs doing properly.'

'Somebody'll have to get up to Beaufre to fetch a couple of oxen with a cart so we can shift him.'

'What about the poor murdered boy? Will the monks send someone to sit in vigil with his body through the night?'

'That's their job.' He turned for the doors. 'Let me go on to Beaufre to bring the ox cart back. I'll send somebody from there to the abbey.'

'Why not let Allard do that? He needs to get involved with something practical and it's a service he can perform.'

Chad nodded but hesitated. 'You'll be here by yourself?'

'I can take care of myself but you are both needed and must leave as quickly as you can.'

A little later, after further reassurances that she could look after herself, the two left, the shepherd and the boy. Hildegard went to sit beside the sleeping patient. His breathing was loud and sounded stronger than before. After a while, feeling less anxious about him, she went to look outside.

Stars stippled the dark-blue vault while in the west behind the trees the sun had earlier declined in a last flourish of luminous gold. It was beautiful enough to make her stand in awe, words automatically on her lips . . . *O lord who art the night and day, Bless us all this night I pray* . . .

She stood on guard near enough to hear if Mark called for anything and watched as the lustre of the moon was wiped from the sky.

The men had had to take the flare with them. It was now darker than dark. Allard had mentioned that the moon would be at the full. The tides had confirmed it but there were clouds now and the pinprick stars began to disappear. Soon not a scintilla of light penetrated the yard or the woods that surrounded it. It was like being wrapped in black velvet. Night enveloped the Great Close.

Impatient for the ox cart to emerge onto the track she listened intently for the noise that would herald its appearance but heard only the usual sounds of the open land, the scuffling of wild creatures in the long grass, the ruffling sigh of the trees, and further off an owl calling to its mate. The mate's reply.

Its echo. Nothing else.

She returned to sit beside Mark. Time passed.

She imagined the riders reaching the grange, their explanations, the return with the cart.

\*     \*     \*

She might have slept for a moment or two because when she opened her eyes it was because something had alerted her. Hoping it was the cart she listened while she peered through the darkness.

It was difficult to make anything out at first. It was a sound too distant, scarcely audible, but it had a steady rhythm and seemed to be coming closer. It came from the direction of the Forest track but it was no horse and cart. Not the carter, then, having struggled from his sick bed. She held her breath.

There was definitely something approaching.

She got up and, feeling her way through the pitch darkness as far as the gate, she expected to hear a lone horseman emerging from the woods. The sound grew in intensity until it was certain it could only be the muffled drumming of horse's hooves.

Still she could see nothing to cause it. No one appeared. No rider. No horse. Despite this the sound became a galloping roar and then, as if passing invisibly by on the track, it began to fade and soon it was no more than a distant drumming, fading, and then gone.

The silence that followed almost made her believe she had imagined it but she worked out that there must have been only one horseman and he must have taken another lower road through the woods, like the side path to the chapel she had not known was there. Even so, without thinking, she had drawn her knife and was still holding it when she returned to the barn.

The night was once more under a prolonged shroud of silence. Mark slept on.

She had been sitting on the ground inside the doorway for a good hour before the unmistakable sound of cartwheels creaking over the ruts could be heard from the direction of Beaufre. Lights flickered between the trees.

She rose eagerly to her feet. Moments later a cart pulled by two massive oxen swayed into the yard. Several men on board were carrying flares. Everything was lit by a lurid glow. She tucked her knife inside her sleeve and went to meet them.

The carter backed his cart up to the barn doors with a lot of shouting and much cracking of a switch.

After the solitude of the last few hours the place seemed to be swarming with people. In fact it was only Chad, the driver of the ox cart, his lad, and Allard, and one other. It was a shadowy figure who kept out of the light.

The driver jumped down and came over to Hildegard. 'Nobody else here yet?'

She shook her head.

'We were discussing whether anybody had brought in those murdering devils yet.'

'Sadly not. But I did hear a rider on the lower path galloping by in a hurry. You must have met him?'

The driver stared at her. Chad and he exchanged surreptitious glances and the carter's lad piped up, 'There is no lower path.'

'I heard a rider going by. It was so loud I could not have been mistaken.'

Chad brushed it aside. 'We're here now. Let's get on.' He marched into the barn, calling to the carter and his boy to follow and shouting, 'Is that the closest you can get that cart? We don't want to disturb him much with the wound he's got.'

Hildegard turned to the fellow lurking in the shadows just as he stepped forward into the dazzle of the flares. First she noticed he was barefoot. Then she saw his hair. It was almost white. A gleaming silver making his young face look even younger.

Sharp features, an ironic tilt to his mouth, and eyes that swept her in a disparaging fashion at once set her against him. He wore a russet tunic and a broad leather belt with a large pouch hanging from it. *Why no shoes?* Then she remembered what the porter had said about the sanctuarymen.

The stranger gave her a sardonic smile. 'It was no horse of this world,' he announced in an oddly inflected accent. 'That was a ghost rider you heard. Look how quick they've disappeared. You've frightened them.'

Did he think her a fool? 'I don't believe in ghosts.'

'Nobody believes in this one until they hear it riding by in the dead of night.'

He went, silent on bare feet, into the barn without another word.

When she followed after a pause he was bending over Mark and feeling along his arm for broken bones with long, sensitive fingers and when she said, 'There's nothing broken. It's a deep knife wound,' he glanced up.

'I noticed. Did you fix it?'

She nodded.

'Good work.'

The others prepared to heft Mark into position so they might carry him out to the cart.

It was a longer drive back towards the grange at Beaufre than the track that led on to the bergerie but it was a shorter distance from there to the abbey. It would make it easier for the infirmarer to come out to have a look at him. At least, that's what Hildegard was thinking as she jogged along with the rest of them through the night, with the other horses tied in a string following.

It seemed, however, that the sardonic fellow, whom no one had introduced, had other ideas. He was first to slide down off the cart when they arrived at the grange.

'Take him inside. I'll have a look at his stitches before we move him again. Let's see if we need to attend to them after all that tussling about in the cart.'

In fact, Mark had lolled peacefully between them, out to the world, his head resting first on one shoulder and then on another, sleeping as comfortably as if he'd been in his own bed. His strong breathing was a reassurance all the way although the carter's lad was given to fits of giggles at the variety of sounds emitted by someone he usually held in awe.

Chad and Allard seemed to agree about what should be done. They lifted Mark off the cart and carried him between them into the grange. The long table in the hall where the labourers ate was soon cleared by the lay-brothers who ran things and the limp body in its bloodstained garments was laid out while the stranger set to work.

Hildegard stepped out of the way as he seemed to know what he was doing. She watched carefully as the lay-brothers clustered round. They had not seen the horsemen with their captive and seemed unbothered by the thought of such ruffians at loose in the Forest. They were mostly muscular field-labourers, in their prime and believed they would overcome any such men should they appear.

It was only when the stranger asked for a knife to cut off the sleeve of Mark's blood-stained undershirt that there was sudden ice in the atmosphere. One or two men stepped back. Ignoring the sudden hostility, the stranger persuaded Chad to hand over the knife in his belt and the sleeve was soon a bundle of bloody rags on the floor. Mark slept on.

Chad held out his hand for his knife and quickly re-sheathed it.

The stranger beckoned to Hildegard. 'I intend to remove your stitches in that coarse thread and replace them with finer ones. I'll need your help. Will you hold the flesh on both sides of the wound as I work?'

'I will.'

'We'll leave the tourniquet.'

The group who had been standing around watching left them to it.

Hildegard glanced at the stranger with a smile as sardonic as his own as they bent their heads over their task. 'You seemed to ruffle a few feathers when you asked for a knife?'

He didn't look up. 'That's because I've killed a man.'

Hildegard felt he might be trying to intimidate her. 'Recently?'

He glanced up. 'You sound unsurprised.'

'Nothing men do surprises me.'

'Heard it all?'

'Many times. I'm always ready to hear it again, however.'

'Well, I'm a sanctuaryman so ask me why I did it, most folk do.'

'If you insist.'

'Go on, then.'

When she didn't answer, he lifted his head and their eyes locked.

He dropped his gaze first and muttered, 'It happened six weeks ago. I have an ungovernable temper. I sought sanctuary here when I realized I would not get a fair trial by the cold, gold-loving administrators of the law.'

'Doubts about the justice of the law must be a view held by a lot of sanctuarymen.'

'Not without good reason in many cases.'

The stitches Hildegard had hastily put in to staunch the blood were removed and the stranger turned to pull a fine thread from a reel he drew from his pouch. He also took a couple of needles from a little book-shaped object which he replaced with care in the pouch. Comparing the needles he chose the finer of the two and stuck the discarded one in his sleeve.

'You're well prepared,' she remarked.

'I have my uses.' His concentration became focused on stitching together the bloody edges of the blade-thrust together leaving only the smallest gap between them. He worked deftly until a line of stitches closed the wound.

'I expect you're sick and tired of telling your story.'

'With new embellishments every day? Yes, you've got me right enough, sister.'

'If there's more I'm sure you'll tell me some time if you want to. Let's focus on this wounded man. Are you thinking of covering his wound with honey when you've finished?'

'I think so.' He added, like someone holding out an olive branch, 'What do you think?'

'It's an obvious precaution against infection.' She turned away from the stranger's intense gaze and called to Chad.

He had been near enough to observe the neat job the sanctuaryman had made. Overhearing what they said he now addressed the cellarer, who in turn cuffed a lad on the head to fetch the honey pot.

Hildegard had a further look at the repair to the blade slash. 'That's a neat job. I can't imagine the infirmarer from the abbey doing any better. Shall the patient stay here this night or shall we take him on? What do you think?'

The stranger asked for water to clean the needle and only after he had replaced it in its exact place in the little cloth book did he answer. 'Best ask the master here. I have no powers of decision.'

Hildegard raised her eyebrows.

Chad turned to a well-set-up fellow standing beside him. 'You heard. What do you think, master? Shall we take him on?'

'I don't want a body here in my keeping. Let the monks have him.' He added, 'I don't mean that harshly. This sanctuary fellow and the nun seem to have patched him up well enough to get him into the infirmary. I don't doubt his survival. But you know the prior, especially with all the trouble at present. I'd prefer to keep out of it.' As if continuing an earlier conversation he said, 'We're masters of our own destiny, as God wills. But we need to know where we stand. That's my view. And I don't see what Avignon has to do with us.'

'Couldn't agree more, me. Sick to death of it we are. Let 'em wrangle if they so will – so long as it don't affect my sheep. I'm not sitting up all night in the cold and rain at lambing just to fill the money chests of some French earl who'd as soon cut the throat of our good English King Richard as look at him.' Turning he said, 'Right, lads, you heard! Let's get him back onto the cart and take him to those responsible for him.'

While the lay-brothers knocked a stretcher together and gently carried Mark out to the cart to put him inside on a pile of feather pillows Hildegard observed that this was the first time she had been able to obey her Prioress's orders: discover what Beaulieu think about the Schism.

Well, from what she'd heard just now it seemed the lay-brothers at least were against the intrusion of Pope Clement into their affairs. But what about the monks themselves? Were they really going to support an opponent of King Richard? The forthcoming attempt to appoint a new abbot to replace Abbot Herring would give the answer to that.

Instead of the straightforward reception of a child heiress into her keeping and safe transportation north with the added knowledge of Beaulieu's allegiance, Hildegard saw that she had been thrust into the drama of an abduction, with a wounded man, a body and a murderer, and the added danger of an armed band at large in the purlieus of a royal abbey. It was not what she had expected.

Her anxiety over Elowen returned with full force and, head bowed in thought, she followed the others out to the ox cart and climbed up beside them as soon as it began to move off.

She happened to glance up. The light of the flares fell full on the stranger's face. His eyes bored into her. When he caught her glance he turned his back. The cart plunged off between the close-packed trees.

# SEVEN

The glimmer of dawn was visible by the time they reached Beaulieu. As they approached the bridge the stranger put a hand on the carter's shoulder. 'Let me down here, if you will.'

The cart slowed and he dropped to the ground, still barefoot, and vanished into one of the hovels near the waterside.

Nobody said anything for a moment afterwards then, over the rattling and banging of the wooden wheels as the ox cart crossed the bridge, the carter said, 'At least you made sure you got your knife back, Chad.'

'You did that right quick,' perked the carter's lad.

'So it's true, is it, what he said about why he's a sanctuaryman?' Hildegard asked.

'True enough, by all accounts. I wouldn't trust him.'

'Does he have a name?'

'He has but whether it's real or just one he gave us, who knows?'

Allard, half asleep, murmured, 'He said he was called Locryn, like the King of the Britons.'

'Told you that, did he?'

'It's what they all call him over there. I had to take his gear across when he arrived.' Allard went back to sleep.

They rolled up to the gatehouse and the noise must have roused the porter because he appeared, spry as ever, to wave them inside after a couple of his men dragged the gates open. The ox cart edged in under the archway.

'Got a wounded man for you, brother. He needs taking to the infirmary right quick.' Chad jumped down from the cart.

'A messenger was sent on to us from the Beaufre,' the porter explained. 'We've already heard about Godric up at St Leonard's. It's a bad business.'

Hildegard alighted. 'Did they find the kidnappers and the lady Elowen?'

The porter shook his head. 'Not a sign. Said they lost the trail in the woods beyond St Leonard's, then the hounds led 'em into a swamp. Those devils must have found they were trapped inside the walls and needed a refuge, so doubled back to St Leonard's and did for Godric.'

'What about the others?'

'Came straggling back around Lauds. If they hadn't been with that Jerusalem monk of yours – Brother Gregory is it? – they'd have been swearing and cussing. Instead they were like lambs – though in mood as sick as dogs.'

'We saw no sign of them.'

'That's because they were advised by one of Sir William's men that he'd heard horsemen out the other way up towards Abbot's Copse. But what a night!' He paused for effect. 'After that, we had one of them sanctuary fellas. Dead drunk he was. Got into a dispute over some point of law that turned into a fight. Glad they're housed over the bridge these days. The prior's all for turning them out for good but he can't until the King agrees.'

With all this information ringing in their ears the men from Beaufre had lifted Mark onto the stretcher again and were carrying him carefully into the precinct through the main gatehouse where Hildegard had to be left behind.

She felt tired out and as soon as she was inside the dormitory she curled up on the straw and shut her eyes. It was not much good. Tired though she was she could not sleep. Where was Elowen and was she still alive? She feared for her even more, knowing that her abductors had murdered Godric at St Leonard's.

At Prime, after hardly any sleep, Hildegard joined the lay-brothers and one or two overnight guests – a merchant and his wife from Hampton, and a group going on to Romsey Abbey – in the impressive church where the daily Offices were conducted from behind a screen to separate the lay congregation from the choir monks.

Hildegard thought she could hear Gregory's tenor voice soaring above the rest but was not sure. She hoped he and Egbert would have the sense to come out of the inner garth to find her as she was desperate to discover what had happened to them during the night.

They must have been enraged at failing to track down the horsemen. In the dark windings of the Forest paths, however, it was no surprise that they had been unsuccessful.

After the last amen, a familiar figure appeared round the screen. Egbert.

He strode towards her down the echoing nave. 'So what happened?' she asked straightaway.

'You heard we didn't find her?'

She put a hand on his sleeve. 'The porter told us. He said something about a swamp!'

Egbert tried to bring a smile to his face but it was more like a frown of disgust. 'Just as bad for Gregory – riding in pitch dark through mud and through briars on a wild-goose chase! It's not his idea of time well-spent. That poor child must be going through hell. But I hear you had a time of it at St Leonard's? A couple of the brothers were dragged out in the middle of the night to go and sit in vigil with a body.'

She told him more of what had transpired after they reached the Great Barn.

He said, 'I'll look in on this other fellow in the infirmary later but we go out again now this very morning. Everyone is desperate to find the child. They're already mustering in the stable yard. You might want to join us? On the other hand, you might well stay warm and dry in the guest house.'

'Will I be any help if I do come along? I don't know this country and if the pony I rode yesterday or something similar is all they can allow me I'll find it difficult to keep up.'

'Stay in the guest house. That's best. I'll inform Gregory.' With a nod he left.

Hildegard had no intention of staying in the guest house. She needed to fulfil two purposes, one, to find which way the wind was blowing in the matter of the Great Schism, and two, to find out if what the horse master had told her made sense. Were the sanctuarymen involved?

So it was, after going up to her quarters to don a thick cloak, she set out. The porter looked worried when she told him where she was going. 'Take Allard with you. He's a handy young devil should there be trouble.'

'I'm sure he's going out with the men in the hunt for Lady Elowen,' she told him.

'Here they come now!' He peered over her shoulder to where a growing band of riders was spilling out of the stable yard. Sir William was at the head. He was looking determined and in as black a rage as ever. She saw him dig his rowels into his horse's flanks and yank at its mouth as it lifted its head. The bit was being pulled so hard it was already making the horse froth at the mouth. Hildegard gave him a black look as he approached but he ignored her.

'Come on, porter. Get those damned gates open, will you!' he roared. 'No time for lolling around. We've a young maid to rescue.' He stood in his stirrups and called back to his men with one arm raised. 'Follow me! A prize of gold to the man who finds her!'

The horses piled past, urged on with varying degrees of force but in fact needing little encouragement as the excitement of the occasion incited the herd instinct and it was a crush to force a way through the bottle-neck that formed at the gates. Allard came up near the tail end, riding a neat little pony not much bigger than the one he rode the previous day, and for a moment Hildegard imagined she might have got her priorities wrong. Maybe she should be out with them after all.

Her misgivings were allayed when he leaned down as he approached saying, 'I can't imagine what we can do in a mass like this. He's called for every able man he can muster to join his own mercenaries and our lay-brothers. There'll be so many of us we'll give these kidnappers such fair warning when we ride up they'll be off before we catch a glimpse of them.'

'Do your best, Allard. God be with you.'

Outside the gates the pursuers began to mill about while it was discussed which way to try first.

'It stands to reason,' Sir William's first-in-command announced, 'they'll have had to stay on the other side of the river where most of the granges are because otherwise we would have heard them pass the gatehouse.'

'Has anyone heard them pass the gatehouse?' William demanded.

Of course most of them shook their heads because they had either been out searching the Forest most of the night or else tucked up inside the Close away from the road that came over this side of the bridge. No one had heard a thing.

'So is it back into the Forest, my lord?' one of his captains was foolhardy enough to ask.

Sir William turned on him. 'Where else, you dolt? You're not such a sotwit you imagine they came this way, are you?' He gestured up the hill where a single track wound round the abbey walls and eventually climbed up towards more heathland and, after many miles across country, went on to the great inlet of water that led to Hampton.

Chastened, the speaker examined his gauntlets as if considering buying new ones.

'We keep to the common-sense side of the river with regard to the incontrovertible fact' – William paused to let his words sink in – 'that the abbey itself stands as guardian against anyone trying to escape to the east.' He gave a supercilious glance round his small army. 'Any objections?'

Gregory and Egbert happened to ride up at that moment, accompanied by a little band of three or four burly monks. They rode right into the silence that followed William's statement of intent and therefore missed what he said. The army began to move off towards the bridge and they had no choice but to follow it.

'Where's he taking us?' Gregory asked when he reached the place where Hildegard was waiting to go out.

He shrugged. 'Mayhap there are some tracks that weren't trampled into nothing last night.'

'Mayhap,' Egbert said, riding alongside him, 'these miscreants will accidentally come into view as we ride randomly about the woods.'

'Mayhap,' Gregory added, 'pigs will fly.'

With carefully blank expressions they rode on.

The sound of hooves clattering over the bridge drowned out the words of their farewells and Hildegard followed thoughtfully in their wake, stepping through the churned-up mud with as little detriment to her boots as possible.

\*     \*     \*

The whole cavalcade had already swept through the hamlet on the other bank as she began to walk towards a crooked line of wattle-and-daub dwellings leaning awkwardly over the water. Outside one was a stall, in truth no more than a three-legged stool with a few small wooden toys laid out in two neat rows and a hopeful though ragged child sitting on the ground nearby. She looked up when Hildegard appeared and gave her an eager smile.

They discussed things for a while and coins were transferred from Hildegard's pouch to the child's sticky fingers and a couple of roughly carved wooden toys followed in reverse. A woman came out with a crust for the child and she and Hildegard passed the time of day.

Before Hildegard could broach a useful question or two they were interrupted by a volley of oaths from a cottage further along the row. Something crashed to the floor within, further oaths followed and then a man came catapulting out of a doorway to land in a heap on the ground. Undeterred he picked himself up and threw himself back inside the cottage. Seconds later two men locked together came roiling out into the lane, first one then the other pounding their antagonist in the face with bunched fists.

The women stopped to stare and the child snatched up the rest of its toys and scuttled back inside the cottage to peep from behind the door.

Hildegard went to shout at the men to stop behaving like brutes but neither paid any heed. To her astonishment she recognized one of them. It was his silvery hair that gave him away even though the other fellow had him in a head lock. She could scarcely believe her eyes. So it had in no way been bravado yesterday when he mentioned his ungovernable temper? As she watched he shook himself free but before she could remonstrate he grabbed his opponent round the shoulders, slammed him hard backwards onto the ground then lifted his fist to deliver an intended knock-out punch.

It was then he noticed Hildegard standing open-mouthed over them and for a second it put him off his stroke. His opponent took his chance, wriggled free, aimed a kick, then ran off down the lane, clutching his ribs.

Locryn, if that was his name, rose to his feet. His face was bloodied and his knuckles were bleeding. He had a red eye that would be black by morning. He straightened his tunic, pulled down his sleeves and with a glance at Hildegard from the corners of his eyes, gave an exaggerated shrug.

To be fair he looked shamefaced. Hildegard did not know him well enough to decide whether this was because he had been caught out, brawling like a brute, or for some other deeper reason.

He was the first to break the silence. 'Well,' he said. 'There it is.' He kneaded his fists and licked the blood off them.

'So I see.'

'I doubt whether you see, sister.'

He dusted himself off and made to go inside the cottage but she stopped him. 'You've alarmed this little child here by your violence. See? She ran inside for safety.'

Two frightened eyes peered at them.

He swivelled his head to stare and his lips curled, 'So you want me to crawl on my knees in contrition?' He gave a sneer. 'It's a lesson to be learned. Violence rules. She needs to know that. I'm not one of your milk and water monks praying for help from the angels. There is no help. We help ourselves or die. Tell her and your monks that as well. It's a lesson they themselves might put to good use in their battle with the false pope. I don't care one way or the other. They can all go to hell for all I care.'

She turned away. 'The monks are too fine for someone like you.'

This made him stop. 'Too fine?' He looked thoughtful. 'So that's how it is?' He paused. 'Come inside and have something to drink with me and explain.' When she hesitated, he added, 'If you dare.'

The hovel amounted to one small square chamber with a bed of straw in a corner, a stool, a pail, and a hook on which hung a grubby cloak. A pitcher of something or other and several clay drinking pots stood next to the door. There was no window.

Although Hildegard sorrowed that anyone should live in such

squalor she set it against the alternative, hanging by the neck, and concluded that he was fortunate enough.

He made no apologies for his condition but poured some water into a cupped hand and dashed it over his face then asked straightaway how the wounded lay-brother they had brought back from St Leonard's was faring.

'I'm not allowed into the precinct so I haven't seen him but I'm told he's beginning to make a good recovery. The infirmarer admired your needlework.'

'And so he should. I'm not a master broiderer for nothing.'

'Is that what you did before the misfortune that brought you here?'

'I was a member of the Guild of Master Broiderers but yes,' he scowled, 'events led them to throw me out.'

'Because of your ungovernable temper?'

'I see you're quoting me quoting them.' He gave that lopsided, satirical smile. 'In my opinion my temper was justified. They did not agree.' He shrugged. 'I should not have used his own dagger on the losel. I give you that. But enough of me, what about you? I hear you were expecting to chaperone the missing heiress back to the North?'

'It's a disaster. The poor child must be in terror of what's to happen. Sir William feels cheated. We have no idea who could have kidnapped her or how to find her until their ransom note is delivered.'

'Raptus. It's common enough in the towns where the daughters of rich men flaunt their purity, along with their jewels.' He added dryly, 'It's one way of getting a husband.'

Stifling her immediate response she asked, 'Is there an opinion on this side of the river about who might have abducted her?'

'Oh, so that's why you're risking your honour by venturing into this den of sin – you're cadging for spies?'

'Who would not? You people are more free in some ways than the monks in their cloister.'

He put his head on one side. 'Do you want me to find out if anybody knows anything?'

'Can you?'

'I expect so.'

There was a long silence while Locryn, so-called, thought things over. He gave Hildegard a straight look. 'In return will you do something for me?'

'If I can.'

'I don't know whether you can but the reputation of you Cistercians may aid my cause.' He gave a desperate glance round the hovel. 'I can't spend the rest of my life here. Every day is purgatory. I must get out and the only way I can do it is if the Guild reinstates me.'

'So how can I help? Surely it's up to them?'

'Put in a good word for me. Anything. Say I was entrapped.'

'A man-at-law would be more useful.'

'Ach!' He threw his hands up in disgust. 'They're not worth the air we breathe. Mine ruined me, taking money from both sides, from me and from my accusers. A lying cheating devil, deserving of hell fire.'

'We're a powerful Order.' Thinking of her abbot, Hubert de Courcy, she said, 'There are many astute law men who defend our interests without recourse to fraud. Maybe one of them can be found to assist you. I make no promises. But you must tell me more about your crime.'

'In case I'm not worth defending?'

She smiled. 'Yes, if you want to put it like that.'

'Let's go and sit on the bench outside, otherwise your reputation will be in tatters. I'll tell you exactly what happened. And then,' he added, 'you can assess whether you want to be mixed up in the affairs of a criminal such as myself.' He spoke with the same satirical edge as before. *Criminal* might be the word he used, but it was a token. He clearly held no belief such a label applied to himself.

The neighbour with the little child selling toys was standing outside her door when they emerged. She gave a black look at Locryn then turned her back.

'See what I mean? I've caused you to be damned already.' He gestured to the bench and when she sat down he placed himself as far away as he could, half-turned as if looking out into the nearby Forest. 'For your sake I sit with my back turned. I'm growing to be wary of women. Once bitten as they say. Well, it's true. I don't trust anyone these days. You're different because you're half out of this midden but outside your sacred walls you'd find a different world.'

'I should say that I have been married and have two grown children. Only when my husband was believed killed in the French wars and I became a widow did I decide the better course would be to join the Order. I did not relish the thought of being some shire knight's wife, unfree, powerless – oh, all that, the midden as you call it.' She smiled. 'What I mean is I'll give you a fair hearing. You will not shock me whatever you say.'

'That's what you told me when we first met. Very well. This is it. I confess, I made a stupid mistake. I believed the woman had some feelings for me. I believed her lies about the nature of her marriage. I felt compassion for her. But it was all a game. Her deepest emotion was boredom. She was bored by her fat old husband and wanted someone to lie with. When I was fool enough to ask her to come away with me she revealed her true feelings. When I foolishly insisted she became frightened. Her brothers set about me one night. Intending, they said, to teach me a lesson . . .' He paused.

'And that's when you—'

'That's when I grabbed the knife one of them held at my throat and turned it on him. I admit I saw red. I did not care about him. I wanted to kill him.' He gazed at her in astonishment at himself. 'I wanted in that one blind moment of fury to wipe him from the face of the earth and pitch him into the pit of hell.' After a pause he added, 'They're right. I'm not fit to live among good folk. It was her I wanted to kill. Not her brother.'

'What happened next?' she asked softly. 'There were witnesses, I suppose—'

'Plenty.' He grimaced. 'Not only her brothers but other guildsmen, among them her husband, the Master of the Guild, no less, his ignorance shattered the moment her name was uttered. He knew in that little flash of time that he had been deceived. His life was a lie. Being who he was he could not admit it and his cronies gathered round, smiling behind their hands – how could the old fool not guess his wife had put the horns on his head? Did he flatter himself that such a young and' – he waved a hand – 'beautiful wife would remain faithful? Only he could imagine it. The rest of them knew the truth. He must have seen it on their faces. It made his need for revenge sharper. He was determined to have me hanged.'

He got up and walked a few paces. When he turned round again, his expression was bleak. 'Heavens, I want to get out of here. I'll do anything to be free.'

'There are ships to France.'

'Yes and I could get work at my old craft over there with no questions asked. *Opus Anglicanum*? They'd bite my hand off. I know my worth. But something makes me want to go back and . . .'

'Reinstate your good name?'

His old smile returned, bitter and sardonic. 'Maybe I want to make sure I murder the right one next time?'

'If that's what you think, I can't help you . . . Obviously.'

He laughed. 'One threat of hanging is enough. Two would be . . .' he lifted an eyebrow, 'greedy?'


# EIGHT


Hildegard heard the bell for Lady Mass, drifting its call to prayer across the river and got up to go. 'Let me know if you hear anything about the little lady Elowen. I'll do what I can about finding someone to represent you.' She was already thinking of Gregory. 'And by the way, unless you want a black eye tomorrow you might apply a leaf of cabbage to your right eye.'

When she reached the end of the row of hovels the woman with the child was gossiping to a neighbour. She looked across at Hildegard and demanded, 'So what story has he been peddling this time, sister? I hope you know he's a liar through and through.'

Hildegard looked directly at her. 'My gratitude for your concern, mistress. We all sin in our own way.' She walked slowly back to the gatehouse deep in thought.

\*     \*     \*

The old couple staying in the lodging house when Hildegard arrived the previous day were now on the point of departure, bags packed onto a patient sumpter pony, the husband astride a cob with his wife behind him. They were on the last leg home after a pilgrimage to Compostela and were keen to get back to their family and friends.

When the wife saw Hildegard leaving the church after Lady Mass she called out. 'Our three days here are up, sister. With regret we must leave. I do hope the problem of the little heiress is soon sorted out. It must be so worrying.'

Hildegard agreed, how could she not, but it was kind of the housewife to show concern. 'I don't suppose you've heard any more this morning?'

'No, but we saw the men leaving. Maybe they'll be in luck. If not, my dear, what will you do? Will the prior allow you to stay longer until she's found?'

'Let's hope that won't be necessary and we find her safe and well this very day.'

'We heard some nonsense about the horsemen who stole her away.' She lowered her voice. 'It is said they went galloping off towards an enormous opening in the ground that suddenly yawned in front of them and there they dragged her down to hell, kicking and screaming. Although,' she added in her normal voice, 'what great sin to warrant such a punishment a mere twelve-year-old girl could commit leaves us wondering.'

'I'm sure there's a more prosaic explanation,' Hildegard replied.

With a click of his tongue her silent husband put an end to this exchange by urging their steed to follow the pony loaded with belongings and soon they were at the gatehouse having a final few words with the porter before leaving.

It was a depressing thought to imagine what Elowen, a prisoner, might be going through in reality and that her ordeal continued.

Later in the day during that characterless period after Nones and before Vespers, the search party was heard clattering back again. Hildegard flew down to meet them. A crowd was already downing tools and flocking into the garth to see if Elowen was with them. Peering over their heads she was disappointed when she could see no sign of a blue cloak.

The mercenaries were jostling ahead of everybody else, followed by Sir William, looking as black as thunder, with no pale-faced rescued girl beside him, only his usual captain and a few other armed men. Then came the Forester's men, grim and silent, and last the cohort from the abbey, Gregory and Egbert still looking quite fresh, while the rest of the brothers were clearly on their last legs. Every horse was up to its withers in mud.

Gregory noticed Hildegard at the back of the crowd and gave her a shake of his head. He gestured towards the stable yard and she began to weave a path through the crowd towards it. He had already dismounted when she reached the corner of the yard where he and Egbert were handing over their mounts to a couple of stable lads.

Egbert gave her a frustrated glance. 'A complete and utter waste of time, before you ask. That man will not listen to reason.' He frowned. 'He insisted that he had some special knowledge and took us through a vast wood where we were immediately lost and eventually, after much fruitless casting about, we found ourselves back where we started. Not only that, he claimed he had secret information that she was being held in a farm there but of farm nor captive not a sign. After that—'

'After that, Hildegard, we spent some time wallowing among mud banks and aimlessly following the paths around the salt-ings looking for a place where a boat might come in to take her off. Of course no landing place was discovered which was not more easily reached by the usual route. Again of boat or prisoner, nothing.'

'And to cap it all a horse was lost. The Prior will not be happy, as it was one of his.'

'What did William hope to achieve by such randomness?'

'He kept saying that his instructions came from an informant who could be trusted, that time was of the essence and if they found her before the ransom note was delivered, he would save himself a heap of gold.'

'Tomorrow,' Egbert told her, 'we are again bidden to ride out. This time we'll quarter the Forest to the north-west of here, up beyond the heath. He says he might have misunderstood what his informant told him, being a stranger to the Forest, and the farm they seek is in this different direction not the other one.'

'Who was his informant?' she asked.

'Nobody knows. William is the only one who saw him.'

She gave him a sceptical glance. 'And I take it you will be riding out with him in the morning?'

The two lads had unsaddled the horses by now and were vigorously rubbing them down and Gregory, glancing in their direction, indicated that they were going indoors. Clearly they had something private to impart. 'We'll come to your guest house and be able to find a drink and a bite to eat, shall we?'

'Indeed.'

One thing that Egbert had inadvertently told her was that at least the absconding maid and her swain had not tried to make their escape by sea. It made sense. If their escape was as unplanned as it appeared they would stick to a route more certain of safety. Any day now they would probably appear seeking sanctuary for their misdemeanour.

'Nothing helpful turned up here either?' Egbert asked as they sat down away from the others at one of the trestles in the guest refectory.

'Not in any sense,' she replied.

'We may have something to tell you about the Schism and the impending election of the new abbot,' Gregory told her. 'Having spent a day riding alongside supporters of the English Chapter it would be odd if we'd learned nothing about abbey affairs.' He gave her a long look. 'Thank heavens for Meaux,' he murmured.

'Is it as bad as that?'

'You won't believe how entrenched they are – neither side is willing to compromise. We were told their discussions are continuing. The Prior wants to assert his right to be in charge but because he is so virulently Clementist the English side won't accept anything he says. Everyone else is too self-effacing to put themselves forward. They prefer to cluster in a group and agree with their companions. No other natural leader has emerged to challenge the prior. He has his coterie among the obedientiaries, which of course puts him in a strong position. The bursar is on his side so they have the cash to call the shots. Meanwhile the ordinary choir monks, the English faction, sit

it out in the hope that someone will step in and tell them what to do.'

If he had had long hair he would have torn at it at this point.

Instead he gave a weary smile. 'The best thing would be if the King issued his orders and told them to do what he says or get out. There will be no other solution.'

'I can't imagine my Prioress at Swyne putting up with such dissension. "Go and pray for guidance," she would say, "let's all find a way to work together. And don't come back until you've found one."'

'But about the girl,' Egbert asked. 'Has her governess any ideas? Have there been any threats or did this attack come out of the blue?'

'To be honest I haven't seen Mistress Goda. She's confined to her chamber with an indisposition, or so I'm told. First thing this morning I went over to the sanctuary to see if I could pick up any rumours from that side, given that they're more free in their contacts than sometimes happens to us monastics – but it was not much help.'

'But?'

'Is my face such a giveaway? I did in fact speak to the fellow who stitched up Mark's wound last night. I've asked him to keep his ears open. You know how rumours fly in these small communities? Sometimes there's a grain of truth in them.'

'But?'

'Again, but, indeed.' She grimaced. 'He's alleged to be an out and out liar, so whatever he happens to tell might be of little use. He also extracted a quid pro quo promise to find someone to help him plead his case in the courts in return for information.'

Gregory poured wine into their beakers and stretched out his long limbs with a weary sigh. Despite the urgency of the situation he drank deeply before lifting his head. 'I might think about that when I've recovered from the day's travail.'

'Was it so bad?' She gave him a soft smile.

His gauntly handsome face relaxed. 'What a ride we had. Interesting country. Good hunting. Deer abounding. William looked as if he wanted to ride off in pursuit. He restrained himself long enough to keep saying, "We must find my son's betrothed. The future of my estate depends on it."'

'Is he in such dire straits?'

'After a year away in Outremer he had a hard time when he took up the reins again. His steward turned out to be a swindler.'

'But that was years ago.'

'Since then bad harvests, those endless floods, the Humber continually breaking its banks. It takes time for land to recover if you want to make a profit from it. I understand he lost a lot of sheep. I admit he's not a man I'd trust but you have to feel sorry for him if it's true, second son and all that. He needs to prove himself.'

'So what do you think has happened to Elowen? You must have a theory. She can't just vanish along with those horsemen.'

'This is my supposition, Hildi, so shoot it down if you wish. I find it hard to believe that she has been taken out of the Great Close,' he began. 'It's not practical. There are gatemen and besides, unless they knew the tracks exceedingly well, they had only a couple of hours' daylight to make good their escape through the woods.'

'But,' she objected, 'they could have lain low somewhere and escaped at dawn, just as you and William's men were setting out from here.'

'True.' His lips turned down. 'We rode out that way but no one at the gate leading on to Lymington quay where they might have hoped for a ship saw anyone.' He turned to Egbert. 'You were listening when that forester came riding back to tell us he'd been out there earlier to quiz the gateman, weren't you?'

'I was. I feared for the fellow who brought such news. I thought there was going to be blood. His information drove William to a fury. "How dare you! Did I tell you to go out there? No, I did not! It's me to give the orders! I want discipline in my followers. I can't have men doing what they want. No one takes the initiative unless I tell them so." That didn't go down well. You should have seen their faces. Somebody muttered about their master being Guido, the Chief Woodward, and they took orders from no one else, especially in their own Forest. Luckily William was too busy shouting to hear this insubordination.'

Both men chuckled though in a rather lugubrious manner.

'Then we checked with the gateman ourselves under Sir

William's direction of course and no one had approached the outer gate for several days, it being Lent and distribution of produce being stopped for a while.'

'Nor had anyone heard horsemen in the night,' Gregory added.

Hildegard remembered how Chad, out at the bergerie, had also told them that he had heard no horsemen passing by on the road.

'I heard one horseman,' she told them, stifling a shudder. 'It was like a dream but I'm sure I was awake. I thought I heard a horseman riding in the same direction as Chad and Allard but no one caught up with them. You must have passed by the Beaufre today?'

'We did,' chipped in Egbert. 'Not that it was any use to us. Nobody admitted to anything we don't already know about.'

'Who was this lone horseman?' asked Gregory.

'According to the sanctuaryman, Locryn, it was a ghost rider!'

The two monks laughed out loud this time. 'I see what you mean about him. He prefers fantasy to fact!'

'It was unnerving,' she was forced to admit. 'I thought the rider must have taken another path nearby, maybe lower down the bank, but the carter's lad from Beaufre said there was no lower path.'

'It would be some local fellow up to a bit of poaching, I expect.' Gregory frowned. 'We've drawn a blank today then, haven't we? Have either of you any idea where best to look next?'

'Aren't you going out with William's men again?'

'I don't think we need to do that. The others might feel it has a purpose.'

'They won't turn out if he's going to lead them such a dance again, surely?'

'There might have been some grumbling and sniggers but obedience prevailed when it came to it, apart from that one spokesman for the foresters.'

Egbert looked thoughtful. 'I had a good talk to them. They told me that the Great Close includes both banks of the river as well as the granges. What if they've whisked her over to the side where William hasn't deigned to look?'

'He sounded adamant that it would be a fool's errand,' Hildegard pointed out. 'He was emphatic.'

'As usual,' grunted Egbert. 'But maybe he'll change his tune if he draws another blank tomorrow?'

The two monks got up to go. 'Come with us after Prime, Hildi. There's no reason why we shouldn't explore the other bank, as Egbert suggests. We're told there's a grange called Otterwood up there on the hill. Maybe it's worth having a discreet look at it?'

# NINE

The remaining guests at the lodge were treated to another rumour going the rounds. That evening as the story was told and retold it was that the little household from St Keverne, intending to swindle Sir William over the dowry, had staged the theft and abduction themselves.

Soon, the story went, the girl herself would be found wandering in the woods but without her casket of treasure. It would be found, if anyone cared to make a search, in the keeping of the St Keverne men-at-arms.

There were murmurs of agreement when this view was expressed. 'That seems the most likely explanation,' agreed a townsman travelling back to Hampton and his glove-making business. 'Given human nature you need look no further, in my opinion.'

'Poor child,' someone else muttered. 'Without her dowry she's got no chance of getting a husband to her father's liking after this.'

'No husband at all, given what might have happened to her,' murmured one of the merchant's wives with a hypocritical little shiver of distaste.

'Isn't her father an earl?' somebody else asked. Someone in the know agreed that he was.

'Perhaps,' said another newcomer wearing a scarlet capuchon, 'we ourselves should join the hunting party to see if our local knowledge might help? I expect this Sir William will be offering a reward?'

Murmurs of agreement rose from some of the visitors while others speculated on their chances of finding her.

As Hildegard left them to go up and get some sleep she heard them planning to join the search party early next morning with an air of open pleasure, as if it were no more than a chance for entertainment. Clearly the abbey had risen in their estimation by providing the opportunity for such unusual sport.

One thing, she thought, as she took off her outer garments, unlaced her knee boots and shuffled them off before lying down in her shift, the St Keverne household were keeping out of things.

On the day before they had been sitting as usual at a trestle placed at a distance from the rest and, as far as she could see, they were as gloomy and anxious-looking as one would expect from servants in these circumstances.

To suggest, though, as the newly arrived guests did, that the household was implicated in the abduction made little sense. It was in their interests that such a marriage between the two families could take place as it would only benefit both. She remembered how Mistress Goda had said she regarded Elowen with as much love as if she had been her own child.

Besides being illogical it wasn't practical. Men would have had to be engaged and where would they come from? How could strangers, not yet landed on the shore, acquire such contacts? It would be nigh on impossible. Unless, she ruminated, sleepless as ever, they already had contacts up here. It was coincidence that William and Earl Richard had met overseas and made their ill-fated vow.

Staring into the darkness she pondered the matter from every angle. Could the monks be involved? It seemed even more unlikely than the household's involvement. What would the monks get out of such an arrangement?

She sat up.

What did they need now they were in such dire financial straits with the pope's new demand for tribute?

They needed cash.

In other words ransom money.

You're thinking wildly now, she warned herself, lying down

again. Go back to sleep. In the morning you'll realize how sot-witted you are.

But she could not sleep. Her thoughts roamed about and would not be shut down. She felt besieged by unanswered questions.

Who gained from the abduction?

Answer: anyone who deemed it worth their while to damn their soul to hell for the sake of a casket of gold and a bride price.

Firmly closing her eyes she decided that for once the question 'who gains?' was one that led nowhere because it led everywhere.

Poor little rich girl, she thought as she drifted off, where is she at this moment? Is she cold and frightened? Is she weeping?

Her thoughts stopped there. The rest of it was too horrible to contemplate.

# TEN

Prime. The outer gatehouse. Rain.

'Never have we seen such weather,' said the monk who was handing out the dole to the sanctuarymen huddled in their worn woollen garments under the arch. 'They call it February Fill-dyke, and rightly so. Let's hope it presages a fertile spring.'

The men took the bread that was being handed out without much of a word beyond a mumbled snatch of prayer in thanks and made off across the river to their own side as rapidly as they could. It was no weather in which to linger and even the leaking hovels on the other side were better than being outside in the full brunt of the rain.

Gregory and Egbert joined Hildegard on the way to the stables as arranged earlier. All three were wearing waterproof cloaks.

Despite that they were reluctant to set forth.

Before they could even reach the stables, however, a voice hailed Hildegard from the gatehouse.

'Domina!'

When she turned the fellow who had spoken lifted his hood a little and she recognized Locryn, or whatever his real name was.

'You asked me to do a favour for you, domina.'

'Yes?'

'I may have news.'

'Can you not come inside out of this rain?'

He glanced at the porter dry inside his lodge. 'With the lady to vouch for me, master, what do you say?'

The porter jerked his thumb over his shoulder. 'No further than the guest house entrance.' He glanced at the two monks. 'You see to him, brothers?'

Hildegard turned to them. 'This is Locryn. I mentioned him to you.'

'We'll vouch for him, porter.' Egbert took Locryn by the arm, 'Come with us, fellow. Let's hasten to find some shelter. Your cloak is wringing wet.'

Together they made their way back into the entrance of the main gatehouse and when they were sheltered from the sweeping gusts that scoured the foregate Hildegard asked, 'So, what is it?'

'Maybe not much,' he replied, pushing back his hood to reveal his startling silvery hair. With rain streaking his face he looked eager to please. 'It's this. A word from someone I will not name—'

'Then why should we trust you?' Egbert interrupted.

'You may not. That's up to you,' replied Locryn. 'I'm simply doing as my lady here requested. See me as a go-between.'

'Let's hear it, then,' urged Gregory, impatient as ever.

'It's only a whisper. Last night when the search party returned, the suggestion was floated that the young lady Elowen might not be hidden in a specific place as your Sir William imagines, but may be kept on the move to make it more difficult for her to be found.'

'And does your rumour-monger suggest anything more?'

'I'm not sure. I think he might have had the idea that she could be moved like the queen in a game of chess.' He hesitated and then added, 'They may be thinking that after you've searched

one place and moved on to another, they can return her to the place already written off. One jump ahead of you, see? You might keep ahead if you return in secrecy to where you've already searched.'

'So not only are we looking for a needle in a haystack but a haystack that keeps moving?' Gregory scrutinized the young man. 'Did you intend this to be helpful?'

'I hoped it might be.'

'Do you know where we looked yesterday?' Egbert asked.

Locryn shook his head. 'How could I? I was not of the party.'

'And no one mentioned where we went?'

He shook his head. 'This talkative fellow didn't stay around long enough to go into details. The day had exhausted him in spirit if not in body. He was for getting off to his bed.'

'Likewise,' grimaced Egbert.

Hildegard was looking askance at Locryn. 'So you're here to suggest that the search party retraces its steps?'

'It will not be as bad as you seem to think as they will only need to search the farmsteads they have already searched to see if anything has changed.'

'The farmsteads, the barns, the bushes, the blades of grass, in fact anywhere where a child of twelve might be hidden?'

Gregory's derisive tone was not lost on him. Locryn turned to Hildegard and heatedly reminded her what she had promised. 'You told me you would try to find an attorney for me!' he shouted. 'One who is not corrupt!' He glared at her and bunched his fists. 'I thought it was a promise but I see that you monastics are all the same! Sweet words, no action! What else should I expect!'

'All is not lost,' she soothed. 'We'll consider what you've told us just as my brothers here will consider your grievance with the law to see if they can help you. Why don't we meet again later today at Compline?' She glanced at the meagre dole in his hands, thinking he might welcome the chance to eat in the refectory. 'You can explain your situation to Brother Gregory. He's trained in the law. If anybody can help he will.'

Locryn's anger evaporated as quickly as it had arisen. 'Is there a chance?' He glanced uncertainly from Egbert to Gregory and back.

'Let's do as Hildegard suggests. We'll inform Sir William of this rumour before he sets out and let him decide. We'll tell the porter to allow you entry at Compline. How's that?' Egbert spread his arms.

After Locryn nodded his thanks he dashed out into the rain again and they watched him sprint as far as the gatehouse with the meagre tatters of an old cloak held above his head. The porter glanced over to the monastics and Egbert raised one hand.

'I see what you mean about him, Hildegard. What is it?' He turned to her. 'Something not quite on the level?'

'It's his adopted name, for a start,' Gregory replied. 'King of the Britons? I take it that's not his real name?'

She shook her head. 'I haven't told you the story he gave me either. But to our main task. Are we going out now or not? We should. The poor girl is still missing and her rescue is our only purpose.'

'Let's find William before they leave.' Egbert began to wrap his cloak more closely round himself. 'I'll tell him what we've heard. Maybe he'll split his army into two, one half to quarter the heathland, as intended, the other to revisit those farms we looked at yesterday. You wait here. No point in us all getting soaked.'

'Now, Hildi,' Gregory said after Egbert left, 'what do you think about this latest suggestion concerning her whereabouts?'

'That it is entirely alleged? One thing in its favour, she'll need to be close by when they deliver the ransom. If that's what they're planning. We're only assuming that, though.'

'True. But without it why take her?'

'Yes, we have to believe in the ransom. His story, Locryn's I mean, sounds plausible. It's true he could have made it up to get what he wants – expert help from a man-at-law.'

'At no cost to himself.'

'What a web, Gregory. How do we work out what's true and what's not?'

'I trust your good instincts in this. What do you really think of him? I imagine he might be found attractive to women?' His dark eyes fixed closely on her expression.

'Possibly,' she agreed. 'It's what got him into trouble at the start, if his story is true.' She thought a moment. 'He might appeal to women who like enigmas!'

'Women like you?'

She ignored the last remark. 'I want to believe in him because there's got to be a solution to the mystery of Elowen's whereabouts but I'm guarded against giving him my trust too soon for fear of being deceived. Something about him makes me feel he's had a rough time and deserves a little help. Let's wait a while and see what transpires. Remember what they say – by his deeds shall ye know him? Meanwhile, despite the weather, and despite William's intentions, I think we should get on up to this farthest grange to spy out the land as quickly as we can.'

Holding their hoods against the driving rain they hurried towards the stables in the expectation that Egbert would soon catch up with them. He did so.

His face had the resigned expression of someone being coerced into a commitment they did not want. 'Orders from Sir William but before I tell you what they are the first question to ask is, do we owe him support or not? He's not our lord. Above him is our allegiance to our Order.'

'Of course we don't owe him allegiance, let alone loyalty. His reputation would preclude that,' asserted Gregory. 'What does he want us to do? I can tell from your face, dear brother, that it's not something to your liking.'

'You can guess,' Egbert told him with a gesture of dismissal. 'He expects us to muster the monks from their cloister and set out to revisit the farmsteads we searched yesterday. It seems he had already heard the rumour Locryn told us about, or so he pretends.'

'I'm inclined to think we should pretend too – that we haven't got your message. We need to search this bank next. We're first for Otterwood.'

'In that case so am I.'

Their hired horses were not yet saddled and ready to go and while they waited rain lashed in at the stable doors.

Egbert gave a grimace when he looked outside. 'This isn't going to let up.'

Just then a small figure came running across the yard with a square of oiled cloth over his head. It was one of the novices. His sandals slapped on the shiny wet pavers as he approached and the hem of his gown was soaked through. He came hurtling in through the stable door and nearly fell at their feet. 'Brothers! Sister! Quick! Praise the Lord I found you before you set off. Come! As quickly as you can!'

'What is it, lad?' asked Egbert, pulling him to his feet. The boy was breathless and could scarcely get his words out.

'We are threatened with excommunication! All of us! Every lord abbot in England, Wales, Scotland and Ireland! And everybody in every abbey therein! We are done for!'

He gripped Egbert by the arm as if he were his saviour and began to sob. 'Brother, save me! I don't want to burn forever! I've tried to be good but that bird's egg was mine. It was I who climbed the tree and found the nest. And I've said I'm truly sorry—'

'Hold still, lad. It can't be so bad. Excommunication? You must have got it wrong.'

'No, no, I haven't. The papal messenger rode in at the gates early this morning. As soon as he finished his ablutions he had audience with the lord prior, seeing as our poor, dear abbot, save his soul, is dead and in his tomb. We shall pray to him for help but they're saying we're still in dire jeopardy of our souls!'

'Let's get this straight. The papal envoy has arrived? Now, first thing to ask – is he from Rome or Avignon?'

'He's not the pretend one. He's the real one in Rome, from Pope Boniface IX!'

'Worry not, lad. Why would he want to excommunicate us?'

'It's because we won't pay his taxes.'

'The law says he can't exact payment from us. We're protected by something called the Statute of Carlisle. It's been in force for decades. He can't go against that. It's the law of England.'

Gregory crouched down and asked the boy, 'Was it a papal envoy who arrived?'

The boy looked confused. 'That's what I'm saying, brother.'

'Or was it the Collector of Taxes from London?'

Bewildered by the question he shook his head. 'I know not, brother. *Mea culpa.*' He began to sob again.

'It's not your fault, lad. We won't let him excommunicate you. Not even for a bird's egg. Now who told you to fetch us?'

'The lord prior. He said, "We must fight this together," and then some of the monks walked out in a rage.' The novice added, in a forgiving sort of tone, 'I suppose they were afraid of being excommunicated and finishing up in hell forever despite all their praying.'

'Have you instructions to go elsewhere after informing us of this new turn in the quarrel?' Egbert asked him.

'No, only to fetch you to the prior so you can support us because your abbey must be an ally of ours.'

'Aye, must we, despite you being allied with Cîteaux and its daughter houses in France.'

Gregory frowned. 'Come, fear not. We will do our best to save you from hell fire, with all your convocation of monks besides.'

The two monks gave speaking glances to Hildegard and began to go out into the rain while pulling up their hoods and making sure their waterproofs were tightly gripped against the weather.

As they left, Hildegard hesitated. 'I cannot come with you. Will you let me know what they decide?'

'I can tell you that now,' affirmed Egbert. 'If they have any fight they'll resist paying the subsidy. How much is it, all told? Six thousand gold florins?'

'Do you believe they'll risk excommunication? Even when they'd be compelled by the seculars to pay up to keep the peace?'

'King Richard will never allow that!' Hildegard was adamant.

'The statute forbids payment of taxes to the mother houses in France,' Gregory added. 'Come, let's go and find out how they're going to resist such an outrageous demand.'

With a horse already saddled up she considered what it was best to do while the monks were in chapter. Allard had been hovering nearby ever since he heard the novice excitedly warning the monks about the possibility of being cast into hell's flames. Now he approached her.

'Are we conversi threatened with hell fire as well, domina? I don't relish that!'

'I expect you'll be safe enough, Allard. It's only the tonsured monks and probably us nuns who expect to be fleeced by the pope. Lambs of God as we are.'

Her dry smile elicited a wide grin from the youth despite his recent grief. 'While I'm sorry for you all I'm relieved to hear we might escape!'

'Are you able to ride out with me as my protector again?' she asked.

His face lit up. 'I'll go and bend my knee to the master. Where are we going?'

'I'll tell you as soon as we set out.'

While the monks had been talking she had been turning over the rumour Locryn had heard and how it seemed to have some sense in it. If the kidnappers hoped to have payment for their ransom demand, if they were indeed hell-bent on such a plan, then they would clearly need to stay somewhere within the Great Close. It was plausible that they would hit on a cat-and-mouse game to stay one jump ahead of their pursuers. Whether Locryn could be trusted was a question to be put to one side for now. William's informant seemed to confirm the plausibility of the rumour.

Allard returned, beaming widely, and without a word went at once to one of the stalls and brought forth a dappled grey that side-stepped in a delighted fashion when he put the saddle on her back.

Hildegard readjusted her cloak as they rode out into the brunt of the rain. 'We'll stop off near where the sanctuarymen live and ask more about the rumour that's going the rounds.'

'If you mean the one about the kidnappers' game of hide and seek, the foresters were groaning about it earlier. All they want is to chop down a few trees, not go chasing about their own woods in what they believe to be a humiliating pursuit that will only serve to turn them into a laughing-stock. They're beginning to say the little heiress brought her own fate on herself.'

'How so?'

'By carrying a casket containing gold without several armed men beside her. What folly, they say. It was an open invitation to every robber around. And of course, domina, you know who they mean by that.'

'These renegades we're about to meet. Yes, I know. They do get the blame for much, deserved or not.'

'The world,' he added with childlike sagacity, 'is a most sinful place that such men should live in it and so often prosper.'

As he was speaking it crossed Hildegard's mind once more that it was slack of the armed men on board the cog bringing Elowen to Beaulieu not to have disembarked first as protection before she even set foot on dry land. If they had done so this whole sorry mess would have been avoided.

When she asked Allard if he had seen much of the Cornishmen he replied in the negative. 'They're not much trusted and are also held to be partly to blame. When they tried to hire horses to join Sir William he ordered us to refuse as he did not want such men riding with him.'

'And Sir William has already left?' she asked, surprised.

'He left by the north gate. It leads up to the heath. He's getting his men to quarter it so that, as he says, "no stone is left unturned." He's also sent a small group to go through the places they searched yesterday.'

'What's it like outside the north gate?'

'Apart from one or two isolated farms it's mostly marshland and with all this rain it's going to be a quagmire – I fear for my horses,' he added on a different note.

The first of the sanctuarymen they came across was an elderly fellow with the bearing of a Roman senator. It would have been intolerable to ask him for what reason he was having to flee the law for the loss of what might have been a venerable old age. He agreed at once when she asked if the rumour she had heard was believed among his fellow sanctuary-seekers.

Standing in the shelter of his doorway he hooked two thumbs into the bands on his cotte. 'The folk here know nothing,' he told her, 'but they know how criminals think. These abductors have made no request for a reward for the safe return of this young woman. Why not? Answer that and you will probably have the identity of these devils.' He began to chuckle despite

having to screw his eyes against the rain that suddenly blustered in through his doorway. 'Mark my words, love will be at the bottom of the whole thing. The young have the misfortune to think of nothing but love. Where does it ever lead? I'll tell you. It leads to perdition.'

'My gratitude for your help,' Hildegard said, about to continue up the street.

He saluted her with all the rigour of an old soldier. 'Bless you for your compassion, my lady.'

Doubtful about whether she deserved the compliment, she handed over a few coins. She was beginning to believe that Elowen must be partly to blame for her capture and felt irritated by such naivety if it were so. Was life so different down at St Keverne that they imagined people could walk the world in safety with all their wealth on show? What was the earl thinking to allow his daughter to venture forth in so innocent and unprotected a manner?

'So now,' Allard turned his head, unaware of her thoughts, 'which way, my lady Hildegard? North to join the quartering of the heath or back towards St Leonard's?'

# ELEVEN

Later she apologized for bringing him out in such vile weather on a fruitless and ill-judged quest.

A few miles along the track in the direction of the Great Barn they had come across a group of three or four horsemen emerging out of the slanting rain. Recognizing Hildegard, the men stopped to tell them they had been instructed to search all the places they had searched previously. 'If,' their spokesman added, 'the hostage has been returned to one of them as Sir William believes, we'll find her – and if not, not.'

They seemed sceptical about the whole endeavour and she wondered how thorough their search was but riding along with them she was glad of the extra protection they afforded as they reached St Leonard's. Swept by gusts of sleet and rain it was

desolate now. The great doors were shut and, as they discovered, locked against intruders.

When they went on to the chapel they found two monks in vigil with the body of Godric covered by a white shroud lying before a little altar aglow with candles. Allard was stoical and knelt before the cross for some time in the mellow light with his head bent. When he got up to re-join her she noticed the glint of tears on his eyelashes.

The two vigil monks stopped their prayers long enough to assure them that no one unknown to them had been near the chapel since the previous night when, they said, they had had the body carried to the place where St Leonard might be hoped to offer his protection in the difficult transition between this world and the next.

She repeated their words to herself. *No one not known to them?*

Ever suspicious she doubted, even so, that it would be worth questioning them further.

It was inconceivable that the abbey men themselves were implicated in the plot but even if they were they would hardly be betrayed by an incautious word from their own monks. With little to see here and no chance of learning anything afresh they turned away.

The men in Sir William's search party were soon satisfied that no twelve-year-old girl along with an indeterminate number of horsemen were concealed about the place and they too began to ride off. Hildegard and Allard decided they were best left to it.

'I fear this is going to be another wasted day,' she observed. 'My heart bleeds for the little captive. Nobody seems to have any idea where she might be.' They sat astride their horses at the roadside and looked both up and down. 'What about these farms you mentioned, Allard, the ones on the heath? Shall we have a scout round there?'

They retraced their steps along the straight track past the ox grange at Beaufre and further, skirting the hamlet near the bridge at Beaulieu and on again, deep into thick woodland with the track dwindling until it was no wider than a deer trail between mature oaks.

Eventually Allard spurred his horse forward and urged
Hildegard to hurry as he emerged from the woods. 'Look! There
it is, Black Down.'

It was a barren gravelly stretch of tufted grass as far as the
next distant treeline, and Hildegard gazed across with a sinking
heart. One or two hovels appeared, no more than hastily thrown
up gamekeepers' huts, and interspersed between them, over-
grown and mysterious, lay dozens of grave mounds.

'Those are the burial places of the ancient folk,' he explained.

'Britons? The ones who first lived in these parts.'

He agreed. 'We keep away from them out of fear of their
magic. They protect their graves with fiendish spells that can
mean death to we invaders if disturbed.'

A quick glance at his expression showed that he was genu-
inely wary. Hildegard herself shuddered. The memory of the
invisible horseman came back to her, alarming because no one
else had heard it. When she mentioned it again Allard looked
thoughtful.

After a pause he said abruptly, 'Come, let's go down to have
a look round and see if the graves of the ancients can tell us
anything. Hooves in the night?' He gave a nervous smile. 'Maybe
we can risk them.'

Reassuringly she added, 'It's the sort of thing to suggest
mortal men bent on poaching the king's venison.'

So far, despite the vast expanse of open country, they had seen
no sign of Sir William's men quartering the area. It might have
already yielded the fact that it held no secrets. When they
reached the first hut it was as desolate as it looked from afar.

A fire pit, a small one in the middle of the earthen floor, was
full of dry ash showing that no fire had been laid for some time.
There was nothing else to see.

They rode on. Rain was still slicing down but somehow, up
above the Forest as they were, the air seemed fresher, open to
the great skies and less heavy with the accumulated fumes of
decaying woodland.

Avoiding the grave mounds they approached one or two
other huts but they were clearly only temporary shelters.
Riding on, however, they eventually came to a more substantial

stone-built farmstead. It was not big enough to be classified as a grange and although it was protected on three sides against the prevailing south-westerlies by a few stunted and wind-bitten ash trees, it had little else to safeguard it, no ditch, no palings. It looked derelict. A door creaked back and forth on its hinges.

Hildegard thought it unlikely that Elowen would be hidden here.

It was too open, too undefended. But while they were still screened by the trees she got down from her horse and threw the reins over a branch. 'Let's approach on foot as discreetly as we can. Just in case.'

Allard did as she suggested and together they made their way through a copse at the back of the building. A lean-to against one side had a rather fine black horse within. Its noble head peered over the stable door and lifted with some imperiousness as they approached.

Hildegard and Allard exchanged glances. Intending to fondle it with the hope of keeping it quiet while they looked round, the moment she set foot in the yard the back door flew open and a man came out.

She froze. He was big and broad-shouldered and walked with a self-confident swagger. At first he did not see her but strode out, whistling, and went to the stable to re-emerge a moment later with a bucket. A spring trickled into a stone trough nearby and she watched him dip the bucket into the water then re-enter the stable.

While he was out of sight she faded back into the trees but to her horror Allard seemed rooted to the spot. He was standing in full view and made no move to get out of sight.

Before she could call to him the man came out again, glanced across the yard, and noticed Allard at once.

With a genial smile he took stock then began to stroll towards him, calling distinctly, 'So who have we here? An uninvited guest?'

Allard seemed unable to find an answer.

The stranger smoothed his left hand down the length of a prodigious black beard.

Allard did not move.

The stranger came right up to him, suddenly dropped the bucket to the ground, and grasped the young stable lad with both hands round the neck.

'You skulking spy! Did the prior send you?'

He shook him to extract an answer and Hildegard, enraged, was about to go to him when Allard came to his senses.

With a swift knee into the man's groin he butted him in the face as he jerked forward then did what Hildegard herself would have done and ran for his life.

She was already pulling free the horses' reins and was in the saddle at once, leading Allard's mount so he could jump astride as it broke into a gallop. Before the stranger could reach them they were galloping at ferocious speed in a wild flight without direction and were soon in among the grave mounds, skirting the wallows where the deer went to drink and putting as much distance between themselves and the stranger as they could. The hooves of their horses squelched through the bogs caused by days of rain and became the only sound above the desperate panting of their horses.

Eventually Hildegard gasped, 'Where are we going, Allard? Slow down!'

Allard carried on with gritted teeth. 'We're going as far as we can. Stay with me!'

They were almost at the treeline on the other side of the heath and as soon as they were sufficiently far from the farm to get in amongst the scrub slowed and eventually drew to a halt. He was white-faced and breathing heavily with fright.

She exclaimed, 'What is it? You look as if you've seen a ghost!'

'And so I have! That man is dead!'

'How can he be dead?'

'I saw him dragged away in chains by the sheriff's men myself. He's a notorious gang-leader and they say he murders anybody who gets in his way. Only the Devil knows what crimes he's committed. He sought sanctuary with us and ran things as he wanted but then, incautiously, stepped outside the Close to carry out yet another crime when the Sheriff of Hampton and his men were lying in wait to take him to the gallows.' Allard was shaking. 'I've never had such a shock in my life.' He got his breath back

enough to add, 'If anyone is leading the sanctuarymen in any evil-doing it'll be him. His name is Black Harry!' He gave her an astonished glance. 'How many of those felons at the gates of Beaulieu know he's back? It shows one thing, we cannot trust them in any way whatsoever!'

# TWELVE

Giving the farmstead a wide berth, they walked their horses in the direction of Beaulieu when they thought it was safe to do so. It gave them chance to talk.

'Why would the sanctuarymen not announce that he's back?' Hildegard asked. 'Surely for their own sakes it's best to hand him over to the sheriff?'

'He's a great lord among the criminal fraternity. He has men who will do whatever he asks. I believe they would die for him. Even in sanctuary he was able to deter his rivals from taking revenge. He has more than the power of an abbot because an abbot has to appear to follow the law and yet Black Harry can arrange everything to suit himself and his own dark needs with no law on earth to stop him.'

'He did not seem so vile – until he grabbed you round the neck.'

'That's his method. He is affable enough until he has his victim where he wants them. Then,' he slit two fingers across his throat, 'God help you.'

'In that case we're lucky to have made our escape.' She narrowed her glance. 'I take it you believe he's behind this abduction, then?'

'I haven't had time to think about it,' he replied. 'But now I know he's back on the scene I can think of no one more likely.'

'To get wind of the arrival of an heiress, to organize her kidnap, and then, possibly, to demand a ransom. And all under the protection of the ancient right to sanctuary. I see.' She turned to him. 'And because he has spent time within the Great Close he will know the lie of the land as well as anyone?'

'That's about it.' Allard looked terrified. 'I'm afraid for that poor little heiress now. I can see no way of saving her from the claws of two such men as Sir William and Black Harry, the one careless of her welfare and with no proper plan, and the other with intentions as black as any conceived in hell.'

'It sounds as if her life hangs by a thread. The good will of Sir William when he receives a ransom demand cannot be counted on.' Poor little Elowen, she thought. An innocent in the midst of such venery.

'We must let Sir William know about this,' she said despite what she felt about him. 'He's probably unaware of the existence of this Black Harry, so-called. We'll return to the abbey in time for Sir William's return. Come, Allard. Let's get back.'

It was another ride through thick woodland and somehow or other Allard mistook one indistinct trail for another and they suddenly found themselves in a clearing they hadn't seen before. A rough shelter partly hidden by thorn brakes was built among the trees. A meagre fire sputtered under a roughly woven canopy of branches.

Tending it was a smoke-stained lad, his hood up, and when he heard them crashing from out of the undergrowth he sprang to his feet and ran back a few paces towards the shelter as if to hide. When Allard rode up he backed off with one arm raised to protect himself from the blows he obviously expected.

'Good day, young sir,' Allard greeted in amiable tones stopping a little way off so as not to alarm him further. 'I beseech your help. We have strayed off the path back to the abbey. May we encroach on the kindness of your heart and beg you to set us right?'

The lad pointed dumbly back the way they had come. Before he could ask for further explanation a second lad, taller than the first and maybe an elder brother, burst from behind the shelter and addressed Allard in a forthright if not threatening manner.

'Leave him alone! He has lost the power of speech,' he told him. 'If you want the abbey go back the way you came then where the path breaks into three take the one on your right

hand. Keep on for a couple of miles and you'll come to the path you seek.'

He went over to the younger boy and put an arm round his shoulders to urge him under the shelter out of the rain. Before following him inside he lifted his head. 'Who are you?'

'I'm a stabler from the abbey and my companion is a guest with us. We seek a girl-child taken by kidnappers but two nights since. We're in fear for her safety. Have you happened to see or hear something that will lead us to one such?'

The lad took a pace forward, his brother hanging onto his arm as if to pull him back, and he patted him to reassure him and asked, 'Has she not been seen since then?'

Allard replied, 'No, they seem to have spirited her away. Might you have spotted something to lead us to her?'

'We may have. We were with our woodsman father not long ago and saw horsemen out yonder.' He pointed in the opposite direction to the abbey.

'You mean near Hawk Hill?' Allard narrowed his glance.

'Yes,' replied the boy at once.

Allard raised one hand without asking anything further. 'My thanks.' He wheeled his horse round to re-join Hildegard. They rode on a little way until he stood up in his stirrups to gaze back towards the glade as if to penetrate the screen of trees.

'Did you hear that?' he exclaimed. 'He's lying through his teeth! There is no way he could have been out at Hawk Hill or anywhere near there this morning and be back here now. Not on foot. Not in all this rain and with the delay of having to skirt a hundred new ponds and wallows. Not unless he flew like a hawk. Did he look like a hawk to you, Hildegard?'

'Why would he lie to us?'

They exchanged glances.

'We'll stay around for a while and see what happens next.'

She rode her horse deep into a thicket and Allard followed.

After a while the woodland settled down after the disturbance made by the presence of human beings. Birds, forgetting they were not alone, now began to call to each other. A rabbit scuttled across the path. A fox followed, distracting itself by the

beguiling scent of other creatures worthy to be hunted. Rain continued to fall in a drenching pock-pock of drops landing on the winter leaves.

'This might be a long wait,' she murmured. 'What would a woodsman be doing out here this morning?'

'A question I cannot answer. He ought to be with the search party, surely?'

With the steady roar of the rain in their ears they were lulled into a prolonged wait and Hildegard was beginning to feel she might easily fall asleep if only it wasn't so cold when a vibration rising up from the ground alerted her. 'A rider?' she whispered.

'Must be the woodsman,' he whispered back. 'But mounted?' He raised his eyebrows.

Thinking it wiser to sink even deeper into the undergrowth they did so and after a moment or two a single rider became visible, following the same path they had taken themselves after rousing Black Harry. He wore a gambeson under his cloak and carried a hawk on his wrist.

'That's no woodsman,' murmured Allard, bringing his lips close to Hildegard's ear to prevent himself from being overheard. 'He must be a poacher.'

Nobody followed. Only a brindled hound loped sharp-eyed after his master.

Allard slid from his horse. 'I'm going back on foot. It's not far. I want to see what happens. Is that their father, do you think? Are they a family of poachers?'

Without waiting for Hildegard to persuade him otherwise he disappeared but was back in no time. His look of confusion was soon explained. 'He rode right past.'

'So you didn't recognize him?'

Allard shook his head.

'My guess is he's come from the abbey.'

'He's no one I know.' Allard was certain. 'A guest maybe?'

'Or one of the Cornishmen? Given that they were forbidden to ride out they're kicking their heels.'

'So he procured a horse from somewhere? And that was a falcon no less, a peregrine. And the keen-looking pointer was of good lineage too.'

Leaving the implied question hanging in the air, they remounted and clicked their horses on.

Before they reached the gatehouse Hildegard asked Allard again if he was still certain the man they encountered at the farm was Black Harry. He knew he was right, he told her and he was going to warn his master that he was back.

Rain was keeping everyone on the sanctuary side of the river indoors but the porter put his head out when he heard them arrive at the side gate.

'Wait on, I'll let you in.' Then Allard told him whom he had seen. At first the porter did not believe him but Allard wasn't known for lying and his honest outrage was convincing.

'Get on and tell everybody you meet. We don't want that sort round here again. He had some of them other sanctuarymen scared half out of their wits for going against him. We want none of that. The sheriff needs to be informed right away.'

As a monk he was able to hurry up to the cloister to find somebody in authority while one of his assistants held the gates.

Hildegard and Allard returned to the stables and Allard, after pouring out all his fears to his master, stood by while one of the younger lads tended his horse. He was looking so far away Hildegard asked him what was on his mind.

'Nothing,' he mumbled. 'Just thinking. I'm amazed he could be so brazen to turn up here again, that's all. It's obvious what has brought him back. He must have heard about the dowry and thought he would get in and steal it as soon as those poor folk set foot ashore.'

With the porter's efforts and the presence of several determined-looking monks, a band of lay-brothers drawn from the granges for Lent was soon assembled in the yard. They wanted Allard to show them where he had encountered the man they all referred to as Black Harry and when he described the farm they knew of it straightaway and assured him he need not bother to ride out with them having just got back, but to stay in the dry.

As they moved off, armed for the most part with cudgels, he still wore a thoughtful look.

Hildegard said, 'I'll go and find out where Gregory and Egbert are and let them know what's afoot.' She thought it

strange that they had not appeared as soon as the call for help was made.

Stepping round puddles, hood held tight, she went over to the guest lodge to glance into the refectory in case they had decided to come over after their meeting about the exactions of Pope Boniface but there was no sign of them. She went as far as the church door and poked her head inside. A sacristan was going round putting out the candles after the last Office.

She ventured as far as the screen and as soon as the sacristan disappeared she stepped through. At the far end near the altar a group of monks were discussing some matter with much heat. She knew none of them.

Returning to the yard she was in time to notice Allard leaving by the postern. The porter shouted something after him but he didn't even turn his head.

When she reached the archway she asked, 'Brother Porter, do you know where Allard is off to?'

'He'll be hell-bent on getting the truth from those scoundrels in sanctuary. He believed all their stories about repentance. He has too much compassion. "They are paying their penalty," he kept saying but he's learning the hard way that you can't trust 'em. They mean no good to anybody. He feels they've betrayed him, I expect. "Why did they not say Black Harry had escaped the hangman? Did they not know?" I told him, "You'd have to be an angel to imagine they had no knowledge of his escape." Probably all Hampton knows he's free! He'd have the hangman in his pocket, that one. Such is his reputation.'

Hildegard crossed the bridge. Allard was standing outside one of the hovels remonstrating with someone inside. As she set foot on the bank a large fellow, familiar as the one Locryn had been exchanging blows with the previous day, loomed in the doorway. He was twice the size of young Allard but no concept of chivalry coloured his actions. He went straight up to the youth and knocked him down.

For a moment Allard lay curled up on the ground. Hildegard began to run towards him. Then, as he slowly staggered to his feet, another figure came sprinting from further down the row and hurled himself at the big fellow.

She was not surprised to see that it was Locryn. He grabbed the man by the hair then swung him round and got him in an arm-lock and, despite his curses and brute size, began to edge him towards the riverbank.

A brief skirmish followed when it became obvious what Locryn intended but it was too late. With a hard shove and a kick to his backside he pushed the man into the water.

He made a loud splash but did not go under. The tide was too low, the sandbanks numerous, and he could only rear up, slipping and stumbling in the mud with river water up to his waist and hard rain lashing down on his head. When he tried to clamber back Locryn kicked his hands off their purchase and shouted something. The man argued and then apparently gave in. He was covered in mud. He floundered about while Locryn marched back towards his hovel.

As his rescuer drew level Allard made as if to thank him but Locryn turned his head and stalked past without a word.

By this time Hildegard was near enough to see that Allard's nose was streaming with blood.

His assailant waited until Locryn was off the scene before he climbed back up the muddy bank then he shuffled off towards his shack with as much dignity as he could summon.

Gregory caught sight of Hildegard and Allard as they were re-entering the Close. He observed Allard's bleeding nose with interest. 'What have we here? Another battlesome lad?'

Allard mumbled something defiant and it was left to Hildegard to explain what had happened. 'But,' she turned to Allard, 'I'm confused about what caused him to punch you like that.'

Gregory patted Allard on the back. 'Here, clear the blood with this.' He drew a cloth from one of his sleeves and insisted on Allard doing as he was told. 'Now answer the question. Convince us our sympathy is not misplaced.'

'I accused him of being a liar,' Allard replied in a muffled voice. 'I told him he must have known Black Harry had escaped the gallows and had set up camp at the farm near the burial grounds.'

'What did he reply?' Gregory bent his head.

'Hildegard saw his reply. It was this.' He indicated his face. Already he was beginning to get over the shock.

'You misjudged your man there,' Gregory reproved.

Hildegard defended him. 'He was twice Allard's size!'

'All the more reason not to be impetuous. It could have been worse.'

'It was Locryn, coming out of his house, who saved me. He gave a shout when he saw him punch me and that's when the brute met his match.'

'He got a well-deserved ducking for his aggression,' Hildegard concluded. She gave Allard a close look. There was more to this, she was sure of it, but maybe now was not the time to probe too far.

'I'll get off to the Domus and get this seen to,' Allard mumbled. 'Thank you for your concern.'

Before they could restrain him he walked off.

'Locryn again!' exclaimed Gregory. 'He's quite handy with his fists despite being a broiderer.'

'Maybe that's why he developed his skill?' Hildegard suggested. 'You know what bullies are like if they believe they have a victim in sight?' She gave a half-smile. 'I can imagine what your average man-at-arms thinks to a fellow who spends his days sewing!'

'All I can say is what an eventful morning you've had, Hildi. You must fill in the details later. Now we need to tell you about how we stand in regard to excommunication.'

# THIRTEEN

They met Egbert as they reached the guest refectory. 'It got quite heated in the Chapter House just now.' He was grinning as he followed them inside saying, 'The astrologers doubtless have a theory of conjunctions and trines to explain it.'

Gregory pulled out a bench for Hildegard before sitting down on the other side of the trestle and Egbert climbed onto the bench beside him. Wine was brought.

When they were alone again Gregory said, 'I'm only glad

no monks carry arms! Dissension has now broken out in the Roman camp and the faction that align themselves with Clement are swooning with delight!'

'Some,' Egbert chipped in, 'are calling Pope Boniface names we will not sully your ears with, Hildegard, while others believe we owe it to him to pay up whatever and whenever he demands it.'

'He's being as rapacious as anti-Pope Clement in his tax-gathering. If taxes to Rome then why not to Avignon, they're asking. They say they may as well offer themselves in humility as lambs and let both popes fleece us till our hides bleed.'

Shuddering at such a picture, Hildegard replied, 'I don't think they fleece lambs, Gregory. Not enough wool. Sacrifice them, I grant you.'

'Either way,' he gave a morose chuckle, 'these Beaulieu lambs won't surrender.'

'The vote was cast unofficially just now and it confirmed the earlier one, much to the opposition's chagrin. They were hoping for a clear reversal of the recent vote. Sadly for them it didn't happen and we're back to where we were. It gives a clear mandate to an English abbot from Hailes to lead them – if he'll take the job.' Egbert looked doubtful.

'The rival faction will not accept him,' Gregory took up the thread. 'They're saying that what they call "a charitable subsidy" – in other words a tax on the English abbeys – is supported by the Abbot of Morimond in France—'

'Abbot Conrad?'

'—Yes, him, as well as by the Abbots of Clairvaux, Pontigny and La Ferté. What this means for us is that among the mother houses we have only Cîteaux on our side and then only because Pope Urban had the foresight to issue bulls releasing us from obedience to what he called "the pretend abbot of Cîteaux", a few years ago.'

'Oh, those Clementists are really delighted now they see us in such disarray.' Egbert sounded as disgruntled as he looked.

'So what happens next?' asked Hildegard. 'This concerns we nuns as well, even though we have little say in what chapter decides.'

'Chapter has little say here when it comes to it. They've chosen their Abbot of Beaulieu but it will not be ratified by the Clementists. The abbey here is a daughter house of Cîteaux and so under the thumb of Clement but ours along with other great abbeys of the North like Rievaulx, Fountains and so on are daughters of Clairvaux.'

'To complicate the network of allegiance further, the little abbey of Quarr across the water on the Isle of Wight is a daughter of Savigny – which itself is a daughter of Clairvaux. You see how complex the problem is?'

'What will happen if Cîteaux and Clement don't ratify the elected abbot?'

'He won't be allowed to set foot here and they'll put their own unelected man in place.'

'The same thing will happen everywhere unless it's stopped,' Egbert contributed.

'And then what? The supporters of the ones who have been elected and then passed over won't accept that!' She frowned. 'How do the numbers work out over the whole country?'

'Ten daughter houses of Savigny, plus half a dozen with Clairvaux, excluding Dore which belongs to Morimond, then there's Tintern on our side and – oh, I'll work it out properly later. Suffice to say twenty of the seventy monasteries here and in Wales are daughters of French houses.'

'They seem outnumbered.'

Gregory's comment brought only derision.

'You don't expect Clement to concede, surely! Beaulieu might find itself on its own except for the power and good will of our lord King Richard, save his soul.'

Hildegard widened her eyes.

'He will never accept French taxation of his own loyal English subjects,' Egbert predicted. 'And certainly not of a royal abbey like this one.'

'You don't mean he'd go to war over it?'

'Better than that. He'll go to law.'

'He has already issued mandates to his sheriffs and bailiffs to protect the monasteries of the English chapter and to safe-guard them and their servants as they travel about the realm on their lawful business.'

'Provided,' Egbert added, 'they don't attempt anything to the prejudice of the crown.'

Gregory finished the matter by adding, 'Or to the prejudice of the king himself.'

A few lay-brothers were beginning to come in from the kitchens to prepare for the next meal for the guests and the three of them got up to leave.

'And all this time that little heiress is suffering who knows what hell.' Hildegard must have looked so distressed Gregory put an arm round her. 'What can we do?' she asked helplessly, leaning against him for a moment.

'Let's see what happens when the sheriff and his men come to arrest this felon Black Harry. They'll prise information about her whereabouts from him by fair means or foul.'

'If he is involved,' she added, moving away. 'And if the sheriff isn't in his pocket. And if the chapter here allows his right of sanctuary to be broken.'

They exchanged looks.

At midday a courier was seen riding his horse at a gallop up the long hill on the abbey side of the river, heading through the woods in the direction of a place called Hythe. There he could take the ferry to the main port of Hampton and the sheriff's headquarters in the keep.

When the constant Lent services allowed, the three from Meaux met briefly in the lane outside the church and Hildegard muttered, 'I wonder what Sir William thinks to all this? He's out of his own county and must be at a loss.'

'Not knowing who to bribe, do you mean?' Gregory sounded unexpectedly cynical.

'Talk of the devil!' Egbert pointed across to where Sir William, accompanied by a small band of his own militia, was leaving by the west door now the rest of the congregation, conversi, guests and others of lesser grandeur, had already poured out into the rain.

'I must insist he acknowledges me before he disappears with his men again.' Hildegard left the monks and moved towards William, blocking his path with a deep obeisance he could not ignore.

'My esteemed lord,' she straightened. They were on a level, eye to eye. 'I crave audience with you on the matter of the lady Elowen and her abduction.'

He raised his eyebrows at being addressed so directly and she added before he could refuse, 'May we speak in private, my lord?'

Glowering he nodded to his men but put a restraining hand on the arm of his lieutenant. 'Continue, nun. I remember you. You're Hildegard of Meaux, so-called.'

'I am, my lord.'

'And you are the nun assigned to escort this troublesome future daughter-in-law of mine to the priory at Swyne?'

'That is so—'

'Then you can have no useful knowledge regarding her abduction, can you?' Having settled the matter with himself he was about to hasten away but Hildegard moved first.

Blocking his path she said, 'I beg leave to remind you, my lord, that I cannot take lightly the authority of my lady Prioress when she has laid a special responsibility on me to safeguard the young betrothed on her journey. I dare not fail. I would deem it a great boon to confer with you on the latest developments and perhaps find a way through to a satisfactory outcome resulting in her rescue?' When he seemed about to dismiss her she threw in her strongest card. 'My Prioress – and indeed the lord Abbot of Meaux who has a care for the interests of we nuns at Swyne and everyone with land in the proximity of his abbey – will expect no less.'

'Where is Abbot de Courcy now?' he asked abruptly.

'He is, I believe, on the way to the General Chapter at Cîteaux.'

'He's not going to be much help here then, is he?'

'In the matter of our allegiance to Pope Boniface and the possibility of war with France?'

William gave a start. 'Oh that. That as well,' he added quickly. 'I meant in tracking down this wench.'

'I'm convinced that if he were here his advice would be worth following. He would expect it to be so followed.'

William pondered this for a moment then, briskly, 'Well, as he's not here we can only second-guess him and assume our understanding equals his. I don't suppose you have any ideas, sister?'

His deliberate slight to her status when he knew better did not deter her. 'I crave a private audience with you, my lord. This inclement weather—' She gave a mock-shudder even though the rain was lighter than before.

Cornered, William covered his boorishness by striding towards the small building reserved for guests of such status as himself, calling over his shoulder, 'Come. Let's pool our information then if you have any.'

The hall was heated by a pile of logs burning energetically in a wide fireplace. A youth sprang to his feet when the door was banged open to herald his lord and master.

William glared, noted who was taking advantage of his absence, and clipped, 'Wine.'

To Hildegard he said, 'Be seated.' He indicated a hard-backed wooden armchair by the fireside and took an opposite one for himself. He stretched out his legs to the flames and steam began to rise at once from his riding boots, filling the air with the stench of pig fat.

Hildegard asked him as a prelude how his search had gone that morning.

'It washed our armour and irrigated the horses.'

'And no sign of Lady Elowen?'

'No sign.'

'Do you believe she is still within the Great Close?'

'Has to be. We've had men posted at the gates into the Royal Forest ever since she was snatched.'

She told him about that morning's brief encounter with Black Harry at the abandoned farmhouse.

'I heard about all that.' He glared into the flames. 'He has some notoriety. Next time he's caught he'll hang. I'll make sure of that.'

When she told him about the rumour of Black Harry having the sheriff in his pocket, stressing that for all she knew it was a baseless lie, his eyes sharpened.

'He's the man around here, is he? We'll see about that.' He smiled rather easily as if it were of little importance. 'These self-made brigands get above themselves. To whom did he owe allegiance? Do you know that, sister?'

'I'm afraid not.'

He sniffed and thought things over. The wine came. He lifted his goblet first and drank deeply. Hildegard took her less ornate goblet, smaller, fit, she supposed for more ladylike drinking, and murmured, 'May God guard her,' before taking a sip.

'I suppose,' he growled when he had thought things through, 'he's a militia man, detritus from the French wars, one of those who feel cheated by their commanders? I hear some have not been paid and have taken matters into their own hands. One can but applaud their initiative. Even so, I will not have my property stolen without a strong response.'

He downed his wine, gestured for his servant to pour another, made a cursory flick of his fingers towards Hildegard's more or less untouched goblet, then waved him away.

'And apart from this Black Harry fellow did you see anyone else when you were up there in the woods?' He looked her full in the face.

She omitted to mention the two lads in the makeshift shelter for fear of what might happen to them if they were caught poaching.

They were too young to bear physical punishment for their trespass. By the look of them they were probably driven by hunger, not greed.

'I saw a falconer,' she admitted. 'My servant said he was a stranger but we decided he was not a poacher as he was so well set up.'

'In what way?'

'Costly peregrine on his wrist. A good horse. A disciplined hound at his heels. If a poacher then a wealthy one.'

'That's my man Bagsby.' He grimaced with smug content-ment. 'I'm glad to find he was carrying out my orders. Not being needed in our quartering of the heath he went off to see what he could fetch back for dinner. God knows, the food here is plain enough. Do these monks never eat the bounty offered to them in their own domain? They could eat meat every day of the year and not notice any diminution in their game stocks.'

'I expect they remember it's Lent,' Hildegard remarked mildly.

'Oh, well, there's that, I suppose. Although why they imagine a man such as myself can get by without good red meat every day I've no idea.'

He seemed about to enlarge on the paucity of the monks' free provision of victuals to their guests but Hildegard interrupted, not without an apology. 'And did your man Bagsby see any unusual activity while he was out, my lord?'

'He reported that he noticed an abandoned farmstead on the heath but did not approach. I already had it on good authority that it was unoccupied.'

'So he kept his distance?'

'Why? Do you think he should have entered, unarmed, and stirred up trouble for himself?'

'I have no opinion on such matters, my lord.' She wanted to cry out, *But the girl might be imprisoned there, you dolt*, but held her tongue.

'So tell me more about this reptile, Harry.'

'I know very little. No more than I've already told you. The story goes that he escaped hanging recently for a string of crimes for which he sought sanctuary here. A man, I'm told, who has Hampton under his thumb as well as its sheriff.'

'More?'

'That's all I know.'

'Or all you're willing to tell me at this stage?'

She did not deign to answer.

'You nuns,' he ruminated. 'It's true what they say.' He settled back. A reminiscing smile came over his face. 'My grandmother, a bed-bound corrodian as she was, knew more about my followers' sins and allegiances than I did. I used to visit her as often as I could for all the latest. I have to say the old witch was usually more right than wrong.'

He rose to his feet and yawned. 'When you choose to inform me of anything else I shall be ready to listen. In return I can tell you we've dredged the heath from end to end as thoroughly as if we were dredging for partridge but found neither hair nor rag of the wench. Soon I shall have to send somebody by ship to Cornwall to tell his grace the sad news about the dowry – and about his daughter's disappearance.'

He gave a heavy sigh.

'All we can surmise is that if no demand for ransom is made in a day or two she is dead and her dowry lost forever. All that gold!' he added as he strode to the door calling for his captains. 'It would make me weep to think an undeserving renegade had got the lot.'

A few moments later as she was being shown out she heard him shout to his men to get out after the lay-brothers. 'Head for the farm Bagsby mentioned. Then tear it apart!'

Before the door closed behind her she heard him add to his lieutenant, 'Rouse my falconer from his nest, not for sport but to keep the men on the right path through the woods. Follow him. He knows the way.'

Hildegard could not help thinking that with so many bands of armed men – albeit the lay-brothers armed only with cudgels and their own courage – Black Harry would, if he cared to raise his glance to the horizon, have fair warning that his bucolic idyll was about to be shattered.

The pack was closing in – with enough fanfares to awaken the dead.

# FOURTEEN

Once outside she almost ran into the stable block to search among the stalls for the horse master and when she found him she begged a horse. 'Is Allard free?'

'I sent him to lie down before he falls down. His nose isn't broken, he says, but it's causing him a lot of pain.'

'Oh, poor Allard.' She made a decision. 'I'll be back in a moment.'

'I'll get something saddled up for you then, shall I?'

Thanking him she ran back to the main gatehouse and asked one of the brothers on duty if he would take a little cure she had to the Domus to hand to Allard then hurry and find Gregory and Egbert for her. 'No problem. They've just left here and gone into the cloisters. Wait here, domina, I'll fetch them.' Catching some of her haste he did as she asked then hurried off across the lane into the inner precinct. Moments later both monks appeared.

'What's happened?' Egbert asked.

She asked them if they were ready to ride out to the farm with her.

'Ready, willing and able,' he replied. 'But why the hurry?'

'William's men are converging on the abandoned farmstead. I fear for Elowen's safety if she's held captive there. Harry will never give her up without getting something in exchange, if we're to believe what they say about him . . . And William won't give a groat, not even to save the girl's life.'

Without need for further explanation the two monks quickly followed Hildegard to the yard and were soon riding over the bridge into the woods before William's men had even turned up to saddle their horses.

'Where's your shadow?' Egbert asked Hildegard as they cantered through the trees.

'Allard? Lying down with a suspected broken nose.'

They continued in silence until they reached the fork in the track where they had lost their way earlier. Hildegard slowed to a trot. 'It might be a good idea to warn those two young poachers I told you about. If William's men discover them it'll be the worse for them. It won't take a moment.'

Leading the way down the twisting track to the glade where the boys had been sheltering, Hildegard halted in dismay.

Someone had got there before them. The little shelter was smashed to pieces, its wooden stakes strewn in the grass, white wood-pulp lying like dead flesh. Of the two boys, no sign. She dropped down out of the saddle and ran over to rummage through the ruins.

Gregory appeared beside her.

'It's all right,' she told him, sitting back on her heels with a sigh of relief, 'there's no one here.'

'But, here, look at this.' He pulled out some newly cut staves from under a mound of last year's leaves. 'Somebody has made a bow and was starting on a few arrows. I wonder what he thought he'd use as fletches?' He glanced round. 'I suppose it might be possible to find a few feathers suitable for your purpose.'

'So they were poaching after all?'

'You sound disappointed?'

'It was just – I suppose boys will be boys.' She shook her head. 'Let's get on. I think I can hear horsemen.'

A faint jingling of harness penetrated the woods and now and then a gruff voice barked a command.

Egbert had remained at the entrance to the clearing and now all three, in unspoken agreement, cantered ahead of the approaching band of William's men-at-arms.

When they arrived at the place where the man said to be Black Harry had been discovered they came to a halt as they took in the scene.

The farm looked much as before: peaceful, serene even, and in the unexpected sunlight that had followed the rain it had the aura of a place that would look well with children playing in the yard, with washing spread on bushes to dry, a farmer's wife singing as she fed some hens, and a bluff countryman busily fixing a piece of farming equipment.

Gregory broke into her thoughts. 'How long has it been empty?'

'I don't know. It's simply known as the abandoned farmhouse.'

'See those men surrounding it?' He pointed.

Egbert followed his glance. 'Lay-brothers.'

Hildegard eyed them with misgivings. 'I see they're all armed with cudgels. Such a large number of men. How did the conversi master manage to rustle up so many in such a short time?'

'Lent,' replied Gregory briefly. Then, added, 'They're obliged to leave their granges and come up to the abbey for so many days a year. A few remain behind to ensure the safety of the animals and see to the crops. It can't be onerous to have to stay in the Domus for a time. It must be a welcome break from farm work and the relative isolation of the granges.'

'It looks as if they know what they're doing, surrounding the place like that. Is it William's idea? Do they expect this Harry fellow to come marching out of his own accord, right into their clutches?'

But it looked as if the circle of lay-brothers, staking out the farm, only intended to make sure no one left until Sir William's armed horsemen appeared. They did so now, crashing from out of the undergrowth and making a great noise.

'They're giving him a good warning,' remarked Gregory.

'You can't say fairer than that,' agreed Egbert with some sarcasm.

'What now?' Hildegard asked.

'There's certainly no sign of him. What would you do, Greg, if you were in there and didn't like the look of your visitors?'

'I hope I wouldn't be so lax as to get into such a situation but if you're really asking I'd—'

But they didn't find out what Gregory would have done because at that moment the captain of William's forces rode out in front of his men and drew up in a prominent position in the yard.

He stood in his stirrups so he was visible to everybody and shouted towards the house, 'Come on out, you black devil! And bring the girl! We know you're in there!'

Unsurprisingly no one appeared.

The captain shouted again, in a less friendly manner, and waved for some of his men to move down into the yard. The rest of them, a dozen or more, spread themselves round the farmstead, guarding all ways out.

When warnings, blandishments and downright threats brought no response the men were instructed to kick in the doors and fetch forth anybody they found within and if they resisted, 'You know what to do!' roared William's captain.

At a signal, men could be seen swarming inside and tumult followed as they could be heard rampaging through the building. Eventually, in ones and twos, they began to reappear. Their evident confusion and dismay were soon accounted for.

'Nobody here, Captain! He's flown the coop!'

The three Cistercians, watching as if at a joust, exchanged glances. Nobody uttered a word of criticism. There was no need.

'That's that then,' Hildegard concluded, beginning to turn her horse for home.

But it was not so. The captain, still astride, leaned down to speak to one of his men who, calling a couple of others to go with him, tramped back, shoulder to shoulder, towards the house.

Everyone watched as they went inside.

Suddenly they streamed out again and only halted when they reached a fair distance away.

In moments smoke began to coil from a ground-floor window.

Inside the main chamber flames were suddenly seen, brilliant and unpredictable. They erupted as something more combustible caught and the fire spread rapidly to the upper floor. The thatch was ignited. Flames began to devour the roof. Violent and stoked by seasoned wood the heat could soon be felt across the mead to where William's men stood watching. Horses rolled their eyes and snorted.

With a crack the main timber was grabbed by the jaws of the flames and slowly twisted like a broken limb. It began to writhe in agony before collapsing in a whoosh of sparks. The walls caught fire. Doors twisted off their hinges and toppled into the conflagration. Flames shot skywards trailing streamers of black smoke.

Hildegard had forgotten the conversi and now she saw the ring of men move forward as if in thrall to such destruction. They were helpless to put the fire out. One or two made as if to rush to the building to rescue it but were held back by their more cautious brothers.

Smoke, pluming into the air, eventually descended in black wreaths, causing coughing fits to those nearest. The house faded from sight under a pall of smoke.

'Did William instruct them to destroy it?' Gregory wondered. 'I imagine it's quite his style.'

'No Black Harry inside, that's for sure. And no Elowen.' Hildegard felt an irrational sense of relief as she registered that there were no boys with bows and arrows either, for why should she imagine the boys would hide out in such a place after their hidden shelter had been discovered? Surely they would get as far away as they could?

The three of them left when it was obvious there was nothing they could do. Behind them was a milling group of William's armed men and a somewhat stunned circle of lay-brothers appalled at the deliberate destruction of abbey property.

On the way back she said as much to the monks. They were silent. There would be too many repercussions from today's work to make assumptions about anything.

Back at the stables they had already seen to their horses before the two separate bands, mercenaries first, followed eventually by lay-brothers on foot, began to troop back. The militia wore sheepish smiles which did not conceal their air of triumph. The lay-brothers were tight-lipped and said nothing.

William came out to greet his men. He could tell by their faces they had had no luck in cornering their prey but had followed his orders to their own satisfaction and wrecked the place.

He asked for a verbal confirmation, glossing over their failure to find Elowen with a mere, 'Keep up the good work, men. That's one less place we have to bother with.'

Overhearing him Gregory asked, 'Does that mean he intends to burn down every building where they fail to find anyone? The Great Close will be nothing but a waste of bonfires. The lord prior will have plenty to say.'

'A clumsy day's work,' grunted Egbert. 'Best if he'd kept his men away if that's all they're capable of doing.'

'They were following instructions.' Hildegard gave them both an enigmatic smile. 'That's what they were doing.'

The two of them glanced at her then at each other. Gregory gave a faint smile. 'And your meaning?'

'Give me time to see if my theory holds.'

Her suspicions were two-fold. One: why, if William wanted to find Elowen and her casket of gold, did he allow his men to go storming up to the farmhouse to give Black Harry time to escape?

And two: why had he ordered his captain to fire the place, thereby destroying any clues it might yield?

It was almost as if he didn't care.

A brief look-round might have told how long the place had been used as a refuge and how many people had been camped out there and maybe whether in fact the unfortunate lady Elowen had been held captive there. A dropped kerchief, perhaps. A give-away fragment of a velvet kirtle caught on a doorpost.

Something.

Anything.

Sighing at such dolt-headed folly, if, indeed, that's what it was, she left the two brothers to their duties and went into the church. She knelt on the patterned tiles and put her hands over her eyes the better to think.

From somewhere distant came the high voice of a chorister practising a difficult phrase. Even when he went wrong it sounded impossibly beautiful. When he got it right the notes belled up into the vault, fading, and drifting, and finally leaving only a melancholy echo to express the transience of all things living.

She wondered why she didn't stay here forever, wrapped in peace and harmony, at one with the great mystery none could solve.

By the time she rose to her feet and let herself out into the Close the light was fading. I could stay for Vespers, she told herself. But there were things to do.

# FIFTEEN

B ack to the stables. The horse she had ridden earlier was brought forth.

Once in the woods it felt strange to be alone. Her senses seemed sharper. The shadows lengthened. A stand of trees were transformed into silhouettes. The sun sank low in violent splendour.

It was a hard ride to reach the place she was aiming for before the light finally went but she rode with reckless haste. There was still light, lingering and luminous, enough to allow her to do what she wanted.

Slipping down from the horse she left him on the edge of the woods and walked firmly across the mead towards the still smoking farmhouse.

*       *       *

The muddy ground was a confusion of prints around the blackened buildings but casting further off and with the patience worthy of the fabled Griselda she eventually found what she was looking for.

Footprints.

The two sets, human and animal, were clear further away from the confusion of prints kicked up around the house where the lay-brothers had been milling.

The man's prints were made by riding boots. Was he alone, or had someone been sitting astride the horse? For some reason she was glad there were no boys' prints running along beside him.

She followed as far as she could until it was too dark to make them out. Then she took a bearing on a group of trees, assessed the probable direction horse and rider must have taken as best she could and, praying that it would not rain in the night before her brother-monks could return to trace them to their destination, rode her horse back into the woods, leaving the smouldering wreckage of a once comfortable farmhouse to the night.

Flares were already alight in the precinct. As soon as she entered the guest house Egbert left the group of St Keverne men he was talking to and came over.

'We're to meet Locryn for collation before Compline,' he reminded. He gave her a closer look. 'Have you been out?'

She nodded. The candlelight seemed glaring after the darkness of the woods. She blinked. 'I had an idea. Nothing much.'

She told him about the trail of footprints in the mud. 'They were a man's prints, leading a horse away from the burned farmhouse. Black Harry had a horse. Tomorrow first thing we must follow them. They must belong to him.'

The main door swept open as the porter's assistant entered. He came straight over to them. 'I have someone to deliver to you and beg you to return him to the lodge when you've finished with him.'

'Ah,' Egbert nodded. 'We know who this is. Bring him in.'

Locryn did not shuffle inside but moved with a certain cautious swagger. Like everything about him there seemed to be a double edge. He gave a swift glance round, taking it all in at once, the hall busy with guests, merchants and their wives, the sellers of goods from the port, a couple with a child, a mixed bag of people from around the area visiting for their own different reasons, both secular and spiritual.

Locryn made no comment but a variety of thoughts flew across his face. He followed a respectful couple of paces behind Egbert but in even this he seemed to make it into an ironic game of servant and master.

Most guests were sitting in a convivial group round the long trestle in the middle of the hall and it was easy for the Cistercians to find a corner table without attracting attention.

Gregory pulled out a bench and waved a hand for their guest to sit. Hildegard smiled a greeting. Locryn returned her smile with a wary glance and sat on the bench opposite with both hands resting where they could all see them on the trestle top.

'Let's eat first while we exchange views on today's failure to find the little lady Elowen. After that you can tell us about yourself.' Egbert, bluff and genial, hitched up his robes and climbed onto the bench next to Locryn, and Hildegard couldn't be sure that his practised eye didn't run over their guest as if checking for weapons.

Surely he couldn't imagine the sanctuaryman would be so witless as to bring arms inside the abbey! Egbert caught her glance and smiled as innocently as a baby and she knew she was right. She poured some wine and water into their beakers and let them begin.

Egbert came straight to the point. 'Tell us about this fellow Black Harry. What's he supposed to have done? Why Black?'

'Not for his deeds. The widows and children wouldn't agree with you there. It's because of his beard. A great curling thing he takes much pride in.'

Hildegard interrupted. 'Locryn, how long did you say you'd been in sanctuary?'

'I believe I told you I'd been here six weeks?'

'Yes, I thought you said that too.' She gave him a cool glance.

Why could he never give a straight answer? 'When did this Black Harry find himself in the hands of the sheriff?'

'Shortly before you arrived.'

'So you were here when he was taken in?'

'I was living in the precinct so did not witness it. Then I blotted my copy book and they threw me out – to where you saw me, domina, living in such splendour.'

'You do seem to find trouble. Was it your temper again?'

He smiled but didn't bother to reply.

Gregory asked, 'Why would widows and children approve of him?'

'He finds food for them, repairs their leaking roofs, asks a paltry rent to keep said roofs over their heads – you monks could do more, given all you've got.'

'It might be because of all we've got that we can do anything at all,' suggested Egbert. 'Should we be like the masterless men, roaming at will, bestowing largesse on our favourites at random, with no order to our giving nor any legal source for our wealth?'

'They give to those folk they know are in need because they live among them.'

'As do the monks here to some extent. Are you suggesting there's no value in daily prayers on behalf of the seculars?'

'What value is there in praying like the most helpless victim of lady Fortune for what you will never have? Who listens to these prayers? Some old monk who has never lived in the world, who has never wanted for bread to fill his stomach, some old praying fellow who has never suffered except in his imagination? Empty words to a being no one has ever seen or heard? A trick played on us to keep us in our place—?'

'Look,' Gregory leaned forward to stem the flow, 'this is not the time or place for a dispute about God and justice. I will happily engage you in such dialogue some time if you wish. At present we need to find this girl. You're hinting that Black Harry is a saint and would never abduct anyone for gain. So we can cross him off our list and leave him to roam – in your opinion?'

'He's no saint!' Locryn gave a sudden laugh. 'I met him when he was here and saw what he did. But some of those sanctuarymen should look to themselves before judging him. They're not as innocent as they imagine. Harry isn't a man to prey on the innocent. Some of them don't understand that. Everybody is prey to them. They'd sell their own mothers if it brought them profit.'

'He might deem the girl's father is legitimate prey. An earl? More wealth than Croesus? How does that fit with his view of justice?'

'I am reproved,' replied Locryn with an expression that showed he would never be reproved by anyone.

Hildegard broke in. 'So you don't believe this Harry is involved in Elowen's abduction?'

He shook his head. 'Forgive me, I know not. I was not present.'

Hildegard widened her eyes. Didn't he realize an innocent girl was missing? 'I understand that,' she replied coldly, 'but you claim to hear the latest rumours before us monastics on this side of the river. You said he doesn't prey on the innocent. Are we to leave it there? The returning lay-brothers must surely have said something about the man they were trying to entrap this morning?'

'I believe they probably think much as I do.'

'What? That he might abduct her in the name of justice?'

Her anger seemed to amuse him. 'I think what I'm saying, domina, is that I can't help you except in the matter of my opinion about him. It seems to me he's blamed for many things which are not his doing!' He sat back to let the heat out of his words and added quite calmly, 'That's all I'm saying.'

'All? It seems you're saying rather more than that. You're hinting that Sir William is after the wrong man.' She raised her eyebrows when he failed to respond.

Gregory spoke. 'I gather you want my help in some litigation?'

'Only if you're able to give it willingly. I cannot pay you.'

'And I cannot do anything for you until I know your real name, Locryn.'

They sat and held each other's gaze. Gregory did not blink.

Eventually Locryn mumbled, 'It was the first name that came to mind.'

'King of the Britons?'

He looked surprised that Gregory knew its significance. For a brief moment he was disconcerted. 'It's from something I was working on as a broiderer,' he excused, glancing away to the guests passing round the wine jug at the main table as if he would like to join them. 'It was a commission for a wealthy man near Romsey. A battle scene.'

'Locryn was known as Locrinus to the invading Romans because they could not get their tongues around his Welsh name. He's famous for rousing an army against them.' There was an odd melancholy in Gregory's voice when he added, 'The Romans, being wealthier, better equipped and well organized, defeated him. He and his army were utterly destroyed, killed to a man. So much for the leader of the people you find buried in the mounds out on the heath.'

'I was working on a depiction of his final battle,' Locryn admitted. 'The man who commissioned it thought everyone should know about it.'

'So now, back to your name?'

Scowling like a child, as Hildegard judged, he admitted in a small voice, 'Will Smailes.'

'Which shall we use?'

'Whichever.'

'Do you know you have a rather exasperating manner?'

'So I'm told.'

'Then heed the tellers.'

Locryn sneered, 'For sure, we're all here to learn, as I understand you fellows believe.'

Gregory was about to get to his feet in irritation when Locryn quickly laid a hand on his arm. 'Help me.' He hesitated. 'If I hear anything I'll tell you . . . if you help me in return.'

Gregory took his seat again, steepled his fingers in a way Hubert de Courcy sometimes did, and asked in measured tones, 'So, Will, tell me about your situation and what led you to seek sanctuary.'

Afterwards Hildegard could not help observing while Egbert escorted him back to the porter's lodge that despite the caustic remark about Locryn being a liar made by one of his neighbours in the shacks the story he told to Gregory was in no way different to the one he had told her, except perhaps, for the fatal beauty of the young wife who had led him on, which he described in more detail. Gregory's eyes had gleamed as Locryn described her and he nodded as if knowing all about the lure of female beauty designed to entrap unsuspecting and innocent men.

'The danger to Locryn,' Hildegard remarked somewhat tartly

to Gregory after he left, 'arises from the jealous husband, not from the wife. The old fellow should have thought twice about marrying a much younger woman and not stepped outside his little realm.' She narrowed her glance. 'Do such men not consider the feelings of their young wives? Moved by financial necessity, these girls have scant choice in how they keep the roof over their heads and so they make these unfortunate marriages – and live to rue it. Then they receive the opprobrium of the Church if they seek solace elsewhere.'

'Are you defending whoredom, Hildegard, because that's what it sounds like?'

'What do you think?' she asked with a touch of sarcasm.

His eyes gleamed again and he held her glance. Eventually he said enigmatically, 'What do I think?'

'Well?' Her eyes flashed.

'I think many things.' He watched her carefully. 'For one thing I think she broke her vows.'

A pause hung between them.

She lowered her glance. 'Vows, yes . . . Like me you haven't always been a monastic. Do you find them irksome?'

'Do you?' Another pause.

Eventually Hildegard, avoiding his glance, said, 'Shall we leave it there?'

'To my rue.' His generous mouth tilted in an ironic smile and before he left he lowered his voice. 'You force me to my knees in prayer every night. I believe only Hubert de Courcy stands in our way.'

He went out before she could register shock. She stared after him.

# SIXTEEN

When Allard appeared next morning his face was bruised but the swelling was much reduced. He greeted Hildegard with a grin then winced and put his hand up to his face. 'Ouch! It hurts when I smile.'

'Have you run out of that arnica I sent?'

He shook his head. 'No, I forgot to use it this morning. It's so much better than yesterday.'

'It was quite a blow. You clearly didn't expect it. What was it about?'

'He wanted to stop me asking him about Black Harry. Which he did! I'll tell you about it later, Hildegard. There are too many rumours flying. I don't want to add to them.'

'When my brothers have finished their duties within the precinct we're going to ride out to see if we can pick up the trail of some prints I saw when I was out at the burned farmhouse.' A somewhat derisive expression made her ask, 'What is it?'

'Did Locryn suggest that?'

'No, I found them myself, why?'

'I thought it sounded like him. You never know with him.'

'Why?'

'His wickedness? Or he confuses himself because he can't make up his mind about his allegiance?'

'Was it over him that brute punched you?'

'It was a misunderstanding. He's one of those types who act first and think later. He used to run errands for Harry. You know what I mean?' He bunched his fists at an imaginary opponent. 'He's one of Harry's enforcers.'

'Maybe I should have a word with him myself?'

'How's your right fist?'

They both laughed but there was no real humour in it and Allard touched his bruised face. 'Shall I escort you to the sanctuary?'

'I have to speak to Mistress Goda first.'

'I'm taking a string of ponies out for exercise. William's men will only ride destriers. They don't realize how smart our Forest ponies are. If you're going over there I'd better come with you. He won't hit me twice in the same place!'

Agreeing to meet later, Hildegard went to find the clerk she had seen coming out of Prime. There had been no sign of Goda.

She found him sitting with a few servants, the maid who had showed concern on that first day when Elowen had been snatched and her companion who had shown only defiance. One or two others were idly finishing off some pieces of pie.

'Any news, master?' were her first words.

A glum shaking of heads round the table followed his own denial and a caustic comment or two about New Forest dwellers was added by several others. Clearly none of them could wait to go back to Cornwall.

'No wonder those two ran away,' somebody else threw in. 'I'd have gone with them if I'd known it was going to be like this.'

'What do you mean?' asked Hildegard. 'Say what you like. I'm not from round here either.'

'It's just them,' the servant explained. 'What help have they given us? None!'

'It's no wonder that Sir William's roving round like a headless chicken,' another one added.

'Mebbe kidnappings are commonplace in this part of the world,' another commented. 'No respect for folk. And those monks—' He broke off and stared at Hildegard's white robe. 'Not your ones, domina. They're doing their best. It's them others. Praying isn't getting her back, is it?'

'Meanwhile,' burst out the maid who had exclaimed the most about Elowen's abduction, 'we none of us know one single thing about what's happening to our poor dear mistress. It's beyond all bearing!' She began to sob.

'Worry not, we northerners are doing our utmost and with the help of your St Keverne men I'm sure we shall soon find her safe and well.'

When she asked about Goda the clerk replied, 'She's not down yet, domina. She's not feeling well.'

She made her way up to the next floor and stopped a passing page to lead her to Goda's chamber.

He ran on ahead and knocked on a door at the far end then turned, 'I'm afraid you're out of luck, domina. She appears to be out – or maybe sleeping?'

Hildegard tapped on the door herself but the page was right. There was no answer. Cautiously she opened it and peered inside. The chamber was empty, the bed made up. Closing the door she thanked him and returned to the main hall.

\*     \*     \*

A babble of excited voices reached her as soon as she entered. The guest master came over. 'We have news, domina. Sir William's servant has this minute brought it over.'

'Has she been found?'

'Sadly no, but Sir William has received the terms of the ransom!'

Hildegard was astonished. William? It cast doubt on her own suspicions. 'When did this happen?'

'Some time during the night, we believe.'

The St Keverne steward joined them. 'Is it true? I pray so! To get our lady back unharmed no price is too high!' He turned to the rest of the household. 'Hear that, friends?'

Cheers went round the chamber but a sceptic asked, 'And is Sir William arranging to pay it – or will he haggle over her price?'

'I understand that he is considering it very carefully,' the guest master replied with delicate diplomacy. 'I'm told he wishes to keep the lord Earl Richard informed before he takes a further step into the morass.'

Hildegard exclaimed, 'That might take weeks!'

'Indeed.' The steward's eyes began to water and he looked directly at her through a film of tears. 'He has failed to find the sweet child and is now prepared to leave her in the clutches of her captors while he haggles with them? It does not augur well for the marriage.'

'Her betrothed is a child of nine, so far not in his father's mould . . .' She spread her arms. 'But I can understand your dismay.'

She was beginning to think it was best if the whole contract could be reassessed. William did not deserve such a well-beloved bride for his son. 'I feel for you and your entire household. If you find there is anything we might do for you please do not hesitate to let us know.'

Her sincerity impressed him because he drew back his paper-thin lips in a sorrowing smile. 'We know nothing of this country, its byways and secret places where someone might be held prisoner. Our men were forbidden horses by Sir William again. They feel helpless and the more helpless they feel the angrier they become. I cannot guarantee anything on their behalf. They're being shamefully treated.'

'I agree. Let me talk to my two fellow Cistercians on this sorry mission. I'm sure I can say on their behalf that they feel as angry and helpless as your men.' She paused. 'Maybe together we can hasten her rescue while the matter of the ransom is being discussed between the earl and Sir William?'

'First see your brothers then return to me, if you will. I'll summon our captain.'

Gregory and Egbert were in the cloister garden. It looked as if they had been waylaid by one of the brothers in charge of the herbs because he was explaining in painstaking detail about the growing of elecampane. 'We have planted it in profusion,' he was explaining, 'because of the high incidence of lung problems suffered by our elderly brothers.'

She lingered on the threshold until they noticed her and came over. She explained about the ransom note and what the St Keverne steward had told her. 'We cannot sit by, we must take matters into our own hands. We must find her.'

'This ransom?' Gregory looked stern-faced. 'How did it reach William?'

'No one said.'

Egbert told Hildegard that the sheriff and his men, summoned by the prior the previous day, had ridden in shortly after dawn.

'He confirmed that this Harry fellow recently escaped hanging by some subterfuge. He thinks that after being flushed out of his cosy farmstead within the Great Close he'll now go to ground somewhere else in the Forest.'

'Find him,' concluded Gregory, 'and Sir William expects to find Elowen.'

'That must be why he's holding fire with the ransom note – despite having waited for it for so long.' Hildegard looked doubtful.

'About these footprints you saw last night—?' began Egbert. 'I hoped we might go and have a look at them ourselves this morning—'

Gregory gave her a reproving glance. 'Were you out there alone or did Allard go with you?'

She ignored Gregory's question. 'Will you both come?'

With another reproving glance, Gregory nodded. 'You know

we will.' He began to move off. 'The sheriff had better be informed about them.'

'Wait,' she told them, 'the men in the earl's little household are becoming restive. Not being allowed horses has angered them. I said we would talk to their captain. Shall we do that first?'

In agreement the three of them made their way back to the guest house and soon rooted out the St Keverne steward. He was talking to a tall, broad-shouldered man-at-arms saying to him when he saw the Cistercians, 'I believe we have allies.'

The man nodded to them. 'We are fighting men. We cannot sit by while our lady is held captive. Without horses we may as well be in chains.'

'We'll get you horses,' Egbert promised. 'We're guests from a northern abbey. Our Beaulieu brothers cannot refuse a reasonable request from us. The problem is these monks have no abbot. No one is leading them. They're in complete disarray. How many men do you have?'

'Three men-at-arms and myself.'

'Then we'll have four good horses ready for you as soon as you muster.'

Hildegard glanced at her two monks to include them as well as the captain. 'Unless you have another plan I must tell you that I found a track last night. It led away from the burned farmhouse. I believe it may lead us to your lady's captor.'

'If your brothers can obtain horses for us, we're on our way.' Decisively he strode off.

'Come, let's get the stable master to saddle up eight horses for us—'

'Eight?' Hildegard queried.

'Will Allard not wish to come with us?'

The stable master was full of bustle, shouting his orders, making his stable lads jump to their tasks and chuckling all the while.

'Those choir monks will scarcely register the fact that their horses are being ridden out. It's Sir William we have to dodge but luckily he's in with the sheriff and I'll have more wine sent in to keep him there. It's unusual for Sir William to be roused from his bed so early unless he's going hunting but his visitors got the last ferry to Hythe yesterday and rode over as soon as it was light enough.'

'Is this rumour about Black Harry having the sheriff in his pocket true?' Hildegard felt she was on good enough terms with him to ask.

He replied with a sideways look. 'There is them that say so.' Something got in his eye and he rubbed it away. 'More than my life's worth if that comes from me.' He winked and moved off.

A voice from behind her made her jump. Standing on the other side of the wooden partition between the stalls was the prior.

'My dear lady of Meaux, I trust your lodging is to your satisfaction?' Wearing the white robes of all Cistercians he moved forward with extended hand to draw the sign of the cross in the air between them. 'You have found us at a delicate time since our dearly beloved abbot died. Sadly his successor has not yet been appointed. For the time being you may regard me as the agent of the Abbot of Beaulieu.' He bowed his head a fraction in what Hildegard regarded as the minimum obeisance to offer anyone, even a woman.

She dropped briefly to one knee. 'Most gracious lord.' Standing up straight she was able to look down on him. 'We live in a divided world. It is an added burden for you to have one of your guests taken captive and no one able to track her down. I trust the Sheriff of Hampton will soon have men out in the Forest to trace her whereabouts?'

His thin smile did not change. 'Amen to that.'

He glided away on whatever business had brought him into the stables and a moment later she observed him entering the lodging of Sir William with a couple of acolytes in tow.

The stable master turned to her, raised his eyebrows, then set about organizing his posse of lads. Horses were led out and taken rather swiftly towards the gatehouse. 'We will not disturb the sheriff,' he commented.

The Cornishmen were soon up and riding out under the archway with Gregory and Egbert and Hildegard herself on a lively little palfrey taking up the rear.

Allard rode alongside her. His nose, still bruised and swollen, was evidently not broken.

'You remembered the arnica?' she asked.

'Yes, my gratitude for reminding me. It works like magic.'

'You should have asked Brother Herberer. He would have given you some.'

'They're getting tired of us lay-brothers and our complaints. He says there's always one or other of us putting a pitchfork through a foot or going down with the ague. He's pleased with Mark's progress though – despite the fact that a sanctuaryman fixed him up, and you, of course.'

'I didn't do much. It's lucky for Mark that Locryn was close by.' They started across the wooden bridge towards the shacks. 'Did you find out why he was at Beaufre that night? Does he usually visit the granges?'

'He happened to be staying over for some reason. What makes you ask?'

'Nothing much. I was just wondering.'

Had he been on his way to or from somewhere when night fell?

And if so, why? That was a question.

# SEVENTEEN

The band of riders reached the ruined farmhouse in good time. Smoke was still rising into the damp air even though the fire had died out. Everywhere the acrid smell of burned timbers hung in the air.

The men dismounted and went over to have a look at the damage but there was little to see now. They muttered among themselves then remounted. Hildegard led them round to the other side of the ruins and indicated the prints she had noticed.

'Big feet,' one of them remarked.

'It's the rider of the horse. You can follow them up to the point where he gets into the saddle and sets off eastwards.' She showed them. 'It was too dark when I found them to follow further.'

Allard said, 'If I'd been with you we would have gone on and this whole sorry business might now be over.'

'You couldn't help getting a punch in the face from that brute. It wasn't your fault. Anyway, we wouldn't have been able to see in the dark.'

The whole group began to move off. Gregory and Egbert went in front to make sure no mistakes were made and being more painstaking than the men-at-arms, made slower work of it than they would have liked.

The rain that had luckily held off through the night now began in earnest. It fell in large single drops at first, making everyone pull up their hoods if they wore them, or have them bouncing off their steel basinets in the case of the men-at-arms, but soon it began to gather force, filling all the hollows in the already saturated ground and limiting vision to only a few yards.

Oblivious to it the men carried on following the direction the monks were taking but rain began to stream down their faces, glittering over their chain mail, over the flanks of the hired horses, and persuading the monks to pull on waterproofed capes. They were forced to raise their voices over the sound of the downpour. No one suggested turning back.

A wet light shone on the marsh pools making them glint like hundreds of small mirrors. At first the indentations were easy enough to follow despite the rain but soon they became water-logged, impossible to distinguish from the natural undulations of the ground.

Gregory called a halt.

On every side the heath stretched as far as the trees in an unbroken wilderness where nothing much grew and the distant woods turned to mist. As the rain increased even the horizon became a blur and the world shrank to a small, grey, moist globe.

'I'm going on,' Egbert called back to the men. He was a little ahead of everyone in his eagerness to encounter Black Harry and his captive. 'You all wait here for me. It'll be easier alone. No use getting the horses in a state the first time we take them out.'

'I'm coming with you,' Gregory said needlessly. 'We'll take a look-see. I suggest you other fellows take shelter in that stand

of trees we passed back there near the burnt farmhouse. We'll
meet you there when we've found this devil's lair. If we're not
back by the time the storm passes over, come and find us.'

'I'll come too.' Hildegard urged her horse alongside them.

'So will I.' Allard followed.

The name of the St Keverne captain was Marrek. Now he
looked doubtfully at Gregory. 'We'll give you long enough but
then we're coming after you. I see you want to keep numbers
down. When the clouds lift we'll be able to see you from the
top of one of those mounds.' He gestured with his whip to a
nearby earth mound. 'Give us a sign to come on or stay.' He
turned back. 'To the trees, men, take shelter!'

The two groups separated.

Protected by her waterproof cloak Hildegard tried to remember
what sort of country lay ahead. It was part of the royal hunting
grounds and soon they should reach the abbey boundary. Beyond
that it was woodland, endless miles of it, and a million places
where a man on the run with possibly a kidnapped girl and
some henchman with him might hide out for as long as he
pleased. That is, if he did not need to exchange his human
trophy for ransom gold.

'Our best cover is this storm,' Egbert threw over his shoulder
as he cantered ahead. 'I'll go on scrying out the prints and you,
Greg, keep your eyes open for what lies further ahead.'

Numerous mounds lay on all sides, dark amid lighter green
patches of marsh grass. Bramble vines covered the ground and
a few stunted trees of wild crab apple and plum stuck out like
way-posts. Sedge water made their going a slithery obstacle
race to a destination they could not discern.

Egbert, riding some way ahead, lifted an arm to encourage
them to keep up. Gregory, eyes blinking away beads of moisture,
peered into the distance for any sign of a suitable hideout.
Hildegard, riding beside Allard, tried to assess how far their
quarry had ridden after she found his prints. If he made his
escape from the farmhouse shortly after she and Allard had first
discovered him, as seemed most likely, then he would be well
out of the vicinity by now.

But then there was the offer of a ransom. Where had that
come from? Who had brought it in? How was the gold to be

handed over? Only Sir William would know that and he seemed intent on keeping his cards close to his chest. His purpose, she surmised, was to play for time so that he could ensure the Cornish earl paid his share if not all of the sum demanded.

At least it meant that Elowen was still alive. That was the most optimism she could extract from the situation.

'Allard,' she reached across to attract his attention, 'you know this region. How far could Harry ride from the time we saw him at the farm until now?'

'He could reach the boundary, easy, and if he could get over the wall or bribe a gatekeeper he could get to . . .' he pondered the matter, 'to Salisbury?'

'Have you been there?'

'No.'

Taking his estimation for what it was worth she added, 'Maybe a town like Salisbury is the last place he would want be seen.'

Gregory overheard this. 'Does that mean you think he's hiding somewhere close, Hildi?'

'Don't you agree?'

'Let's see where these prints lead us before the rain washes them out. They might prove your case.'

The wetness rose upwards from the soggy ground as well as cascading down into it from out of the clouds so that it was only when they were almost up to one of the grave mounds that they realized that the prints were leading straight towards it. As tall and solid in height and width as a small house it would have been impossible to miss in ordinary daylight.

Now it loomed out of the mist like something from another world.

A skeletal sapling grew on top of it and as they approached they saw that a curtain of willow fronds concealed what looked like a crevice in the earth.

They dismounted.

Pushing their way forward on foot they noticed how the hoofprints they were following suggested that a horse had been taken right inside the mound.

'It must be a passageway,' muttered Egbert, reining in and jumping down. Without a sound the others drew alongside.

Gregory murmured, 'No sign of a horse coming out again.

We can go back and fetch up the men or take him ourselves if he's in there. What do you think?'

'I'd like to know how many men he's got with him.'

Allard moved forward, keen to have a say. 'Let me scout round to the other side on foot. I've never been this far out before but we used to play among the nearer mounds as little lads. Sometimes there are two entrances. There might be another one on the other side.'

'Are there no lookouts?' Hildegard asked. 'He's surely not alone? It seems strange to have no one keeping watch. Or does he imagine he's so well hidden as to need no one?'

Allard threw his horse's reins to her. As soon as he started out his boots sank deeply into the mud. He disappeared into the mist as he began to skirt the hideout.

With only the whisper of the rain on the grass the magic of the mound washed over them like a physical presence. Everyone seemed to feel it. To make sense of the eeriness that pervaded the place Hildegard mentioned that it was another of the burial mounds where the ancient ones offered their dead into the keeping of their pagan gods.

Some mounds, founded on more uneven terrain and ruined now, provided shelter for the flocks that roamed freely here-abouts in the domain. Others, desecrated by grave-robbers in search of treasure, were now only broken heaps of earth and stone where the shepherds, if they had the courage, could shelter through the cold watches of the night.

Gregory, with his usual impatience, made some caustic remark about Locryn, King of the Britons, and began to stride towards the entrance with one hand already lifting the vines aside when there was a sound of rushing hooves, the thudding of a horse racing over the ground nearby, but nothing to be seen until Allard, white-faced, hurtled from behind the mound with a shout.

'Watch out! It's a trap!' He snatched the reins of his horse from Hildegard's grasp.

At that moment a group of men armed with swords emerged from the burial mound and began slashing at the Beaulieu horses, causing them to rear and prance their forelegs in the air as they wheeled and backed against each other to ward off the blows aimed at them.

'Get out of this, Hildegard!' shouted Gregory. 'You're not armed!'

The monks were armed. Hildegard had not thought to ask them before, and they defended themselves with a force that surprised their attackers but neither side yielded and close-quarter fighting ensued with a viciousness that drew much blood on both sides.

Egbert, one arm held bleeding to his side, mounted his horse and rode it into the thick of the gang, knocking one to the ground to lie winded and groaning until he could stagger to his feet and grasp one of the frightened mounts as it passed.

Gregory fought his way to Egbert's side, aiming with precision at the gorget of an attacker, sending him half falling out of the saddle as his horse bore him away into the wilderness after the others with its reins and stirrups flapping.

Hildegard was not merely watching. Hearing a sound from the far side of the mound she spurred on her mount in time to see a black-bearded fellow with a figure wrapped in a blue cloak seated in front of him gallop off into the mist. All that remained moments later was the receding thump of hooves over the ground.

When she went to summon the others Allard, armed only with a riding whip, was thwacking the rump of one of the opponent's horses, to send it careering after the others while the remaining attackers, seeing their companions leave, and no doubt satisfied that their captain had escaped with the girl, gave up the fight and took themselves hastily from the scene.

The monks were all for following and set off in pursuit and Hildegard shouted to Allard, 'Go back and bring up the Cornishmen!'

Needing no second telling he urged his horse into a gallop to where the Cornishmen waited. Hildegard approached the cleft between the rocks at the entrance to the mound with her knife in her hand.

Inside she discovered a cramped chamber, low-roofed, dank, but with the advantage of another gap in the rock to allow a quick exit as Allard had surmised. There was no one within. Nor was there anything to suggest that it had been used for more than an overnight halt, a fact, she decided, that made it more likely that Elowen had been held at the farmstead when they had flushed out Black Harry the day before.

Cursing the fact that they had made such a mess of things she went to the exit but nothing in the poor visibility hinted at the nature of the encounter between the monks and the kidnappers. Had they caught up with them? Had they met sword with sword again? No sound suggested that this was the case. In fact the only sound was the hissing of the falling rain.

Worried because the monks were outnumbered, she put her faith in their experience on the Jerusalem road. They would not force an attack if they thought they were best to ride away from it.

One thing was to the good about this latest. It proved that Elowen was still within the Great Close.

Allard must have ridden like the wind because he was soon back with the four Cornishmen, and to their captain's gruff command she described as she was sure Allard had already done so what had happened and in which direction the kidnappers had escaped. In a moment they fixed themselves to the trail. Allard hesitated, his eyebrows raised when he turned to Hildegard, but she waved him after the others.

When they disappeared from sight she took the opportunity for a proper look inside the grave mound.

It was a sinister place, shadowy and dank, even though the bodies it had received were long gone. Nothing but fallen stones and sheep droppings met her glance. At least it was out of the rain. She led her horse inside and together they sheltered out of the wind that funnelled through the gaps in the stones.

There was little to note. Dry rock. Some of it covered in lichen. On the earth floor a few horse droppings. She poked a finger in them to discover if they were still warm. They were. That meant the men could not have been there long. She frowned. That was strange. There was nothing else to note.

Scarcely many moments passed before she heard voices. They were distant and accompanied by the faint jingling of harness. About to step outside she quickly changed her mind. It was obvious that one of the voices was that of a woman.

Leading her horse deeper into the burial chamber she was

well hidden by the time two riders appeared at the entrance. They did not dismount but, still talking, carried on round to the other side where they came to a halt. From her hiding place Hildegard could only glimpse the hem of a grey gown, somewhat muddied, and the boot of her companion as his horse shifted back and forth near the opening.

They were discussing something with some heat. The woman was adamant about a matter which made no sense to Hildegard, coming in on it halfway through. The palfrey she rode was as restive as her companion's cob and its random movements brought her more clearly though briefly into Hildegard's line of vision. Her mouth fell open.

It was Mistress Goda, Elowen's governess.

Had the household clerk deliberately lied when he told her she was confined to her chamber that morning? Or had he simply been mistaken?

Hildegard was considering whether to reveal her presence when something made her freeze.

The man growled, 'To be hoped he doesn't ruin her the way Bolingbroke ruined that Bohun heiress.'

'Come now, Robin!'

'Aye, well, we were disgusted. Luckily for her the babe died and they kept Bolingbroke off her until they were both of age. Then it was one visit a year down to Monmouth Castle and one squalling infant every nine months later until the day she died.'

'Heaven forfend that such a fate should ever await my darling Elowen!'

'It will hardly be worth his while, marriage, if he can get his hands on a fortune without that.'

'He can be trusted, quite besotted by her. You're too harsh!'

'It's a harsh game.'

'Aye, 'tis so. I hope you're prepared for that. I, for one, do trust him. Just make sure you don't let on to the men. Keep them keen.'

'I'm a falconer, Goda. I know how to handle wild 'uns with their own ideas.'

'Good, then we'll achieve a fine finale if everybody does what they're told.' Her horse swung her out of sight behind the stone wall and they both began to move off. The mass of hoof-prints led as plainly as the king's highway across the heath, but to what destination?

She edged towards the exit and peered out between the stones to be certain they were leaving, then, keeping well out of range of a casual backwards glance, she began to walk her horse through the mist after them.

They seemed to be in no hurry and it allowed Hildegard to hang back at a safe distance where she only needed to keep in view their darker shadows floating like wraiths in the watery air. Rain fell without end.

Without paying much attention to their direction they seemed to know where they were going and continued in a companion-able manner across the heath. She wondered if they knew they were at the back of a train of pursuers and the pursued. She wondered what they were plotting. Their conversation just now, fragmented though it was, hinted at something that if she could only understand it might be the key to Elowen's abduction. Who was this 'he' they mentioned? Was it important or just some idle gossip while they rode out?

Maybe they had ridden into the woods for exercise, and it was coincidence that they had stumbled across the burial mound, an obvious landmark in an otherwise featureless plain and it had no bearing on Elowen or anyone else she knew? She peered after them but the two shapes were moving before her like will-o'-the-wisps. Increasing her pace she came to the top of a shallow hill and there, down below, the trail stretched on towards a grey, rain-pocked lake, its filmy extent impossible to gauge in the low cloud that limited vision to a few yards.

The other figures leading this farandole had disappeared into the mist but at least Goda and her companion – Robin, was it? Her falconer? – at least those two were still faintly visible. She continued steadily down the slope after them.

A small copse loomed, no more substantial than a cloud. If they were making for that – and she wondered how they knew about it, if so – it made her hang back to give them time to enter the trees.

Then something unforeseen happened.

With a great flapping of wings a pheasant flew into the air with an alarmed screech right under her horse's forelegs. Startled, she felt him rear back under her and thrash about to keep his balance, then he dipped down again and at once reared back onto his hind legs too abruptly for her to keep her seat. She slipped from the saddle and hit the ground with a sickening thud.

After a moment she struggled to her knees. Shaken, she glanced up to see, riding back towards her, Mistress Goda and her companion.

When they reached her they did not offer help. They sat on their horses staring down at her. In an astonished false voice Goda exclaimed, 'Domina! How did you get here? Did the heavenly host drop you at our feet?'

Her companion swung one leg over to get down from his horse but instead of helping Hildegard he reached out for the dangling reins of her horse, still trembling after its shock. He muttered a few soothing words to it. Like Goda he seemed to be waiting for Hildegard to explain.

She rose achingly to her feet and tried not to wince. Brushing down her clothes she chanced to look up. 'My gratitude for holding my horse.'

She reached out but he made no move to hand over the reins. His watchful glance had something ambiguous in it, something threatening she felt, aware now how isolated the heath was and how these two could mean good or ill and – unexpectedly – she had no idea which it would be.

She took the reins but he did not relinquish his hold. 'My gratitude, master,' she prompted. 'I saw you from the brow of the hill and tried to catch up with you to tell you what has happened.'

Both stared at her more intently.

Constrained to say more she said, 'Your men came out with my two brother monks in the hope of apprehending this fellow they call Black Harry.' She spoke in as gauche a manner as possible. 'To their surprise they ran him to earth in one of the grave mounds! Can you believe it! He made off with a captive, Lady Elowen in her blue cloak. We could not believe our eyes. Everyone followed in pursuit.'

'So the blackguard escaped? What a shame,' replied Goda in a brisk tone. 'Let's go on then. We may catch up with them when they bring him down, as I'm sure they will. Do ride on with us, if you can ride after such a fall.'

The man Robin handed over the reins after this covert instruction. She remembered him now. He had disembarked at the haven with the others. He had been in the group that accompanied Egbert as far as St Leonard's barn straight after Elowen had been snatched.

'So you say this Black Harry, so-called, had our poor darling with him?' Goda remarked at last as they set off into the woods.

In similar circumstances Hildegard knew it would have been the burning question on her own lips and would have been thoroughly gone over by now but Goda asked nothing more.

'Now at least we know she's alive and in the vicinity, praise the Lord,' Hildegard murmured.

'And they recognized him but did not apprehend him? Too bad. The sheriff has now arrived—' Goda gave her a narrowed glance. 'Perhaps you already know that?'

'Is he coming out on the trail?'

'We've seen nothing of him since he went in to parlay with Sir William.'

She could not control the quick glance she threw in Robin's direction and Hildegard noted that he responded with a complicit smirk. Surely this was not the 'he' Goda had mentioned earlier? Besotted? Not William then, surely.

'Ah, Sir William,' sighed Hildegard, testing to see how much she could glean, 'he must be incensed that someone should trick him in this way. The dear little heiress and her casket stolen. I'm astonished he hasn't caught up with us already. He must be desperate to have her back.'

Goda's face was set in stone.

Hildegard continued. 'I was attending to my spiritual duties this morning when, apparently, the sheriff and his men rode in, so I'm out of touch with what has transpired since. It is such an insult to Sir William's status.'

'You know how these things pierce the heart?' Goda gave her a sideways glance. 'Even in your priory you must feel a wrench or two when someone mislays a prayer book or enters late for Lauds? So it is in the outside world. Things are felt deeply which, later, are seen as nothing. Not, of course, that this is nothing and—' She frowned and Hildegard saw her stumble towards an abyss and waited for her to fall in but the woman recovered herself to add in pious tones, 'We trust God will be just and the felons punished according to their deserts.'

They rode on until they emerged from the copse onto a wide hillside that lifted them pace by pace through the mist towards a summit they could not yet behold.

'I applaud your knowledge of the countryside,' Hildegard continued in the same slightly wondering tone of someone who rarely left the cloistered sameness of their priory. 'I would be lost here without you. How can you scry which way they've gone?'

Goda's laugh held a smug note. 'My dear, if we only knew which way to go, maybe it would lead us to her. Isn't that so, Robin?

'We are merely following a trail we found, wondering where it might take us. Hoping and praying we find her. Look, see those hoofprints? Now you've told us what happened I believe they must be made by the men as they chased after these renegades. We shall trust Robin in this. He could follow a trail over water, could you not, my friend?'

'Indeed, ma'am,' he spoke for the first time. 'I receive such praise with the utmost humility, save you.' He touched his forelock.

*He called her ma'am*, Hildegard registered. Somewhat different to the way he spoke to her when they thought they were alone.

In a short while some figures materialized out of the mist. It was the white Cistercian robe revealed underneath a cloak and the elegant way Gregory always sat a horse that made her return her knife to its sheath in her sleeve with a sigh of relief.

'Ho!' called the Cornishman, Robin, when he recognized the rest of his fellows. 'I hear you disturbed the prey but have had no luck?'

A few grunted negatives were the only response and the group came to a ragged halt. It was clear at a glance. They were disconsolate. Enraged. Resigned.

'We lost them at a lake,' the captain explained. 'They had the sense to shake us off the scent by going through water. We saw their trail clear enough down to the water margin. All of them must have waded in. Where they came out we don't know. We haven't enough men to examine the entire shoreline.'

'Nor do we know how deep it is,' one of them added. 'They must know of underwater paths to keep their heads above it.'

'They could have come ashore anywhere,' the third man agreed. 'In this rain we can't even see the other side.'

'You must return with more men,' Goda stated with the authority of one used to being obeyed. 'They're not fish. They must have come ashore somewhere.'

Gregory was looking askance at the arrivals but edged his horse next to Hildegard. When he lifted his hood a little she saw him raise his eyebrows as if to ask how she happened to be so accompanied.

'I bumped into them after they turned up at the burial mound,' she whispered.

'Later?' he breathed.

She nodded. 'Are we going back?'

He lifted his head and addressed all of them. 'We monastics have to attend the mid-day Office. I trust we shall be excused further help until our duties permit it?'

There was rough agreement and when they started to ride back the way they had arrived the others followed evidently thinking it a good idea to give up now and return, warmer, drier, possibly fed, and accompanied by more men to help them solve the mystery.

'They seemed to vanish into thin air,' one of the Cornishmen said as the horses picked up speed now home was a prospect. 'What do you make of that?'

Somebody replied, 'They must have had a boat moored nearby, don't you think?'

Goda cut in with an indulgent smile. 'We will find her, men. Of course we will. The sheriff is here now. We have not given up.'

# EIGHTEEN

Egbert was steaming his riding boots by the fire in the guest lodge. His expression was bemused. 'It was a masterstroke to get into the water like that. It was too vast for us to circle without stretching our forces. Leaving only one of us to combat half a dozen of theirs should we come across them was not an option.'

Gregory agreed. 'We don't even know whether we were following this Harry fellow and the girl at that point or his gang. They may have split up in the mist to lure us away while he went in a different direction.' He turned to Hildegard. 'And Mistress Goda and her companion? I noticed a certain froideur between you, if I may put it like that, Hildi.'

She told them about the conversation she had heard between Goda and the falconer. 'His manner changed at once as soon as I was on the scene. They were like allies, as if cooking something up between them when they thought they were alone.'

Egbert put his boots back on the fire rail. 'I may be missing the point here but they strike me as – well, how shall I put it? – oddly unfocused on the problem of finding their charge. William as well. In fact,' he added after a moment's thought, 'William mostly. I mean, where is he now? The sheriff and his men arrived in good time this morning so why weren't they out, lending us numbers? We might have been able to pick up the trail if we'd had more men.'

Gregory's lips curved in a cynical smile. 'As soon as she's found, Sir William will have to give up his free lodging for himself and his men. Have you thought of that? Maybe he wants to hang around Beaulieu for as long as he can,' adding, 'or for as long as it takes to finish his business in Hampton?'

Egbert looked askance. 'The devil. Would he do that and leave that little maid in the midst of such danger and uncertainty in return for some meagre worldly advantage? She must be sick with fright wondering whether she'll be allowed to live or die.'

'As well as other horrors she might be suffering at the hands of Black Harry,' Hildegard felt bound to add. 'We *must* find her.' She turned to Gregory. 'What business in Hampton?'

'Something to do with his wool clip, I expect. It's only something the fellows were discussing. They know no more than I do.'

They emptied a carafe in front of the fire before they remembered they had intended to go into the midday Office. 'Too late now,' observed Gregory. 'And we're no nearer to finding a solution. Are we missing the key to the whole thing?'

'Is there a key – or is it a story of sheer random greed for gold as is so often the case?'

'That's not much help, Egbert. Who gains?'

'I've been asking myself that from the start.'

Hildegard wrinkled her brow. 'The kidnappers gain if the ransom is paid, but if William feels he has to consult with Earl Richard before paying a penny it could take months. And it hardly narrows the list! So many here would gain in their time of need. It doesn't rule anyone out, does it, not even the monks themselves!'

'One thing I know, when Earl Richard, safely in St Keverne in ignorance of what has befallen, learns about the way the betrothal party has been received, you can be sure the monks here will feel the brunt of his rage. They definitely won't gain. I wouldn't want to be them.'

'Come, this is getting us nowhere.' Gregory rose to his feet. 'Let's go and find out what this sheriff thinks if he's still here and whether William intends to pay up. Then we'll persuade them to ride out when the mist clears to see if we can find out exactly where those horsemen went ashore.' Gregory shrugged on his waterproofs. 'I vow to follow the trail if it leads to the farthest reaches of Uttermost Thule!'

They followed Gregory's suggestion and crossed over the garth to William's lodge where the sheriff was last seen.

A couple of the sheriff's henchmen, well buckled into their fighting harness, were on duty outside Sir William's lodge and when the Cistercians appeared they jumped smartly to attention. A couple of lances clashed across the doorway.

Gregory looked down at both men from his magisterial height with a look of exaggerated surprise. 'I say, men, this is strong, isn't it? Don't you see we're only three innocent monastics?'

'We have our orders, brother. Nobody enters.'

'But is there any need for this?' Gingerly Gregory touched one of the lances as if not quite sure what it was. 'Do you fear two unarmed monks and a nun? I think not. Surely,' he added with mock astonishment, 'you cannot believe we wish harm on anyone?'

The two men pretended they couldn't hear.

'Come now, your orders are not to waylay innocent visitors and colleagues of Sir William but to halt felons and others who are here with ill-intent.'

The two men glanced at each other out of the corners of their eyes.

Egbert had his arms folded but remained silent. Egbert at his most dangerous, registered Hildegard, wondering what would happen next if the men refused them entry.

'Now, the way I see it, you're good fellows doing your duty and when Sir William hears about your assiduity—' he stressed the word knowing they would not know it and would therefore feel at a disadvantage, 'he will be delighted that you have proved yourselves such stout men and will no doubt reward you for it.

'However, if he hears that you have prevented legitimate visitors from imparting vital information to him he will not be pleased . . . And we all know what Sir William is like when he is displeased?'

The more decisive of the two henchmen lifted his lance and stood it next to himself. 'Come on, Jack, let them through, he's right. We don't want to get on the wrong side of 'im.' He nodded over his shoulder to indicate the unpredictable lord within. 'Remember when he visited the guardroom last time he was in Hampton?'

'Aye, we're not likely to forget that one.'

Grudgingly, smarting from the memory, the other guard did as his companion had done, lowered his lance then edged cautiously to one side as if he expected Gregory to drag him to the ground in a flying tackle. Gregory gave them an affable smile. 'So the lord sheriff is parlaying with Sir William even now?' He did not wait for an answer but, still smiling, pushed his way through into the porch with the other two in close order behind him.

Hildegard heard the clash as the lances were replaced to bar the door. It made her wonder who they expected to come barging in to see the sheriff and what was the nature of their conversation if he always had to travel with two such dolts in attendance to guard his privacy but then she was following the monks into the hall and saw the usual blazing logs in the hearth.

This time two men, Sir William and a stranger, had their heads together.

The word 'ship' and 'cargo' floated to them as both men turned to see who had entered without warning. Their conversation was abruptly curtailed and Sir William sprang to his feet with an oath.

'My revered lord,' greeted Gregory at his smoothest before William could get a word in. 'We crave audience with you at your convenience and trust that the present moment is such?' He bowed to the stranger. 'My lord Sheriff?'

The sheriff nodded.

Gregory cut in again before William could draw breath. 'No doubt, my lord, your captain at arms informed you of our failure to follow the band of abductors holding your son's dear betrothed this morning but at least we had a sighting—' Sir William opened his mouth to speak but Gregory continued, 'and we are of the opinion that a thorough search of the margins of the lake should be made as soon as the weather begins to clear. I'm sure your captain has already made the suggestion and is even now about to rouse his men from their quarters?'

Sir William blinked. Was this a question, he seemed to ask because if so he had forgotten the beginning of it and for a moment was at a loss until his usual response came to his aid.

'Who the devil let you in?' he roared. 'I'll have them gutted, the useless losels! I told them to keep everybody out! OUT!'

The Cistercians remained silent as if waiting for a storm to pass.

William, in the face of such sublime serenity, recovered himself sufficiently to say to the sheriff, 'I will not have insubordination in my militia.'

'Quite right, quite right,' murmured the sheriff, smoothing the whiskers of his greying beard with one hand. 'These are harmless monastics, however, so I'm sure your men were unable to withstand their request, eh, Brothers? And blessed sister, too.' He gave a genial smile much as a man holding a lion might smile at an audience he wishes to court for his daring.

'Come in then, sit.' William flicked his fingers at his servant. 'Wine.' He continued, 'We were breaking our fast before setting out. So in your estimation, brother, we should scour the lake shore and follow yet another trail over this blasted heath? It's such a damned wilderness, no shelter, nothing but sheep. I envy them their flocks but it's a bitch of a place in bad weather. At this time of year my men need to be somewhere dry where they can practise the arts of war, not trailing about like a disgruntled set of hounds on the scent of a wench.'

'But they will be the better for a little hardship, my lord,' murmured the sheriff, and at the word 'hardship' William's expression brightened.

'So where were we?' the sheriff himself resumed.

William, with a hurried glance indicating the visitors said, 'We'll continue our business later.'

The sheriff replied, 'I can allow you a few men to join the search to supplement the ones you brought yourself. Not forgetting the conversi if they're available – they have useful local knowledge, together with a few of the more physically capable monks perhaps?'

He turned to Gregory but William butted in. 'How wide is this lake?' he demanded. 'How many men will it take?'

'It's not a lake as such, a flood, an overflow from the upper reaches of the river and when the dry season starts it will disappear as quickly as it formed. It was a clever stroke to use it to disguise the direction they've taken.'

It seemed to Hildegard that William listened to what the sheriff said with scant interest despite his questions, but then he glared at Gregory, was about to say something, then dropped his glance as their eyes met. Even William knows he has met his match, thought Hildegard, observing the minute change in his manner.

Now he began telling him in an offhand tone that as far as

he was concerned the hunt for the wench should already be under way again.

'Call my captain!' he ordered his personal servant, giving him a clip on the head. By chance one of William's many rings caught the young fellow's cheek and blood sprang in a line of scarlet down his face. It must have smarted but he did not flinch.

William ignored him.

'Tell them to get him out of his sack, the idle fellow, and hurry up and muster my men. Let them get out again. Are they frightened of a drop of rain now?' He nodded to Gregory. 'How many of those Beaulieu monks are able to come out? Enough, I would imagine. They've nothing to do all day. They're not my problem. They're their prior's responsibility. He'll do as I tell him. He was here earlier and got the message with his whining about the fire yesterday.' He rose to his feet again and gave his servant a push. 'See to it!'

He turned to his guest. 'Right, Sheriff, you and your men join my militia, you monks come along as God wills, and let's find this wench and her little casket of gold so we can have done with the business and get down to what really matters.' He gave a swift sidelong glance at the sheriff. 'It shouldn't be too difficult a task now we've cornered the brute. What's his name? Black Harry? He won't be coming back this way again. Not now he's warned. He'll know we're waiting for him. Let's go!'

'My lord,' Gregory moved forward. 'Our reason for persuading your guards to allow us entry into your presence touches on the matter of a ransom note we are told was delivered here during the night.'

William scowled. 'You've already heard about that in your cloister, have you? I can tell you something. It makes such an outrageous demand I am choosing to ignore it for the present. What are your brothers saying in their wisdom, then?'

'My brothers' restricted conversation does not include such topics.'

'Good, good. Then I'll tell you and you can tell them and they won't have to sully their lips with any idle talk. Everybody happy. It asks me for—' He flicked his fingers at the servant who had returned, blood still beading down his cheek, after passing on instructions for the muster, and who now handed Sir William a piece of parchment which was resting on the stool beside him.

William handed it to Gregory who glanced at it and in turn handed it to Egbert, who did likewise and passed it on to Hildegard.

She was left holding it for longer than the others and had time to sniff it, intrigued by a scent of incense and the neat, educated hand in which the short demand was written. Her eyes widened at the amount requested in exchange for Elowen.

Without massive loans Sir William would not have enough to pay it even if he wanted to, which he clearly did not.

She handed it back to the servant with thanks.

When she turned Gregory was saying, 'I can understand your reluctance to pay up, my lord. It's a huge amount.'

'It's out of the question. We'll run them down wherever they hide. I won't pay a farthing.'

When Sir William said, 'Let's go,' it did not mean that he himself was going to ride out in the teeth of foul weather.

Once his men were reassembled in the stable yard and the few men the sheriff had were brought along to join them, William made it clear he was going to remain in his lodge as the centre of authority.

'All information will pass through me,' he snarled as his captain asked if he should have a horse saddled up for him. 'How do you imagine I'm going to keep tabs on everyone if I'm out on the heath riding who the hell knows where? You sotwit. I'm surrounded by fools!' He stamped back indoors.

The Beaulieu monks were fewer in number after the midday Office, having some other important Lent duties that required their attention, and even Gregory and Egbert made no haste to have fresh horses saddled up.

'What are you planning?' Hildegard asked. They were alone in the peace and quiet of the stables again with only the sound of the horses champing at their hay after the noise and clash made by armed men in such a confined space. It had been a relief when the sheriff gave the command to leave and they roared out under the gatehouse in their usual manner.

'What makes you imagine we're planning anything, Hildegard?' asked Egbert with a cherubic grin after they left.

'I know you both well enough,' she returned.

'I think we all feel we can leave things to the sheriff and you remember you suggested riding up to the grange on this side of the river yesterday?'

'You want to do that now?'

'What do you think?'

'I was going to suggest it. If Black Harry is to elude his pursuers it seems likely he'll avoid the side of the river bristling with William's men. He'll want to seek somewhere less dangerous where he can hole up until he has a reply to his ransom demand.'

'I can see you're about to say but—'

'But – yes, this ransom – what do you make of it?'

Gregory laughed. 'Audacious.'

'An amount unlikely to be paid in the way he would want,' added Egbert.

'And,' she added, 'surely not penned by a man who has been described the way they describe Black Harry?'

'What do you mean?'

'It was in a clerical hand, don't you think? It also held a whiff of incense.'

'What?'

'I held it in my hands for a moment or two. It was not written by anyone living rough in the woods.'

'You think it came from – here?' Gregory for once looked surprised himself.

'It makes no sense. But yes. At least, that's the immediate conclusion.'

'Would it be like one of these fellows to try a fast one? A monk set on making a fortune?'

'Or one hoping to pay the enormous papal taxes that are being demanded from them by means of an exaction of gold from Sir William's coffers?'

'The prior?'

'It would certainly solve their tax problem!'

Gregory, always looking for a loophole in any theory, was doubtful. 'We mustn't jump to conclusions. It may well be a

bluff by Black Harry to keep William on the trail, playing cat
and mouse again, and hoping to maintain a good price for her
ransom.'

Egbert was frowning. 'Hildegard, maybe you might suspect
that this Black Harry has paid someone to write the note for
him?'

'That he has an ally within the abbey?' She pondered the
matter but could come to no conclusions. 'I admit I hadn't taken
it as far as that. Are you suggesting the monks would collude
with a blackguard like him?'

'And don't forget, it's not only tonsured monks who can write
a fair hand. Some of the novices are quite capable of it too.'

'At least it lets the lay-brothers out, poor illiterate saints as
they are.'

'Who brought it to William in the first place? How was it
delivered?' she asked. 'Do we know yet?'

'We weren't given time to find out amid all his bluster.'

'That servant of his told me he found it on a stool in the
guest hall – but who would have put it there?'

No one knew. Hildegard was as puzzled as the others.


# NINETEEN


With no way of resolving anything at present they
saddled up and set out on the long uphill track
towards a place known as the Abbot's Well. After
that they continued riding up through the woods until they came
out near several tracks, one leading straight across the high
moorland to the east, one to the north which Black Harry, if he
had escaped this way after blurring his tracks at the lake, might
have taken, and a narrow one leading down to the farthest-flung
grange on the same side as the abbey.

Otterwood.

It was a suitably remote hiding place. From the crest of the
hill they could see the serpentine bends of the river winding
like silver filigree between the trees. Even the ruffling patterns

of the tide as the waters ebbed were visible from the heights. They decided to hobble the horses among the trees and descend on foot.

It took a little time. The track wound about, at one point seemed to double back on itself, and eventually they found themselves above the thatched building of a small farmstead. A few cows munched the short winter grass in a narrow meadow. Apple trees grew crookedly further off. A heavy silence lay over everything now they were sheltered from the wind. That morning's rain and mist were giving way to pale sunlight.

'There seems to be no one around,' murmured Egbert, eyes narrowed as he searched the domain for a sign of movement.

'The lay-brothers will have been called down to the abbey with all the others. Someone will have been left in charge. The cows need milking for a start.'

'Someone has evidently seen to that duty,' observed Hildegard. 'Shall we go down?'

They descended the hill and crossed the yard to the door.

A knock brought no one forth. Egbert pushed it open. Aware of the possibility of ambush he allowed it to swing wide. There came no response. He edged sideways and peered through the crack between the jamb and the door post.

Whispering to the others he gave the door another push. 'I'll go in first. Seems there's no one here.'

Gregory gave a lazy shrug. 'Certainly no sign of Black Harry and that gang of horsemen.'

Egbert disappeared inside the single chamber and they heard him climb some stairs. Gregory was on the alert but Egbert came down almost at once. He stepped outside. 'We're right. Nobody. But, strangely, there are three bowls on the ledge. All have had pottage in them recently. Is he entertaining guests up here?'

They circled the small stone-built dwelling without seeing any sign of the lay-brother in charge.

It was a well-ordered little place. Hay was stacked in a wooden barn, enough to see out the rest of the winter. A wood pile showed someone had been busy. The thatch on the roof, even that, looked well kept. Then a cat came round the corner and confidently began to brush itself against their legs.

'There was a jug of milk on a ledge inside,' Egbert remarked. 'The little creature knows what it wants.' He went back inside and emerged with one of the bowls containing a drop of milk and placed it in front of the eager cat. They watched its small pink tongue flick milk into its mouth with obvious pleasure.

'So he's a cat-lover, this lay-brother? Look how unafraid it is! No kicks for this little one.'

Bluff, tough Egbert, an indomitable fighter, stroked the cat with one large, capable hand as it purred and Hildegard and Gregory exchanged amused looks as he began to murmur sweet nothing to it in an unexpectedly soft voice. The cat rippled with pleasure beneath his touch.

Gregory was the first to break the spell. 'I'm going to take a walk down the meadow to see where it goes. Mayhap I'll find the fellow sleeping under a tree. He might know something.' He set off.

Egbert stood up and the cat wound knots round his riding boots. To Hildegard he said, 'Let's keep Gregory in view. He's breaking one of our basic rules, going off into unknown territory alone. If it is an ambush – not that it appears to be – he's laying himself open to danger. I've never known him to be so lax but he's somewhat preoccupied today. Haven't you noticed?'

'Not really. I mean, we're all rather preoccupied by the situation, aren't we?'

Egbert's sharp grey eyes met hers. 'Physical danger is not the only danger he needs to beware.'

'I know.'

He held her glance.

'Egbert, I know. I will do the right thing.'

'I know you will. I have faith in you.'

'Then have faith in him also.'

She turned briskly to put an end to an exchange that had suddenly become uncomfortable.

'Let's do as you say, Egbert. I find it oddly quiet here. It fills me with a sense of foreboding. It's as if something we cannot foresee is about to happen.' As she walked away she said, 'I don't usually feel like this. Maybe a storm is coming up.'

She looked at the sky. The pale February sun pushed its way through milk-white cloud covering one end of the horizon to the other.

They found Gregory standing in a clump of bushes gazing down the slope towards the river. Even now from the vantage point of the meadow it lay a fair distance away. Something in that direction though had obviously alerted him. When he heard a footfall in the grass behind him he spun round then, seeing who it was, waved them to silence.

When they stood shoulder to shoulder he murmured, 'He's down there by himself. See? Between those trees? I can't make out what he's doing.'

With some surreptitious parting of twigs they managed to make out the shape of an oldish lay-brother hacking at something on the ground with an axe. He was holding the haft in both hands. The axe shone as he swung it up into the air and smashed it down.

Egbert was not as interested as Gregory. 'It's just some farming task. Chopping wood. So what?'

'I saw him drag something from out of those bushes.'

'Something hidden?'

'I'll go down and greet him, shall I?' Hildegard suggested, beginning to make a move. 'I'll find out if he's on the level, as the masons say. It's probably nothing more than a routine task, Gregory.'

'Let Egbert go. He can do his man-to-man performance.'

She noticed Egbert look across in surprise. 'Do I put on a performance?' he asked mildly.

'You know you do.' Gregory spoke more sharply than usual. Egbert said nothing but seemed put out.

Hildegard had never heard them exchange a cross word before. She thought it prudent to leave them to it but Gregory reached out a hand and pulled her back.

'No!' His fingers brushed the back of her hand and he sprang away as if burned. 'I'll leave you two together. If you wouldn't mind sparing a glance to see if I've managed to flush out Black Harry single-handedly?'

He stalked off.

'What's bitten him?' she asked as he disappeared down the meadow.

'You can guess. He's walking on hot bricks at present. It's no more than a fever. Let's hope it passes. We cloistered monks, you know how it is? I expect you nuns are much the same. It's the usual challenge to our faith. Prospects of hell fire usually bring everyone back to the Rule.'

'Let's keep him in view at least, just in case it is an ambush. Could Black Harry have come out here? We've seen no sign of visitors—'

'He may have found a way to outwit William again,' Egbert answered as he continued to peer through the screen of branches. 'It's a fact we're all feeling uneasy. None of this hangs together in any sense. Someone is guilty of theft and kidnap. Likely they're also guilty of murdering that poor young lay-brother.'

'Young Godric.' She crossed herself.

'We must not give up.' He gave a rueful smile. 'Let's at least imagine how it might turn out as we would wish.' He folded his arms and began, 'William's men have already apprehended this blackguard; the sheriff is grinning from ear to ear to have him in custody; Sir William himself is happy because he's avoided paying a ransom; little Elowen has been restored to her betrothal ship; and all's right with the world!'

'To be more practical—'

'Let's go down and do our best to prevent Gregory from being kidnapped himself!' He added in an undertone, 'Cussed, ill-humoured and brimming with sin though he is!'

He let the branches snap back into place. 'It looks as if he's engaged the fellow in conversation.' He grinned at her. 'He's probably discussing Thomas Aquinas with him, man to man. I'll go down and put on a performance, shall I? You can tell me if I've missed my vocation and should exchange my habit for a cap and bells!'

'Sotwit,' she replied fondly. Together they made their way to the lower meadow beyond the trees.

The lay-brother glanced up when he saw the two of them walk down. He leaned on the haft of his axe and glanced from Gregory to them both and back. 'Quite a congregation. Are there any more?'

Gregory laughed in a way that would never have earned him a place in a players' company, judged Hildegard, and she listened as he went blandly on, 'Brother Egbert and Hildegard of Meaux. And – as I was saying – we happened to be passing and wondered what sort of place was down here, our curiosity piqued.'

Egbert stood a little way off, waiting for his cue and not wishing to upstage the main player.

Despite the anxiety she felt, Hildegard couldn't help smiling to herself. She was fond of them both but sometimes, instead of being monks she could lean on for good advice or for help at times of physical danger, they were like two boys, rivalrous and competitive, despite their dedication to their calling.

Rivals, she thought now, but with less enmity than the abbey monks with their support for rival popes, one of whom, Clement, was known as the Butcher of Cesena, with horrifying accuracy.

'And you are . . .?' Gregory was asking the conversi now.

'Marland, brother. I'm master at Otterwood. But for my bad back I'd be down in church raising my voice in prayer for Lent. We decided it was best I stayed here. It did away with an election over who would have the honour. There would have been several contenders. It's not onerous, seeing to the animals here and making cheese.'

'It's so well organized,' murmured Gregory, clearly at a loss how to play the game of man-to-man.

Egbert would probably have made some comment about the back-breaking work of chopping wood and offered to lend a hand. As it turned out it wasn't necessary as the old fellow, maybe not as old as his stooped back suggested, seemed quite eager to talk.

All the while he was doing so he began to amble casually away from the wood he was chopping, leaving a scattering of laths, something he had been at pains to destroy. They followed him up the meadow towards the house without remarking on it.

Hildegard, not without irony, ceded her minor place as a woman to the authority of men, and took the chance to linger, glancing back, wondering what he had been breaking up and why he wished to draw them away as if to forestall questions.

She remembered the makeshift hide the two young poachers had built on the other side of the river. Then she estimated how long it might take to walk from that side to this. They would have had to cross the river. Not by the bridge where they would be seen. By a ford? But that would have to be higher up near the heath. If they managed to get across to the track along the ridge above Otterwood they risked being seen as they made their way into the woods.

At least they would find plenty of cover here and enough game to keep starvation away. A bow and arrow would be useful. No one would guess their presence unless they stumbled across their shelter – before it was systematically destroyed.

Was that it?

And what if they had not been poachers at all, but armed men, crossing the river with a captive heiress?

Could the monks be in on the plot?

She had another look while the men continued up the meadow towards the farmhouse. Vines woven between the laths suggested that it could have been a shelter like the one they came across yesterday. That had been destroyed too. But it might also have been a coracle.

The men reached the top of the meadow with its view of the river and she joined them – as silent and devout a nun as a hundred popes could have wished – and wondered about her own prospects of joining the players.

The conversi master invited them into his house. Without being asked he poured watered wine into some clay beakers lined up on a shelf and, picking up the milk jug was about to pour a drop into the cat's bowl when he saw there was still some left.

'I thought you finished it off, Mite, you old fraudster,' he murmured.

He picked up the cat which at once nestled in his arms as his master indicated that they should all find places to sit.

Hildegard stayed near the door on a stool. The monks settled on a bench. The lay-brother seemed to ready himself to break into a yarn but Gregory spoke up first.

'Forgive me, brother, but I must ask if you know what is happening at present?'

'With regard to what?'

'The kidnapping of Lady Elowen of St Keverne.'

'Poor dear child,' he replied. 'Yes, they do keep me informed, isolated though we are. I hear that this Sir William is burning every property he finds in order to eliminate them from his search?'

'Not quite all. One only, to our knowledge. One too many in our opinion, if we're allowed opinions on such matters.'

The fellow chuckled. 'But you are under this lord's authority, I believe, being part of the escort appointed to safeguard what he regards as his property?'

'Our allegiance is with our abbot, Hubert de Courcy,' Gregory explained. 'At present he favours Boniface so I should say it lies with the Holy Father. What our prior will concede after the convocation at present taking place at Cîteaux none but God knows.'

Egbert stood up. 'Who's this?' He went outside and they heard him greet someone.

'That'll be Brother Simon,' the conversi master informed them.

A bright-faced young monk put his head round the door. 'Visitors. Our friends from Meaux?'

'Pray enter, brother.' Marland was already pouring out a beaker for him. 'Now tell us the latest.'

Hildegard wondered where the young brother had sprung from. Had he been following them? If he had approached along the steep hill they themselves had climbed earlier they might not have noticed him if he kept to the trees. He looked in no way out of breath.

She waited to see if anyone would say anything and leaned further back into her corner to observe matters.

Egbert of course broached the question at once. 'Greetings, brother. I don't imagine you want to be walking that hill very often. Did you ride up?' He knew very well no horse had been heard outside.

Brother Simon smiled. 'I walked up through the woods,' he replied. 'It's shorter than the track you probably took although a little steeper. I'll show you the path when you decide to walk down again. It's easy to get lost, I warn you, but I'm sure you fellows have a good sense of direction?' His bright eyes fastened on each monk in turn.

Oh, I see, thought Hildegard. Initial sword-play. And he's going to make sure he sees us leave.

Egbert noted the opening thrust and was keen to engage. 'Fair to middling,' he replied. 'Brother Gregory and I were escorting pilgrims on the Jerusalem road for a while. Of course, desert sand is rather different to find your way through than English woodland, but I suppose the homing instinct is much the same.'

Brother Simon raised his eyebrows. 'You must be well able to look after yourselves.'

'It's all in the luck of the game when it comes to survival,' Egbert replied. 'Certain tactics make it more likely you'll come through, but no one lives forever. We hope to continue on our chosen path for some time yet but who knows? Every day is a new day and every day may be our last on earth. We trust in God.'

Simon nodded agreement over these platitudes. 'You must have been in a lot of skirmishes. I admire you. I'm untested in physical warfare.' His sharp eyes missed nothing. 'As for the spiritual battle, I find it enough of a daily challenge for my strength. As God wills.'

Gregory's earlier ill-temper seemed to have abated. 'As adherents of St Bernard the imposition of raising taxes for Boniface seems to be our greatest challenge at present.'

This contribution brought a cackle of derision from Marland. 'You Cistercians. You're like everybody else when it comes to guarding your own. I hope you manage to find an equitable solution. The lay-brothers don't want to find that three-quarters of our hard work goes to keep some fellow in idleness, calling himself pope in some foreign palace when our own people are starving for want of bread.'

'That is a most sacrilegious view, Marland, if I may say so.' Brother Simon smiled without any sign of condemnation and the two men somehow, despite their words, seemed to be in accord.

Gregory had gone to stand by the open door with his back to them as if deep in thought. When he turned he gave Simon a searching glance.

'If I may put our cards on the table – forgive the metaphor – we are at a loss to work out where you fellows stand on the most pressing matter that concerns us, outside the major problem of popes and their exactions. This child, whoever she is, whatever she is, however good or bad or worthy or unworthy, however she stands in the world, is missing. She has been abducted in your purlieu. We need to find her. What suggestions do you have?'

Both Beaulieu men fell silent.

The conversi master continued to stroke the cat. Brother Simon inspected the frayed strap of his sandal.

Even after one of the hens came inside, scratching for grain, made a circuit of the chamber and went out again, the silence continued.

Marland fixed a meaningful glance on Simon. 'You must have some ideas, brother?'

Simon looked uncomfortable. 'As we say, we must trust in God and pray she is found.'

'I can't help wondering,' Gregory continued, brushing aside this nebulous response to a direct question, 'that somebody living within the Close must have seen something that has given rise to suspicion. Horsemen, with no colours to show to whom they owe allegiance, cannot have come from nowhere. Given that the gate-keepers have seen no one enter, or so they say, these men must have been noticed within the Great Close either in some visitor's retinue or going about their usual business here. One of them at least is guilty of the murder of one of your own lay-brothers. It is unlikely that the men marauding at St Leonard's and the abductors of Elowen are not one and the same. But he is your responsibility. Even so I regard it as a grave insult to be lied to by anyone who has the slightest suspicion of the truth.'

Nobody said anything.

Gregory took it as permission to continue. 'I also want to make it clear that I offer fair warning to all concerned that, as men given the betrothed into their sacred charge, we are not likely to give up on what we set out to do. We know where our responsibilities lie. Whatever it takes we shall find her. Moreover, the perpetrators of such an outrage will pay, either in this world or, to be sure, in the next. I suggest they look to their immortal souls and seek a way back from the dark path they have chosen.'

Egbert cleared his throat.

Hildegard waited to see how the Beaulieu men would respond.

A moment passed before Marland lifted the cat down and pushed it away. Not roughly but in a businesslike manner. He looked up at Simon then turned to the others.

'I follow orders. I run the grange here for the benefit of the abbey. I follow the rules laid down for us lay-brothers. With no abbot in place we're left only to do whatever we think best. I mean no ill to anyone.'

He got up and went out. The cat sniffed at Egbert's boots in passing and followed.

'That leaves me, then,' observed Brother Simon.

'So it does,' remarked Gregory.

'It's like this.' The young monk stood up and folded his hands inside his sleeves.

Hildegard noticed the Cistercians tense but Simon was merely concealing his hands in order to look more imposing, not to produce a weapon.

'We are hiding something from you,' he began. 'Not from you so much as from your lord. He must have chosen you to escort the betrothed and her little retinue because he knew you would think as he does and therefore do his bidding—'

'You're wrong in that assumption,' Gregory broke in. 'He did not choose us. We do not think as he does. We volunteered when our abbot asked for two men to accept the mission. We judged we were the best two to undertake such an undertaking.'

Egbert shifted in agreement. 'True. We're not cloister monks. We can look after ourselves and others in most situations. And so can our sister here if it comes to it. Our abbot and the Prioress of Swyne judged us to be the best for the job.'

For the first time Brother Simon turned and had a good look at Hildegard on her corner stool. When he turned back he bowed his head in acknowledgement. 'Forgive me for making such an assumption—'

'Reasonable in the circumstances. How could you know how we arrange things at Meaux?'

'So then, the truth is this. We are hiding someone – two runaways living in fear of breaking the terms of their allegiance. They fear that members of the household who travelled from Cornwall in the betrothal ship will pursue them and drag them back to face the penalty of their actions. Out of perhaps a misplaced sense of compassion we have helped them elude their masters ever since they threw themselves on our mercy. That is all. This has no bearing on the mystery of the missing heiress.'

His open, honest features betrayed no hint of guile.

'Tell us more,' Egbert suggested. 'When did these runaways seek your help?'

'Shortly after the abduction. I understand they spent a night or two in the woods and hunger drove them to steal food from the Beaufre. Instead of remaining in the vicinity fear led them here when the heath was overrun by armed men. They managed to cross the river on a makeshift raft and climb up into the woods below Marland's farm. He found them in a sorry state and took pity on them. It's nothing to him that they've escaped bondage to the earl, their lord and master. He believes they must have good reason and should have a fair hearing. If the Cornish earl is anything like Sir William he believes that might be the last thing they'll get if they're forced to appear at his leet court next quarter.'

'Where are they now?' Gregory eyed him closely.

'They've moved on to a more secret location and asked only that Marland did not incriminate himself or the other lay-brothers by leaving the remains of their raft to be found by the members of their household.'

'We saw him disposing of it just now.'

'Then that confirms what I say.'

'Wait a moment.' Hildegard stood up. 'Did you say two runaway boys?'

Brother Simon considered her question for too long before nodding his head. 'So I believe.'

Gregory broke in smoothly, 'You mentioned a path back to the abbey through the woods? We have horses with us. Is it suitable for them?'

'Indeed.' Brother Simon was not too slow to make his earlier meaning clear. He went to the door at once. 'I have finished here, having nothing you might not have overheard. I called in just now to find out if Marland had done as these lads requested. You say he has. We can therefore leave when you're ready.'

With a confused expression he called, 'Marland? We've finished. We're leaving now.'

When the conversi master appeared, Simon said, 'I have explained about the raft and that you are in no way responsible for any subterfuge concerning our visitors' own quest. They are now ready to be guided along the woodland path back to the abbey. All I have to add is to let you know that the clerk of the St Keverne household has spared a couple of his servants to continue their search down by the saltings. He has convinced himself that the runaway servants are hiding down there and, being a kindly fellow, fears for their safety. Someone among our monks,' he added, 'has instilled in him a dread of our double tide and a fear of the salt marshes. I understand the St Keverne men are more used to rocks and but a single daily tide on their part of the coast.'

As they made their farewells Simon added, 'It grieves me to hoodwink so genial a fellow as their clerk and I will find a way to allay his fears about them.'

# TWENTY

'Apart from everything else that's the smartest removal from the premises I've ever experienced,' commented Egbert when they reached the abbey guest house and followed Hildegard into the refectory to sort through what they had just heard. 'I can tell you, Hildegard, before I joined the Order I had a somewhat colourful life. I don't mind admitting it. Many are the taverns my comrades and I were thrown out of, protesting our good behaviour even as we continued to drink ourselves into the nearest ditch. Nothing as smooth as this, however! Were you ever slung out of a tavern so smartly, Gregory?'

'You know I wasn't. I led a sober and respectable life.' His eyes were dancing.

Hildegard was only half listening. When she spoke she said, 'We've just been subjected to a pack of lies and you two fellows can only talk about the doubtful glory of being thrown out of taverns. Men, honestly!'

'I don't know what to make of it,' Egbert admitted. 'Why the blatant lie about two boys? He must know the runaway servants were a page and a young maid?'

'Maybe he hasn't heard the gossip, or maybe he's too pious to admit the truth?' Gregory looked grim.

'Maybe they are two lads and nothing to do with St Keverne?'

'I'd like to know why he was so eager for us to leave. Was he expecting another visitor?'

'We heard William's horsemen on the road above the woods, howling along as usual when we walked down—'

'We heard what Brother Simon *said* were William's men,' Hildegard pointed out. 'But were they his or not?'

'You can't imagine they were Black Harry's gang?' Egbert looked astonished.

'Well, we saw no sign that anyone was held captive at Marland's as we half-hoped,' Gregory pointed out.

'It was a wild idea,' Egbert remarked. 'What would the master of one of the granges be doing inviting a felon like Black Harry into the domain?'

'An army needs feeding,' Hildegard responded.

'Would he go against the principles of the Order and align himself with such a blackguard?' Egbert was scathing. 'We're clutching at straws. It'd be tantamount to a bare-faced lie. A lay-brother? Pretending one thing while doing another? It's lying by default. He'll need his confessor for that.'

'The whole thing was a pack of lies from beginning to end,' growled Gregory.

'It must have been William's men on the road. As I see it we three are still under suspicion because we were engaged by him.'

'Oh, Hildegard . . .' Egbert continued to wrestle with the problem of the identity of the horsemen, the master's diplomatic silence, Brother Simon's apparent ignorance about the runaways, and these further ramifications of being distrusted by the monks of Beaulieu.

'Apart from William's unmitigated arrogance I can't see why they regard him with such contempt,' Gregory mused. 'At least his rages are honest ones. He's also going to be the firm loser in all this.'

It was Hildegard's turn to say, 'Oh, Gregory!'

Later, an hour before Vespers, some of Sir William's search party returned. The sheriff and his men were downcast, William's militia unruly.

By chance Egbert and Gregory were hanging about the stable yard at the same time and, hailing the men in a generally affable manner, asked them how the day had gone. Grunts, expletives, one or two apologies and a Hail Mary or two followed but not much else.

Meanwhile Hildegard had noted Allard riding in with a couple of lay-brothers with an expression she could only describe as severe. She went over.

With a warning glance and an indication that she should follow he led his horse into the stable block away from the others and when they reached the far end he led his mount into a stall and, under cover of giving it a good rub down, spoke in a quiet voice, 'I have something to tell you.'

'And?'

'We had a look all round the lake. There was no sign of where Black Harry had come ashore. They must have waited under cover of the mist then doubled back. We couldn't make it out. The captain was in a dither because he would have to return with the bad news to Sir William that he had lost them again. Fearing that, he ordered his men over to this side of the river and, bringing Sir William out, rode up to a grange beyond the Abbot's Well—'

'Otterwood?'

He nodded. 'You know it?'

'We decided to have a look in that direction ourselves. What happened?'

'He tried to restrain his men but as soon as they got there and failed to find their prey they used it as an excuse to vent their rage and turn the place over. Needless to say there was no sign of Black Harry or his captive.'

'Where was the sheriff?'

'He peeled off at the lake with his men and only joined us on the way back here.' Allard looked grim-faced. 'This will cause bad blood between the abbey and Sir William. First the attack on the farm and now on one of our important granges. The destruction of our property will not be tolerated. It might even bring together our own warring factions to oppose him. Someone should warn Sir William – he is treading on dangerous ground.'

'Me, I suppose?'

'As you will.'

He gave her a dark and puzzled frown as she was about to leave. She halted. 'What did the master at Otterwood say when armed men broke his solitude?'

Allard looked anxious. 'He came out and waved a stick at them but when they laughed in his face he took himself off. I don't know where he went.'

'What worries you?'

He was hesitant but eventually admitted, 'I only know a gang of three or four followed him and when they returned they were laughing and claiming victory. One of the lay-brothers riding with us piped up, "What? Four of you armed to the teeth against one crippled-up old fellow with a stick? Some victory!" So they shouted abuse at him and it would have become more violent if that useless captain hadn't stirred himself for once and stepped in between them and issued some sharp orders. I was astonished to see them obey. The rest of the men were already moving off with Sir William and I had no choice but to follow them. I'm on my way to the precinct now to inform the grange master what has happened, although I'm sure I won't be the first to let him know.'

'I'll get my brothers. We'll go back to Otterwood and seek out Marland and make sure he's unharmed. Did you not see him after the bully-boys returned?'

Allard shook his head. 'I didn't believe what they told us. I took it as a form of boasting. It's only now, too late, I believe I may have been wrong. The others were out in the yard and did not hear what they said when they returned from their so-called triumph.'

'I'll get Egbert and Gregory to come with me to find out if he's hurt.'

'No!' Allard laid a hand briefly on her arm and to her surprise said vehemently, 'Don't do that!'

'Why ever not?'

'I beg of you—' Recovering from whatever had led to his outburst he mumbled, 'Your brothers are generally liked among the abbey lay-brothers but they're not entirely trusted. I have to say this. It'll only make matters worse if they put in an appearance, however good their intentions.'

'You can't mean that? You know they're devout and decent men and have a wealth of experience in healing wounds caused in anger – I fear for Marland. Armed with only a stick against sword-wielding fight-hungry mercenaries? How could he defend himself? Why on earth did you leave him?'

'I beg of you. This time, let the conversi deal with it. I am at fault. Somehow I thought Marland could defend himself. It was all over in a moment.'

Again one of the Beaulieu denizens wanted them away from Otterwood. Reluctantly she turned to go. 'I'll speak to Sir William, for what good it'll do. It's his responsibility to keep his men under control and to behave as guests should. But I shall do it openly, not in the privacy of the guest hall where anything I say can later be made to mean anything he wants. For this, Allard, I insist on having my brother monks beside me.'

He nodded and, throwing into a basket the brush he had been using on his horse's coat, he hurried from the stall to join his fellow lay-brothers.

She heard a crowd gathering in the stable yard and followed him out. A tight-knit band, united by one clear purpose, was advancing towards Sir William's lodgings. One of the men was urging them on and, with a leader's encouragement, they were joined by others emerging from the Domus where, no doubt, their fellow lay-brothers had told them what had transpired and what they intended to do about it.

Before they could make their intentions clear a burst of

shouting was heard all the way from the outer gatehouse and Sir William cantered in at the head of his personal guards.

'What is this?' he was shouting, waving something in his hand. 'Who dares challenge me?' He glared round.

The band of conversi froze to a standstill.

The rest of William's horses came on at a faster pace once through the archway but reared to a halt when they encountered the lay-brothers standing firm across the yard, all on foot, unarmed, but resolute.

'Who does this prior think he is?' roared Sir William. 'Who is he? Is he king? Have they crowned him while my back was turned?'

He glared round. When no one answered he shouted, 'Or is he pope, eh? Which one? That I'd like to know!' He waved something in his free hand again and Hildegard made out a small piece of vellum.

'This—' he waved it again, 'has just been handed to me at the gatehouse by that benighted porter of yours. This! Look at it! Says he, "Only doing my job, my lord." The lying losel. You're all in on it! Every man jack! There is no abbot here! No one in command. And you think I'm to be reprimanded by a mere prior? Am I to be held to account by an *obedientiary*?' He snarled a jeering guffaw and glanced rapidly round to note anyone who joined in.

Nobody did.

'Maybe he is now the Archbishop of Canterbury?' He waved the scrap of vellum again. 'This is the extent of his effrontery. He sends me an account for payment! He sends it to *me*! Me! Lord of Holderness! He asks me for payment for the firing of a derelict farmhouse! Is this a jest? Are we all meant to laugh out loud?'

William emitted a sound of strangulated derision and it was threatening rather than humorous and everyone else maintained a speaking silence as before.

His horse wheeled and shied and he dug in his spurs and drove it towards the lay-brothers but when no one flinched he jerked at the reins and the horse reared to a stop in front of them, Cerberus, snorting and, hooves flashing, pawing the air.

'Tell him, this prior and his bursar, skulking in their cloisters,

I have armed men at my command. Tell him that! Tell him his days are numbered! Tell him I condemn his impertinence! I'll make you listen, Prior!' he shouted in the general direction of the cloisters. 'Hear me? I will not pay your outrageous demand! I will not countenance it! I would rather set fire to the entire abbey, to every stick and stone, than pay you a single farthing. I am armed! I am a great lord! I am above you in every way! You will heed me! You will dance to my commands! If you do not obey me I shall fight you to the death and bring down hell fire upon you!'

Gregory and Egbert, alerted by William's ranting, had come to listen.

There was plenty to listen to, albeit in similar vein. 'Hear me, Prior?' William was still shouting. 'And you, lay-brothers, illiterate peasants that you are! Hear me! I will not be insulted by such as you! If you oppose me you shall have war!'

Gregory stepped forward to stand between William and the silent lay-brothers. 'My lord, I beg you to heed me. You cannot wage war on unarmed monks.'

'Cannot? *Cannot*, you say? You have the effrontery to address me in such a manner? And why "cannot", monk? They offend me! They will kneel to me! Let them call on God to send angels with fiery swords if they imagine that'll get the better of me! I am William of Holderness!'

'My lord, I beg of you, this is a royal abbey. The King will defend it should harm befall his brethren or anyone in it.'

'King Richard?' William threw back his head and roared with derision. 'He won't defend his own crown when it comes to it. Mark my words! Him? Our king? Our golden-haired, silk-clad child? Those days are gone! He's supposed to be a man now and men go to war! Him? The saintly Richard? Pick up a sword? He's all mercy and no balls! I am a man! When I'm attacked I fight back!'

'Even when your opponent is unarmed?' Egbert reproved, stepping up beside Gregory. He folded his arms. 'That is not within the rules of chivalry.'

'It makes no difference to me, brother! The lord Bolingbroke would support me. King Richard daren't say "boo" to Bolingbroke. And nobody here will say "boo" to me! These

monks offend me with their outrageous demands. Asking me
– *me!* – for recompense! How dare they have the gall! I'll burn
the entire abbey and every grange, barn and stable they possess
to the very ground before I pay them a farthing!'

His horse wheeled suddenly and nearly unseated him. When
he righted himself he kicked it into a fast trot towards the stable
block and they heard him bawling for the master to attend him.

The lay-brothers remained outside the Domus. Gregory and
Egbert waited to see what would happen next but when William's
mercenaries grumbling among themselves followed their lord
into the stables the confrontation seemed to be over for the
moment. In twos and threes the conversi returned to the Domus.

When Hildegard glanced across the foregate she saw a line of
white-robed choir monks assembled at the entrance to the cloisters. They stood, grim-faced, alongside one or two obedientiaries.
The prior and the bursar were nowhere to be seen.


Sir William was later observed leaving the Close when
the sheriff and his men set off back to Hythe. If he intended to
go on to Hampton in his company it explained why no one saw
him again that night.

The men he left behind made the most of their freedom by
singing and drinking in the refectory where the lay-brothers
usually ate before Compline.

While the latter went about their duties and attended the night
Offices, the militia had the place to themselves and tried to
continue carousing throughout the dark hours until the master
of the conversi remonstrated with them. He had a large bunch of
keys with him and was accompanied by several burly lay-brothers.
They made it obvious they were going to clear them out at any
cost and with little regard for their freedom.

Sir William's lieutenant, a fellow used to taking the brunt of
his lord's wayward dealings, and absent during William's earlier
imprecations, stood shoulder to shoulder with the master and
reiterated their desire for the men to leave. Much muttering
followed but, being paid men with the threat of having their
pay docked, they eventually saw their error and the last one
staggered to his hay sack groaning about being a man not a
monk to no avail.

Hildegard, sleepless in the guest dormitory by now, heard the noise in the garth and had got up to have a look. At first she thought Sir William had returned until she made out what it was about.

Soon silence fell.

Wondering what drew William to Hampton and whether it was a tactical retreat after his earlier rage, or whether it had any bearing on their quest to find Elowen, she stood at the window slit for some time but no answers came to solve the mystery.

Maybe he was merely concluding some business with the sheriff?

There was no guessing with Sir William.

# TWENTY-ONE

'This is the third morning we have arisen in the expectation of finding the little lady and continuing our journey back to Meaux,' Egbert observed. 'I'm feeling failed, outwitted, and like a sotwit. I'm beginning to miss the old place as well. I wonder if our beloved abbot is also itching to return home to Meaux?'

'They've hardly had time to greet all the visiting abbots summoned to Cîteaux,' Gregory opined. 'He'll be away for months on end. He won't be allowed back until they've thrashed out their differences and if they fail the Schism will hook in its claws until they do so.'

'Brothers,' Hildegard spoke up. 'In the absence of Sir William are his men continuing the search for Elowen under their lieutenant?'

Egbert called over one of the lay-brothers serving bread and cheese and asked him if he had heard anything of their plans.

'His men are nursing their heads after last night,' he told them, looking smug. 'They never learn, do they? Drink to excess? Suffer to excess. The two go together like night and day.'

'You're right,' Egbert agreed. 'What we're wondering is whether the search will be continuing.'

'I can send someone to Sir William's guest lodge to find out. His lieutenant will be in there now. By the way,' he added, 'you were asking after Master Marland, brother? I can tell you he's well enough but he's adamant that he's not going to be driven from Otterwood by anybody. We've sent someone to protect him.'

The informative young servant returned a while later. 'Sir William's lieutenant is mustering his men despite their green faces. He's telling them that a hard ride to the outer boundary of the Great Close is a known cure for sore heads. They don't believe him but they've got no choice.'

'And this is to further the search for Lady Elowen?' Gregory persisted.

'They did not say but I would expect they will not give up, brother. If they find her abductors they'll also find the murderer of Godric.'

'You have a more optimistic view of them than I have, lad.'

'And what's the latest on poor Mark?' Hildegard asked.

'I know he was yearning to be out and about yesterday but the infirmarer said no because he did not want to see the wound open up again in spite of Locryn's neat stitch-work.'

He hurried off.

'So what leads do we ourselves have to follow?' Gregory was frowning. 'I feel like a useless clod too, Egbert. Is she still within the Great Close? If so she cannot be far away. So near and yet so far!'

'These woods need more men than we have if we're to conduct a thorough search. A hundred men would not be enough. How many acres of woodland do we need to cover?' Egbert matched Gregory's frown.

'They should bring out the hounds again,' Gregory suggested. 'She cannot have been spirited away as if she has never existed. Isn't there a scrap of cloth belonging to her that might set the hounds on the trail again? Lord knows where we'll start from, though. The scent where she disembarked will be cold by now.'

'Egbert, what exactly happened when you followed after she came ashore at the Haven?' asked Hildegard.

'Without horses we were trailing far behind. We lost them shortly after passing St Leonard's. Little did we know that a man had been murdered. After that they must have used local knowledge to keep ahead of the hounds.'

'Local knowledge?' Hildegard queried.

But Egbert's face had softened when he mentioned the hounds. 'Poor little wretches,' he continued. 'They hate it when they lose a scent and have to mill about like half-trained puppies. It hurts their pride.' He got up. 'Let's find that kennelman and see if he wants to give them a second chance. Coming, Hildegard?'

'I'm not sure. Why don't you two go on ahead? I'll catch up with you later.'

Claiming knowledge of her own, albeit of knife wounds, Hildegard obtained leave from the guest master to visit Mark in the hospitium. It was a large echoing chamber lit by a row of clerestory windows down both sides and was situated above a series of connected stores a short distance from the inner precinct.

Mark was sitting up on a truckle bed trying to tie a few knots with one hand and looked up eagerly when his visitor was shown in. 'Right welcome, domina. I'm reduced to playing with twine for want of anything else to do. Yon infirmarer is a harder task-master than the master of the conversi. "No using your hand, not even to cut bread," says he. And then he strapped it up tighter still!'

'It's for your own good,' she smiled.

'Exactly what he tells me.'

'He said you were on the mend. I'm pleased to see it so.'

'I hope you've come to tell me they've caught those devils and put them in manacles?'

'Sadly not. We're at a loss as to know how to lay hold of them. Do you want to tell me anything more about what happened that night now you're able to think about it?'

'The night Godric was murdered . . .' He crossed himself. 'I've been going over and over it, lying here with nothing else on my mind. I've no idea who attacked us. Never seen them in my life, before you ask. But then, I wouldn't know the guests or their retainers up at the abbey and I'm thinking they must have come from there. No cause to know them. We were too shocked, Godric, God bless him, and me an' all, with them bursting in like that. I'm thinking they attacked us because we surprised them. They must have thought they had the place to themselves and were going to barricade themselves in.'

'And they had the girl with them, did they?'

He shook his head. 'I know not. I only found out about her later. Two of them came into the barn and started to lay about with their swords when they found us. They were demanding bread but we said it was sacks of grain we had, they'd need a mill if they wanted to make bread and they'd have to set to themselves and get busy over a fire instead of stealing the labour of other folks, and it riled them – we should have kept our mouths shut. Poor Godric, he didn't take to being pushed about by strangers.' He broke off for a moment and looked down at his hands. His voice thickened when he said, 'Ah, well, this is a vale of tears and no mistake. We expect nothing else. He was a brave lad. I miss his spirit and always shall. He'll no doubt be giving lip to St Peter and his hosts when he gets up there.'

'I wish I'd known him.'

Mark lifted his head. 'You know what? The others must have been waiting by the gate with the girl. We didn't guess at the time though I did think I heard voices.'

'We saw three horsemen when they abducted her. Maybe there were more.'

'I definitely heard men's voices. Arguing among themselves, like.'

'Have you ever met Black Harry?'

'I'll say I have! He was difficult to miss in his time as a sanctuaryman. He kept order down there for the lord abbot, Abbot Herring being alive at that time. When he died Harry made the sanctuarymen come out to pay their respects in the church. He was like a father to those miscreants and they were the better for it. The day he was to hang they moved around like ghosts. Nobody spoke. I had to take some produce down there and it was a place in mourning. Tough though they were, many had tears running down their cheeks.'

'I've heard different accounts of Black Harry's dealings. Some say he runs gangs in Hampton involving extortion, blackmail and worse. Is it true?'

'That's what they say.' He looked away.

'But you haven't found it so?'

'He kept order. Everybody got their fair dole and he sorted out disputes as far as he could. His word was law. You forget, domina, if I'm not too presumptuous, that those felons are not above grabbing and taking what they can get and damn everybody else. They're liars and cheats and bullies and not above slitting a man's throat if they imagine they can gain by it. Not all are like that. But most are. Some are simply unfortunate. Or they've made bad decisions and are living to rue it. The worst don't know how to live among good, kind folk, having no goodness or kindness in them. It takes someone strong to keep them in check. Harry knew how to deal with the worst of them. I won't say he was an angel. You certainly wouldn't want to cross him.'

'So had he got wind of the arrival of an heiress in the purlieu?'

'Everybody knew about it.'

'Perhaps what I should ask is whether it's likely he decided to act on the information.'

'How could he? The sheriff had him in custody by then.'

'Could he not organize his men from jail?'

He hesitated. 'Anyway,' he resumed after a moment's thought, 'it's not his line, kidnapping young heiresses – even though they say the fortune she carried might have tempted a holy man!'

When she was about to leave after asking if there was anything she could fetch for him he called her back.

'There is something. I don't know, it may be an idea prompted by too much imagination after the event—'

'Go on.'

'Don't take this amiss. But when I heard the voices in the night it struck me – as I now seem to remember it – that they did not come from round here. They were strangers, it seemed to me.'

That was all he could say.


While the monks from Meaux were attending Lady Mass after telling her they were going out with the hounds straight afterwards, she took the opportunity to visit the guest lodge. Not because she expected to find Sir William back from Hampton, but out of concern for the welfare of his body servant.

This time there were no armed sheriff's men guarding the entrance. She went straight in. William's personal servant, the same cowed, skinny, pale-faced one as before, was again unaccountably shivering before a well-banked fire. His recent wound puckered blood-red down one cheek.

When he heard the door open he sprang to his feet but seeing Hildegard he made a perfunctory bow and with a look of relief came over to her.

'If you want Sir William he left with the lord sheriff yesterday. He has not returned. That's all I know.'

'Does he often disappear without leaving instructions?'

'He is, I have to admit, a law unto himself, domina. I have no idea how long he intends to be away. Last time he was absent he returned with much mud on his boots.' He shrugged. 'I've learned not to comment.'

'When was this?'

'The day you arrived. He said he'd been out hawking with Master Bagsby but the falconer returned by mid-afternoon. Sir William came in much later, scarcely before Compline with the light already gone.'

'Was he riding alone?'

'He had one of his captains with him. He always does.'

'And has this captain accompanied him to Hampton?'

'I expect so.'

'I see.' She could not see beyond the bare facts. But she would see because she had no intention of giving up.

'Does it help?' the servant asked with an anxious kneading of his hands.

'It will do.' She peered at his cheek. 'That was quite a slash he gave you yesterday.'

'It might have been worse.'

'He does this often?'

When he hesitated she put her head on one side, 'You may tell me, if you will, my dear. Nothing you say will go any further.'

Reluctantly, half-turned as if he could not face his own confession, and with many fearful glances towards the door, he began to pour out a stream of misery in his soft northern voice.

It was centred on how he dreaded the constant clouts on the head and other punishments he could not admit to in her hearing and when most of it was off his chest he offered deep regret for any disrespect to his lord. When he met her eye he clearly feared he had gone too far. 'My lady, I beg you, forgive me. I mean no disloyalty . . .'

'Believe me when I say you have my sympathy. I wonder how you came to work in his household?'

'Both parents and my only brother died in an outbreak of the Black Death when I was twelve. I've been owned ever since by one master or another. I thank the Lord every day that I was spared. For what purpose I know not. So many worthier than I suffered unto death. They were dark days. I do not complain. It's so long since I've spoken to anyone about myself and the purpose of it all—' He gave a diffident smile. 'I sometimes feel like one of those wooden mannikins the jongleurs bring round on holy days! Pull my strings and I jerk to life! "Yes, my lord, no, my lord." There's no more to me than that.' He gave her a shy glance. 'I would live a more useful and godly life if I only knew how to escape.'

Hildegard put a hand on his arm. 'Tell me your name if you will. Sir William seems never to have used it in my hearing.'

'Brigge.'

'Then, Brigge, if I can help in a way that will not bring down more punishment I beseech you to seek my aid in any way you think fit.'

Tears came into his eyes. He was no more than sixteen or seventeen, alone and in the pay of a brute to whom he was bound by law.

Suddenly he fell to his knees and gripping the hem of her robe, mumbled, 'Forgive me, domina. Something is weighing on my mind and I – I cannot hold it back much longer. I beg to make a confession.'

'Your priest is the man to hear this.'

'I dare not. I beg on my knees . . . hear me.' He looked up with tear-filled eyes she could not ignore.

Kneeling beside him, she asked, 'What is it?'

'I am driven to some horror – I know not which way to turn. I cannot beg the Church for help—'

'What is it, Brigge, tell me?'

'It's this.' He took a breath, steeled himself and mumbled in a rush, 'If I stay here much longer I will poison him.' Looking directly into her eyes, he said, 'I know how to do it. Although I fear for my immortal soul should the urge be too strong to withstand, I will do it! I am driven to it! I have discovered something. I know his secret. At first I didn't understand but now I do. I know what he has done.'

'Tell me, I beg you. For your own peace of mind do not hold back—'

'I cannot.' His lips tightened. 'He would kill me if he knew what I'd seen – his evil heart, his coldness, his hatred, his ill will, his impassioned rages and his violence are driving me to reveal it! But I dare not. I ask only why he should live when the good die? Pray for me, domina. I beseech you, pray that God will give me the strength to speak out!'

He sobbed on her shoulder, no more than a child, and when his sobs abated somewhat she held his wrist. 'Can you not tell me, dear child?'

He shook his head. 'I dare not.'

'Then I may do something in the meantime, Brigge. Come with me if you will. I believe you need some respite.'

He drew back. 'I dare not leave the hall. He'll beat me if he returns and I'm absent!'

As he put out a hand his sleeve rolled back to reveal a scarlet welt, oozing pus through a black crust of dried blood on the soft inner side of his wrist.

She took hold of his arm. 'He did this?'

He tried to cover it up. 'I'm shamed by it. It's nothing.' He tried to pull his sleeve down.

'Will you tell me how it happened?'

'He was in a rage over some misdemeanour and said, "You'll do as I tell you. You're my property. I own you. To prove it, here's my brand!" and before I could guess what he was about to do he grabbed the irons from the fire and then—' He tensed.

'Come.' She coaxed him towards the doors.

After some initial resistance he followed with a mixture of fear and daring, stepping outside with a palpable sense of doing something dangerous and forbidden.

'Follow me,' she insisted.

Urging him into the guest lodge she approached the master. 'This young fellow, Brigge, is in the retinue of Sir William as his personal servant. I fear he needs to spend some time in the hospitium. I leave it to your herberer to prescribe something to aid him, a tincture of St John's wort, perhaps? I would also advise none but monks and lay-brothers be allowed in to see him, and least of all his lord. He needs sleep and a place of refuge. He may also like to help Mark?' she added.

The guest master exchanged glances with her. 'I think I understand, domina. Leave him with me.'

'Show him your wrist, will you, Brigge?'

The guest master tutted when he saw William's brand. 'That looks nasty. It must pain you somewhat, lad? You're quite a stoic. A wound like that would have most lads yelping with pain. We'll soon have you right. Fear not. We'll have a bed for you where you can get some rest within the precinct. The brothers are generally hale at present so we have plenty of space. Follow me.'

Bowing to Hildegard and with a complicit acknowledgement of what it was all about he escorted him towards the precinct saying, 'You're known as Brigge, are you, young fellow?'

Hildegard was still within earshot and heard his reply to a question about his knowledge of cures.

No wonder he had thought of poison as an escape from William's vindictive rule: the youth had been apprenticed to a herberer in the Holderness market town of Beverley near Meaux before his previous master had succumbed to the periodic return of the Black Death.

Gregory strode into the guest lodge with scarcely a greeting to anyone and went straight over to Hildegard.

'Come out. Saddle up. We're going to take the St Keverne hounds out to see if they can still pick up a scent. Anything's better than waiting for some sad losel to blurt something to incriminate an enemy.'

Hildegard needed no more persuasion. On the way to the stables she told him about Mark's admission earlier about overhearing the men who murdered Godric and how he now imagined they were not local men. 'He was unsure whether he dreamed it up due to overmuch imagining or whether it was an impression so slight he had forgotten it until recently.'

'What do you make of it?'

'If it's true and they were not local men it throws an entirely different light on things.'

'Couldn't he tell where they came from?'

'He doesn't even know if he imagined it or not. Don't forget he was only half-conscious.'

'Yes, I see that.' Gregory plainly thought it interesting. 'I imagine you're asking yourself, as am I, whether they were northerners or not?'

After a long pause when they had almost reached the kennels he turned to her. 'I believe we have both reached the same conclusion after what you've just told me.'

She returned his glance. 'I'm sure we have. We usually do.'

'That's true, Hildi. No one can condemn the marriage of true minds—' he touched the wooden cross he wore, 'despite all this.' He took a breath. 'Back to the kidnapping. I'm sure you'll agree with me that despite what Mark told you about the men who broke into St Leonard's and committed such a vile attack, it makes no sense to assume they were William's men?'

'A group of other strangers, then?' She looked as sceptical as she sounded.

'Erratic and unpredictable as he is, you surely agree that he is hardly likely to abduct his own son's betrothed. Why would he?'

'My selfsame question.'

'When is he back from Hampton, by the way?'

'Nobody knows.'

They reached the kennels and three or four hounds rippled round them in a stream of brindled gold and silver. Eager to be off they surged towards the wooden gate as soon as they heard it click open and were beaten back by the kennelmen with good-natured oaths and some determined handling. 'Back, Zenobia! Hold fast there, Caesar!'

He glanced up when they appeared. 'I'm taking the St Keverne lead alaunt and her partner and a couple of brace of our own scenting hounds. They've worked out who's lead bitch. If there's anything to find they'll find it.'

Egbert pushed his way over to him and handed over a piece of linen.

Hildegard asked, 'Did Goda give you that?'

'Her maid gave it to me.'

The scent hounds had a good sniff and were keen to get going. After a sign from the huntsman, his servant allowed the gate to swing open and they surged forth.

'Are you going to let them choose which way they go?' Gregory asked.

The kennelman answered, 'They'll lead. Look how excited they are. Faint though the scent now is it's familiar to the Cornish hounds.'

The animals were soon casting around with attitudes of puzzlement however and the kennelman walked among them with his assistants and whistled for the hounds to follow. A few lay-brothers joined them on foot like Egbert but others, including the St Keverne men, were on horseback. They crossed the bridge when the hounds were safely on the other side then there was some more milling about until the kennelman decided to take the track through the woods towards the burned farmhouse.

'Let's see if we can pick up a scent from there.'

'Do you think there's a chance they can discover where those fellows left the lake?'

'Could do.'

Several hours later they had found nothing that satisfied the kennelman. He was looking as puzzled as his pack. They drooped along with their heads low, looking the picture of dejection. They were uninterested in the burned farmhouse and found nothing to excite them at the lake even though they circled it twice.

There was nothing for it but to trail back towards Beaulieu until the kennelman, after much head-scratching, decided to go on in the direction of Beaufre instead. The only sign of interest from them came when they eventually approached the grange but the kennelman didn't see how it could lead them anywhere.

'Probably excited by the stink of oxen,' he muttered. Despite his words he went in to speak to the master with a troop of followers at his heels but the master of the grange, after greeting Hildegard and asking after their wounded man, Mark, shook his head when the kennelman pushed for an answer.

'Nobody been near the place. If we'd seen 'em with the little lass we'd have apprehended them, you can count on that.'

'No hooves in the night?'

The two men exchanged glances.

Egbert, never one to give up, led the way optimistically back into the lane, with the words, 'I trust them. If there's anything to find, these fellows will find it. You said so yourself.'

'We've had rain, don't forget,' muttered the kennelman. He was clearly shamed by his animals' lack of success.

'Even after rain the scent would have been left somewhere – strange, I grant you, that we found nothing by the lake – but she would be riding not walking.' After a moment or two he added, 'I grant you, it's a slim chance in that case.'

As if to state their agreement the hounds slackened their pace although they were still questing until the St Keverne hound began sniffing more urgently before picking up her paws and breaking into a trot. Like a message passed from one to another the rest joined her and soon the pack began to stream from the yard, lifting their heads in a united belling that showed they were on a trail of some sort.

A few lay-brothers came out of the grange at the racket and stood in the yard to watch. Instead of heading towards St Leonard's the hounds spilled in a glinting cascade into the darkness of the woods.

Egbert and the kennelman sprinted after them, followed by other foot followers. The rear was taken up by those on horses, holding back in order not to crowd the narrow path.

Down twisting, narrow deer tracks, through screens of copse-wood, the hunt proceeded at an ever-faster pace.

Gregory rode alongside Hildegard when he could and shouted, 'The scent must be stronger here – sheltered from the rain.'

'I'm mystified as to why she might have been so close to the grange.'

She followed, eagerly scanning the undergrowth for anything that might offer a clue that they were on the right track.

Not for the first time she wondered why Elowen had not shown enough initiative to leave some sign of where she was being taken. Maybe her hands were bound. Maybe she was in no shape to leave any sort of sign. She shivered at the thought.

When they emerged on the far side of the wood they found the pack milling about on the riverbank. One or two pawed at the water. A couple of younger ones rushed out onto a sand-bank and ran back in puzzlement to their elders.

Gregory muttered, 'It's the same story. When in a tight spot he takes to the water. He's making fools of us.'

'He? Do you mean Black Harry?'

'Didn't we see him escaping from the grave mound with her? Who else could it be?'

'Maybe he's sitting somewhere watching us, laughing his head off?'

He grunted with dissatisfaction. 'I shouldn't be surprised, Hildi. We're showing ourselves up as benighted sotwits at every turn.'

Egbert was talking to the kennelman and when he finished he strode over. 'That's that. Another dead end.'

Hildegard slid down from her palfrey. 'Ask him what's on the other side of the river.'

Both monks turned to scrutinize the woodland on the opposite bank. Because of the bare branches it was possible to see to the top of the steeply shelving slope. As the branches swayed in the breeze they couldn't help but see an intermittent flash of something.

'Is that the building I think it is?' Egbert went over to the kennelman where he was calling his hounds in. 'Have we worn them out or will they be game to have a look over yonder?'

The kennelman brightened. 'I reckon we can squeeze a bit more eagerness out of them!'

As they all moved off again, eventually crossing the bridge to the opposite bank and following the river path into the woodland,

Hildegard said, 'This is the trail up to Otterwood. We wanted to look in on Marland after his argument with William's men. Now we can, without drawing attention to ourselves.'

She had already told them that Allard had compounded the mystery that puzzled them by gently warning them off.

They followed the hounds through the woods. And they led without deviation right up to the demesne of Otterwood itself.

# TWENTY-TWO

I t looked different this time. Someone had built a palisade of beech saplings pointing outwards to deter anyone from forcing their way down to the farmhouse. One narrow entrance was defended by crossed branches tied by willow wands to the palisade. It would not deter a deliberate attempt to break in but it would give pause to anyone who thought it might be a good idea.

The kennelman stood on the perimeter and shouted for Marland to show himself. Instead, Brother Simon appeared accompanied by a brawny-looking lay-brother who flexed his muscles and demanded, 'Who wants him?'

'These hounds and the St Keverne men looking for their lost lady.'

'Why come here?' It was Brother Simon this time. He walked up to the palisade. Glancing at the reception committee he gave a benign smile. 'No little ladies here, friends. We shall have to disappoint these valiant fellows.' He gestured towards the hounds. 'What brought them to our gates?'

'Ask 'em yourself,' muttered the kennelman, plainly irritated. 'Are you saying they're mistaken?'

'I wouldn't dare go so far as that.' Simon, unperturbed, looked out to see who else was among his visitors. He noticed Egbert, switching a piece of willow in one hand, Gregory standing beside his horse, and Hildegard, at that moment dismounting. He made a small obeisance to them and smiled kindly on all the rest. 'Do they want to come in and have a look round the place?'

'If you'd be so kind.'

Simon began to untie the barrier so he could pull it to one side. The hounds began to sniff again, keening now and then, slightly confused, but determined not to give up. They spread out as soon as they were through and circled the farmstead, paid much attention to the path leading back down the slope towards the river, then returned in a cluster, certain that they were on the trail of their quarry.

The St Keverne men kept them in sight when they milled about round the side of the farmhouse and followed them when they began to sniff at the path through the meadow.

By now Hildegard was on the threshold of the farmhouse. She called to Marland. Brother Simon walked up behind her. 'Please enter, domina. He has almost recovered from his experience at the hands of Sir William's mercenaries.'

'The lay-brothers thought it best if we did not show our faces. I understand we are under suspicion of colluding with William?'

He shrugged. 'They're unused to strangers so they blame them for everything.'

'Well, he doesn't help much by making himself so conspicuously violent towards those who do not deserve it.'

He widened his eyes at the vehemence in her tone. She did not bother to explain but bent her head under the lintel and entered the small chamber, where Marland was sitting in a wooden chair. He was well provided with blankets and glanced up when she appeared. 'Welcome, domina.' His voice was a croak. He lifted a hand to indicate his throat. 'A touch of rheum. Did they tell you what happened?'

She shook her head.

'Those fellows dipped me in the river! Can you believe it! In this weather! I doubt they imagined I could swim so I lay under a bank of sedge until they left, singing their own praises for so easily disposing of someone they thought to rid from the world. I'm made of tougher sinew than that. So here I am, you see, singing my own praises instead!'

'I'll join you in a descant, if I may!' She gave a great sigh of relief to see him so cheerful. 'When they wouldn't say what had happened, not knowing the details, I was alarmed for you. Luckily we were brought here on the trail of Elowen just now, the hounds believing she's somewhere nearby.'

His expression did not change.

'Poor creatures,' she continued. 'They're beguiled by a piece of linen belonging to her.'

'I'm right glad to see you. By the noise outside it seems you brought your retinue?'

She smiled. 'My brother monks whom you've met and some worried men from St Keverne, together with a few conversi from the abbey.'

He was coughing and sipping at a steaming beaker of what she took to be a tisane of thyme.

'Would you like a tincture of something I've always found helpful?' Delving into her scrip which she always wore on her belt she found a small bottle with a waxed stopper and handed it to him.

After giving it a close look he asked, 'May I?'

She unstoppered it for him and he sniffed, nodding, and added a few drops to his beaker.

'Let me leave it with you so you have it by you when you need it.'

The sounds outside had abated and she went to the door.

Everyone but Gregory and Egbert had left.

'They're still on the trail,' Gregory called. 'Are you coming?' He poked his head in through the door to have a few words with Marland.

They remounted and cantered off through the woods in the direction of the jingling sound of horses' harness and eventually caught up with the tail end of the foot-followers, mostly conversi, stoutly walking along and trying to decide whether the hounds knew what they were doing.

'It's a contaminated scent,' one of them explained as they caught up. 'We've let the St Keverne men and the kennellers go on ahead. Exercise is the best we're hoping for today.'

'I was wondering about Mistress Goda and whether she'd been up here? It's not her scent they're following, is it? I know she likes to ride out with Master Robin, the St Keverne falconer.'

Nobody knew.

Hildegard was about to make some comment about Marland when shouts reached them from ahead. Believing the hounds had found something they hastened towards the sound.

It was not Elowen.

It was a group of armed men.

They emerged from every side of the clearing, pinning down some of the Cornishmen with drawn swords, taking them so suddenly that they had not enough time to draw their own weapons. The kennelman was gripped by both arms while another fellow held a knife at his throat. He was undeterred and continued to shout to his hounds and yelled back in fury at his captors not to harm a hair on their brindled heads.

The attackers kept several other men penned up like prisoners under guard. It was a swift and well-executed ambush. Hildegard wondered who could be behind it.

As Egbert and Gregory took in the scene the men from St Keverne appeared on the far side of the clearing, brought back by the sound of arms. The rasp of their own swords being drawn made the man with a knife at the kennelman's throat freeze. His wild glance flicked in surprise from one side of the clearing to the other. He seemed surprised to find more men on the path.

That one moment of inattention was enough for the kennelman. He whipped out his hunting knife, ducked underneath the other's blade and backed off, knife raised. His hounds jostled round him, making a snarling, defensive barrier.

The prisoners took advantage of their captors' surprise and drew their own weapons in a flash of steel.

Seeing their cause almost certainly lost the attackers were about to flee when suddenly everything changed as a small, tight posse of horsemen rode savagely into the middle of the clearing, knocked over a few unarmed followers and scattered the rest of them into the bushes. A good number returned at once with makeshift clubs.

Egbert dragged the nearest horseman off his mount and kicked him into the long grass then sent his horse careering off into the woods. Gregory brought down another. He grabbed his sword and started to put it to good use. It was the signal for the St Keverne men to join the fray. Nobody knew who their enemy was as the two sides locked but the manhandling of unarmed abbey servants was enough to make the Cornishmen join forces to beat off their attackers.

Blood began to flow.

First one side made the most of the advantage of surprise and then the other. Numbers were even. There seemed no reason for any of it and Hildegard stared wide-eyed, wondering what she could do, who the attackers were and where they had sprung from. There seemed to be only one answer to that. Armed with only her eating knife she could not see how she could help.

At that point, with man against man, horses and hounds mixed up together, they were interrupted by a new arrival.

He came riding into the middle of the brawl mounted on a broad-chested black courser which he drove hard into the general confusion shouting, 'Do not resist on pain of death! You are surrounded!'

He wore body armour over a black gambeson.

What else was black was his long hair and a prodigious beard masking his lower face and curling to his chest.

He cannot be mistaken for anyone else, thought Hildegard. This is Black Harry himself!

To prove that they were surrounded a flight of arrows from several directions came from the cover of the trees to land in the grass as a warning.

Every man held still.

Black Harry cast a careful glance round the clearing. In the uncanny silence that followed he took time to notice the monastics, the conversi, the St Keverne men and the kennelman surrounded by his snarling hounds. He appeared to count the number of his own men and calculate that they outnumbered the others.

With his sword drawn he gave the monastics another glance and then almost laconically, kicking his horse into action as he left the grove, he called over his shoulder, 'Bring the nun. Keep the others back.'

He rode off into the trees and before Hildegard could move she was grabbed on both sides by a couple of ruffians, a rope was lashed quickly round her arms pinning them to her sides, and she was being dragged behind a horse in the wake of their leader.

Protesting, shouting useless oaths, she was hauled into the woods. Gregory managed to elude the swordsmen and grab her by one arm but as the outlaws dragged her away she heard the thump of a fist and a groan as he fell to the ground.

A clash of swords was evidence of more resistance but she could not turn to see what was happening because she was being forced rapidly along behind Black Harry down a narrow, treacherous path into the thick of the trees.

# TWENTY-THREE

They travelled at a swift pace with many frequent twists and turns over the gnarled roots of giant oaks and round standing pools until she felt dizzy. The speed with which she was being dragged along, with the added effort of trying to keep her footing, made her lose all sense of direction.

Eventually they reached a ditch, an outer defence of some sort, and she was forced to slide down into it and wade through the wallows at the bottom before being dragged up the other side and onto a rickety bridge just wide enough for one horse to cross at a time. It jetted them out onto a patch of tree-covered land. Between the boles of the trees she could see water on every side. They were enisled.

She guessed they must be much lower downstream than the landing stage at Otterwood.

At first there seemed to be nobody around. Only the smell of woodsmoke hinted at more. Still in ropes, she was dragged towards a clump of trees and when her captors forced her to the other side she discovered an encampment, at its centre a blazing fire with meat roasting on a spit attended by a couple of men, and surrounding the fire a few logs to serve as benches and a table of a rough sort, and in an outer ring, a collection of shacks, thatched, and a picket where the horses had shelter. The whole camp was screened by high wood that had the effect of prison walls. She had no idea how she was to escape.

Black Harry had already dismounted and now casually threw

the reins of his courser to a stable lad. He bade his men untie
her ropes from the saddle-bows of their horses and gestured
for her to be brought before him. He took his place on one of
the logs by the fire and watched her without saying anything.

She gazed round at her captor's domain and saw how well
set up it was on its islet. Protected on all sides and visible from
neither the bank nor the water, the only way it might be breached
would be by someone having fore-knowledge and mounting an
assault from both the woods and the river.

How would Gregory and Egbert find out where she was? She
had had no time to leave a clue to help them follow her. When
she recalled the sound of the attack and the groan as Gregory
fell she was riven by a terrible fear for his life.

At last she allowed her gaze to rest on the man who held
her captive. Her heart sank. He looked formidable. They eyed
each other with suspicion.

Suddenly his teeth shone white in the thicket of his great
black beard. He was smiling!

'So it's like that is it, domina? You're wondering how you're
going to get away?' He read her expression with amusement.

After a pause she asked, 'Why do you call me domina?'

'Because I know you're not a mere nun of the cloister. You're
educated. I understand you can read and write.'

She forced herself to remain silent. How did he know that?

He was not what she had expected, this great chief who
terrorized the Forest folk and the petty felons of the sanctuary
and divided opinion on the matter of his violations. She recalled
the deeds that were laid at his door. Misdeeds, rather. The
murders and the robberies and the assaults. Well, so much for
him, they had not even checked her for knives.

He was reaching for a jug and she watched as he poured
wine into a goblet then handed it to a man to give to her. He
poured another for himself. He settled for a moment as if
considering his next move.

Still gazing at her with a glance more piercing than inviting,
he put his head on one side and asked abruptly, 'So what brought
you here?'

'You must know that if you've heard about me.'

He slammed his goblet down on the log next to him and she

jumped despite herself. 'I asked you a question. I'm not here to play word games with you. Tell me what brought you into this part of the Forest.'

Thinking it better to tell him what he could probably work out for himself anyway she said, 'We followed the hounds in an attempt to find the captive lady Elowen.'

'Captive?'

'You must know.'

'Why must I?'

About to accuse him to his face she thought it might be prudent to appear more amenable until she saw which way this was going. So far there was no sign of the girl. 'I thought everyone connected to Beaulieu knew that an heiress from St Keverne was to be handed over into my keeping at the haven and escorted by ship up to the homeland of her betrothed in the North.'

'You did? You thought that? I'm flattered you would imagine I have any interest in such matters. My mind does not dwell on issues as to which family of thieves is making treaties with another of the same ilk. Why would it concern me?'

'I don't know why it would.'

'So?' He smiled again. She felt she was being cornered into saying something he could pretend to find insulting. Then the punishment. She had seen men such as this at work before. The smile. Not to be trusted. The affable manner. Not to be trusted.

He was still waiting as if he expected her to give him an answer.

She said, 'I do not know you. I do not know your motives or why you are living like this outside the law. I know nothing about you. I have no idea why you've decided to bring me here. I know nothing of your purposes.'

'That's quite a list but I imagine I can supply some of the answers if you would like to hear them?'

When she did not answer he slammed his goblet down on the log again. 'I will have answers and will give them in return. Silence I will not tolerate. It gets us nowhere.'

'My deepest apology, master. Forgive me. I imagined it was a rhetorical question. I find it difficult to engage in conversation when I know not how to address my interlocutor.'

He almost smiled. 'Harry will suffice. You need know no more than that. And you? Hildegard of Meaux. Well, Hildegard, shall we begin again? You had a list of questions mainly about my motives but also, it seems, why I've bothered to bring a cantankerous nun into my lair no matter how well educated she might claim to be.'

'I make no claims. Reading and writing and a smattering of Latin are enough to be thought educated in the great world.'

'Latin, did you say? Good. You can help me with my translation of some deeds I have in my possession, written in Latin by the law men in the misguided belief that they can pull the wool over their clients' eyes and scrape up a profit for themselves by doing so.'

She couldn't stop her lips from twitching. His views on law men were similar to Locryn's and many others in sanctuary, often with justification.

'I'm sure you didn't bring me here to be your clerk,' she replied. 'May I ask you something that is most urgent at present?' She bit her lip. She dared not put her trust in his word but somehow or other she had to find out about Elowen.

When he nodded, she watched him carefully and asked, 'I beg to know if the little heiress, an innocent young girl . . . is . . . if she is safe and unharmed?'

'How would I know?'

'I thought that was what it meant, this encampment, a safe place in which to keep a hostage?'

'I know nothing about all that. It was reported to me that there were trespassers in our woods. A band of men, poorly armed as I witnessed. With hounds. Obviously looking for something or someone. Am I supposed to pretend I know why you're here? Am I supposed to pretend that you were not caught trespassing?'

'You mean I'm here only because we trespassed?'

'Trespass is not to be mocked. Men can lose their lives when accused of trespassing on the domain claimed by some knight or other. Such is the justice meted out to the poor, for sure it's only the poor who are treated in such a way. Have you ever heard of a high lord being punished because he stepped into a field somebody was claiming as their own?'

Aware that this might be a threat, her right hand tingled. Was she to be a scapegoat for this man's grudges? He could do what he liked.

'The laws against trespass are upheld by the in Eyre,' she replied with as much caution as she could muster. 'Both I and my fellow monastics from Meaux are innocent of any intention to trespass. We saw no sign that this was your land. We thought it was part of the Royal Forest.' Of course it was, she told herself. He must know it had belonged to King John, who gave a large tract of it in law to the Cistercians long ago.

Evidently he did know because he gave a smile of derision and as if he had heard her thoughts said, 'So if a king decides to claim our land from under our feet and invent a few laws so he can give it away, are we, the people of England, to accept it without question?' He gestured to include the entire domain of earth and sky. 'Are we to yield all rights to it – to this land, this earth, these trees that grow upon it, this river, these birds and beasts that dwell here in the Forest? No! Why should we? All are ours. We dwell on this good land and have a right to it. We till the soil. We husband the crops. Our farmers bring in the harvest so that our people do not starve. When invaders arrive and claim it from under our very feet is that justice?'

'It has always happened. We ourselves are a people descended from invaders.'

'My people are the ones who outfaced the Romans. Read the blessed Bede, read Monmouth's history. I'm sure you have.'

'But what do you hope to achieve by living outside the law? Do you believe one man and his small army can overthrow the long-established laws of the realm?'

'It nearly happened during the Hurling Time, remember?' His eyes were cold.

She decided it was better to remain silent.

'Remember the Great Revolt when the people said enough is enough?' More harshly he repeated, 'Remember that?'

His vehemence forced her to hold her tongue.

'Where were you in the tenth year of King Richard's reign?' he persisted. 'Then aye, when the Great Revolt took place and the people held London for four days?'

'I had just taken my vows.'

'So? You were safe in your cloister, were you? Did that stop you from supporting the Revolt?'

She shook her head. 'Four years before that I happened to be in Westminster when John of Gaunt showed his hand at the Bad Parliament – and reversed all the decisions made at the previous one—'

'At the Good Parliament as we call it.'

'Yes, when his cronies were thrown out and forced to hand back their fraudulent exactions from the Exchequer and, because Gaunt had the power to do so – owning the land and the castles and the gold as the richest man in the realm – he imprisoned the Speaker of the Commons and reinstated his cronies—'

'—And with Speaker de la Mare in prison, he permitted the thefts from the Exchequer to continue. Aye, so he did.' He gave her a considering look. 'And he introduced three poll taxes of such severity on free labourers that thousands were forced into starvation and to top it all he forced us to pay him over six thousand marks as so-called back pay for his war-mongering in Castile—'

'I remember all that and I wanted no part in it! It's no surprise that it erupted into a great rebellion four years later.'

'And you comfortable in your priory by then, of course.'

Something about his assumption that she approved of the corruption that had gone on under John of Gaunt, the Duke of Lancaster, when he was head of the King's Council, enraged her and she added, 'For myself I wanted no part in being the wife, the helpmate, to some shire knight who rode out as a vassal in support of Gaunt's heinous greed and his sacrilegious ambition to be king of England.'

'Hence the veil?'

She nodded. 'As a widow what other choice does a woman have?'

He chuckled at some suggestive alternative. 'And you wanted no part in that bully-boy's surge to power?' A disbelieving cackle of disbelief followed. 'What about his son, the great lord Bolingbroke?'

'I wish to exempt myself from the rapaciousness of both father and son. I wish only to teach the children of ordinary folk to read and write because I believe violence in the towns and in the manors will not bring justice. Only a knowledge of the laws that bind us will do that. Parliament will not change such laws unless urged to it.'

'Perhaps the King will do it if he's allowed to be king and not trammelled by conspiracy and hedged in by laws made by the barons in his name?'

'Perhaps.'

'You speak as if we might have something in common. If only we could rid you of this mistaken view that I know about this stolen heiress.' He turned to one of his men. 'Let's eat. Free the nun. If she tries to run off she'll only earn a ducking.'

One or two of his men laughed in a way that made Hildegard smart with humiliation.

Later she discovered that the wooden ramp they had crossed could be pulled up like a drawbridge.

So, this was Black Harry's Castle. And she was a prisoner in it.

# TWENTY-FOUR

There was no doubt that his men were the lowest from the nearby town of Hampton, beggars, thieves, murderers, commonplace fugitives from justice as it was daily enacted by the more comfortable merchants and lesser knights and lordlings who protected their own with all the means they could find within the law. Not that she was able to indulge in the pleasures of conversation. A couple of armed men hung about and were clearly under orders to keep a watchful eye on her.

The rest of the day dragged and she greatly feared the night to come. Such fears were not allayed when she was shown to a bed of straw in a lean-to adjoining Harry's own quarters. That she did not fear him as a rapist struck her as odd. It was something equally dark she feared in him but as yet could not name.

Clearly his law was the only law here. His control of his wild gang was in no doubt. It was not fear, perhaps, but something like respect that made them do as he ordered.

In return they had food, she saw, dry lodgings, a certainty of camaraderie and a definite order to their daily activities.

Observing a group of men going about their chores with no argument, sharing the burden equally, she suspected that it might have been the first time such regularity and order had ever been experienced by many of them.

A casual conversation with the lad who brought her a mug of warm water doused with herbs proved that.

When she asked him where he was from he told her in humorous detail about living on the doorstep of his old home when his parents left without him.

'That was four years ago. I was ten. Too many mouths to feed. They couldn't do it. Neighbours,' he added, 'dropped food onto the step when they passed, knowing I would not eat else.'

He grinned, a wide, innocent flash of guilelessness as if it had been a sort of joke, one of life's little trials which he had, by grace and good fortune, withstood.

'This is the life!' he concluded as he left, whistling.

Whatever her fears for herself, night-time did not herald the bawdy carousing she had expected. There was no drunkenness. The fire was heaped with ash to keep it in till morning not long after darkness fell and, sleepless, she glanced through the open door of her shelter once or twice and saw someone tending it during the dark hours.

From her straw bed she could hear Black Harry talking until late with one of his lieutenants. Despite her fears, the rumble of their voices and the chuckles that broke out now and then were strangely comforting.

She still had no idea what he held in store for her. She saw no way she could be any use to him, apart from the matter of a Latin translation. She would be a liability when, not if, it came to a fight. Surely he did not imagine her capture would go unnoticed by her Order? Even to the highest level, she thought, it would be a scandal that such an event had taken place. She wondered if he had captured her as a provocation. There seemed no other purpose to it.

Wondering if she might escape before it became a matter for serious retribution, she remembered Gregory with a tremor of fear.

Prayers. Fears and prayers and the conversation of men next door were the companions of her dreams through the long night hours.

Something grey seemed to creep into the hut, pressing in thickly from the encampment outside, and when she raised her head, bleary through lack of sleep, she thought instantly of smoke, something on fire, then no, she corrected herself, it's fog, and then she realized it was only, the softly filtered light of dawn penetrating the enclosure.

A nearby rustle of someone in the adjoining hut rising from a straw bed made her tense in fear. A yawn was followed by the slither of a hauberk being pulled on, a belt being buckled, boots stamped into, a splash of water in a bowl, and footsteps moving stealthily to the adjoining door.

She did not move a muscle. Silence. He was looking in at her.

His inspection brought a prickle of fear running over her skin.

A faint movement suggested that he had stepped away.

Opening her eyes she heard a chuckle. Saw the black shape motionless in the doorway.

'I guessed you weren't asleep. Expected to fool me, did you?'

He remained in the doorway. Now it would come, his retribution or whatever he planned.

Instead he told her, 'We help ourselves here. All for one. Bound by loyalty to our cause. If you want to eat and drink before you carry out the task I've allotted to you, better do it now. We're going to be busy.' He was about to turn away but stayed a moment to say, 'Maybe you nuns wash more than my men? There's a pool down behind some bushes where you won't be overlooked. Young Aelred will show you.'

She waited until he left then climbed stiffly out of the straw and went to stand on the threshold looking out. Somebody at the fire was stirring a pot on the gridiron. One or two figures were briskly going about other chores, fetching wood, carrying water in rough wooden buckets from the river, even rolling out dough to bake in the fire in the Scots manner.

It made her wonder why men, some of whom clearly had military training, should be living outside the law and how Fortune might aid or hinder the most honourable intentions.

It felt like a great risk, to take her first step outside into such outlaw territory. Wondering how her presence would be received she set off in the direction Harry had indicated but was stopped almost at once. It was a reminder that she was a prisoner. It was only the grinning lad, Aelred, however, saying, 'This way to the royal bath house, my lady! Follow me!'

He led her to a sheltered arbour on the other side of the wood where an inlet formed a deep pool, brimming with fresh, clean water as the tide flooded in. A few hours hence it would ebb. That would be the best time to make an escape under a pretence of washing or fetching water. She would be carried downriver. She would bide her time and escape like that. Anything would be better than the suspense of waiting for what horror lay ahead.

She guessed that given his views on justice, Black Harry would lay much of the blame on the monastic orders for the way things were. Perhaps he intended her to be the scapegoat to atone for the others.

With Aelred sitting at the top of the bank and turned away to give her privacy, she removed her habit and wearing only her gauzy undershift stepped into the freezing water up to her knees. Making do with a few splashes to freshen herself, she pulled on her robe again then called to him that she was ready to leave.

'Do you do that every day, domina?' he asked as she climbed back up the bank.

So he had been watching.

'I try to. It's not necessary. I know nuns who don't bother. The worse for those who kneel and pray next to them.'

He gave that wide grin again. 'I've never heard tell of it. Maybe I'd be better for a little immersion in God's holy stream?'

'Maybe you would. That's up to you and your priest to decide.'

'Lord Harry don't agree with priests for anything. Nor do I, probably. I ain't made up me mind yet. We'll no doubt have a discussion about it tonight. That's his usual way. Your arrival has changed our routine a bit. He expects them to come after you with swords and that.'

She noticed that he himself wore only a small dagger thrust in his belt.

'Do you know what else he has planned for me?'

'Not really. You're to go to him when you've broken your fast.'

'Is that an order?'

'It's a suggestion. He doesn't believe in orders.'

When he was ready Black Harry indicated that she should get up from her place on the ground beside his men where they were eating from the common bowl of pottage that was being passed round and sit beside him at a rough-hewn table, indicating a seat on the bench beside him. She sat close enough to smell the aroma of woodsmoke that clung to his garments.

Without asking he poured some of the watered wine he was drinking into a beaker and pushed it towards her. Then he fished inside his shirt and took out some sheaves of vellum, laid them on the table between them and leafed through them.

'It's this section here.' He indicated a neatly written page or two. 'Tell me what you make of it. You say you can read,' he mocked.

It was a document concerning a case in Chancery. She glanced up. 'Is this a dispute you're having over some land?'

He shook his head. 'Not me, some poor fellow who's having his land lawyer-ed from under him, been tilling the soil there all his life, as did his father and his father before him, and he would rather like to keep it that way. He asked for my help.'

She read briskly through it, murmuring the Latin aloud as she had been taught. She put the papers down.

'This is land his grandfather squatted after the Black Death over forty years ago. You'll know that much land was laid waste having nobody to work it when so many bonded men died. It was only slowly brought back into cultivation and tilled by free men – or by those escaping bondage under a feudal lord. Later, when the Death was only a distant nightmare recounted by our grandparents, the descendants or distant cousins or others related to the original owners imagined they had a claim to the land. They began to look into the matter of ownership. They were encouraged to believe they had a right to acquire a few acres at the present owner's expense.'

He gave her a glinting look. 'I see you have the gist. What's this fellow's chance of holding onto it?'

'It depends on the acuity of your lawmen.'

He chuckled. 'We'll find one or two of those among our supporters. We'll trust they now come over to the right side of things and will put their knowledge to better use than heretofore.'

He took the pages from her and pointed with one finger at a paragraph halfway down. 'Tell me again how you'd translate this, will you?'

She read it then said it again in English. 'It is ambiguous, I'll give you that, but it's nothing a good law clerk cannot make much of on your man's behalf.'

'How come you know this?'

She shrugged. 'Cistercians? We deal in rights and infringements all the time. Our chronicles are full of them. Land is our wealth.'

'And sheep.'

'Yes, the wealth of the realm. It's not for nothing the Chancellor sits on a woolsack!'

His sigh was heartfelt. 'I wish all laws in hell.'

'So we could live in the chaos of man against man?'

'Ah, that, and so we discuss endlessly around our campfire in the long summer evenings. Are there answers?'

'We're enjoined to believe that everyone is our sister or brother and all things are equal before God.'

'Aye. That's what they say. But what do they *do*?'

Through the day he brought a few more similar texts to have her check against his own reading. They argued mildly about the meaning of certain phrases, what they really meant and how they were to be interpreted, and finished at one point in such agreement their eyes met in a sort of friendship making both turn away at the same moment.

I am a prisoner of this ruffian, Hildegard reminded herself. He means no good to me, I am merely useful to him at present. So he smiles on me.

I'm a captive in a chanson, she decided, destined to spin gold from straw by night and, failing, to be brutally murdered on the morrow.

\* \* \*

A day and another night passed with no violence towards her. Wondering about the fate of her companions, she did not expect a straight answer from any of the men here. She was greatly disturbed, then, when a few odd remarks were made about a skirmish that had taken place in the Forest that very morning.

Her blood ran cold. She told herself it was something from another time. Not now, heaven forfend.

The fact that something serious had happened came home to her in full horror when one or two men limped back covered in blood later in the day. The men gathered in a strangely silent group round the fire after the initial babble of questions died down.

Aware of her prisoner status, it was viciously confirmed by two of Harry's henchmen. From out of nowhere they strode over and without a word of explanation threw a rope round her and dragged her roughly to her sleeping shack and shut her in.

The bar dropped down outside and she quickly gave up pounding on the door to be freed.

One advantage was that the ropes had been so hastily tied they were easy to loosen once she began to struggle against them. Soon she was able to reach for her knife and hack at them in the speckled gloom until they frayed.

Once free she ran her fingers over the rough wood of the door until she found a knot hole she could bore through with the point of her knife.

Soon she forced a hole large enough to give a view of part of the campsite where men were coming and going in front of the fire. Something had disturbed them.

She could glimpse a single boot. It kicked ash over the fire. At a different angle she could see a corner of the table where she had worked that morning alongside Harry and his law texts. Only an elbow, his probably, a rough woollen cloak, again his, some movement she couldn't make out, and then the outside world disappeared as a shadow blotted out the little squint she had made.

Someone began to lift the beam on the other side and she retreated to the back of her prison, unsure whether to attack and try to escape now while the routine was disrupted or to prepare herself for what would happen next for good or ill.

Light flooded inside making her blink.

It was Harry himself. 'Come out now, hurry!'

'Why? What's happening?'

'Shut up. Come!' He turned, expecting her to follow, and she edged cautiously as far as the threshold.

He was already halfway across the site and turned. When he saw she wasn't following he called again. 'Are you deaf? Get over here. We're leaving!'

Without waiting for her to respond he strode back, gripped her by one arm and dragged her powerfully along beside him.

'You're hurting me!' she managed to blurt out.

'Don't be so frail. Would you rather be dead?'

With no time to get into a discussion about what he meant she was forced to run beside him to where his black courser was being saddled up.

'Hurry, lad, follow me,' he said tersely to the groom.

To her astonishment he turned to her, put two muscular arms round her as if to embrace her then hoisted her into the saddle, leaping up behind her as the horse began to move off.

Ahead, at the wooden bridge, the rest of his men were already filing recklessly across and disappearing into the woodland. Black Harry, together with Hildegard and his stable lad, were the last to leave. The lad stopped only briefly in order to pull up the drawbridge and let it fall into the water-filled ditch as if having practised what to do.

No orders were given. Everyone seemed to know where they were going and the gang galloped in single file along a narrow path where it rose with every step to higher ground until at last they came pell-mell onto a road as wide as the king's highway on the ridge at the top of the heath.

Somewhere, down below, among the knotted woodland trackways the shouts of horsemen could be heard but instead of getting closer the sounds began to fade and soon they came from further off and she guessed the riders had discovered the entrance to the camp and were probably even now trying to drag up the drawbridge, throwing it down over the water-filled ditch and clamouring across it in the hope of having chased their quarry to earth.

*     *     *

Hildegard's burning question about where they were going was answered by the time it was nearly dark.

Riding for some time over the windswept ridge, as night came on they found themselves near the coast. Instead of the wind howling through the trees it was the sound of the sea roaring behind a sandbar that surged in deafening fury up a shelving beach while close at hand, within sheltered water, waves surfed onto the shingle and retreated without cease. Seabirds shrieked on all sides as soon as they appeared over the brow of the cliff. Undeterred by the clamour, the horses began to pick their way between piled banks of dry sand spiked with broom and seagrass. They stumbled, knee-deep in the unaccustomed softness, whenever they strayed off the path that had been worn in a winding trail onto the strand.

It would be a terrible place to use as a hideout, she thought, for as far as she could see there was no way off the sands. Once there they would be sitting targets for any bowmen that had followed them. She found she was thinking in terms of Black Harry's gang and how they might hope to survive this latest escape.

Heavens, she thought, astonished at herself, the men who have discovered the island camp will be abbey men, foresters, sheriff's men, the men from St Keverne, and am I in fear of them? They will be my rescuers.

# TWENTY-FIVE

Harry allowed one of his trusted men, his lieutenant should he decide on a hierarchy of command, to canter along the beach under the lee of the dunes with everyone following. It looked as if he knew of quicksands to be avoided, otherwise she could see no reason for such caution. The men seemed to have no doubt where they were heading.

With a start she saw the lead rider vanish behind a sand-bank. In the fast fading of the day it seemed like a trick of the light, a blink and he was gone. Harry drove his horse forward and the sound of the sea was cut off as soon as they passed between the dunes.

In the sudden silence he turned his head to growl, 'Journey's end.'

He dropped down from his horse, was about to walk off, then remembered his passenger. 'Can you get down?'

He looked up at her and opened his arms wide as an invitation to jump.

Throwing one leg over the horse's back she launched herself into the air. He caught her. For a moment he held her in his arms. His beard, like soft black silk, pressed against her brow. She closed her eyes. He tightened his grip. The links of his mail shirt pressed into her breasts. He gave a groan and did not release her but instead said, 'It's an age since I've held a woman in my arms.'

He held her tight and whispered, 'What are you first, Hildegard, a woman or a nun?'

She raised her eyes to his. Her lips opened in astonishment.

He gave a final squeeze and ran his hands over her. 'Maybe we'll find out tonight when we're safe in our bower?'

He suddenly released her and, shouting a few commands, put his courser in the charge of a groom, and set about organizing his men's installation in their new hideout. Confused by the conflicting emotions his embrace had aroused she could only stare after him as he strode away.

The new camp had clearly been used before but of Elowen there was still no sign. Every man had his allotted function: stores were brought in, horses tended, campfire lit, water butts checked, and all the doors of the flimsy reed shacks were flung open.

A stream gushed from the cliffside. It looked shallow and pure and an attempt had been made to construct a basin of knee-deep, constantly running water with an outlet to allow it to flow away across the beach.

Behind the sandbanks formed by nature at the entrance to their secret hideout was a dry cove carved out of the cliffs by a thousand ancient tides. It was capacious enough to take everyone and their horses and baggage with ease and, facing south, could not be overlooked except from the cliff top.

Knowing Black Harry as she was beginning to, she did not doubt that lookouts were posted up there already.

She tried to work out how long it might be before, having succeeded in tracking them to the island, the search party would take to discover this latest hideout. It was certain, they would not find the place in the dark.

And ahead there was the night to be endured.

With the fire blazing under the protection of the cliff and screened from shipping by the sandbanks standing sentinel at the entrance they were as secluded as anyone hiding from the law could wish.

Every evening round the fire as she had already seen it was the custom to hold a moot where the men discussed various matters concerning the running of the camp and where quarrels were sorted to everyone's satisfaction. After that the discussion would move on to more abstract matters. Not everyone could join in at this other level, they were just not interested, but everyone had experiences they could share that made a difference to the views being put forward. On the topic of justice, or lack of it, there was nobody who did not speak up.

The Church, blamed for much mischief with its taxation of births, marriages and deaths, was condemned for taking the best of whatever wealth it could get its hands on.

No matter how carefully she listened there was never any mention of Elowen, nor of Godric for that matter. Had one of these men murdered the youth? Looking at them she wouldn't put it past any of them.

She touched the knife in her sleeve with the tips of her fingers for reassurance.

If sometimes the conversation went on into the night, this night Black Harry drew things to a rapid close and even got to his feet to clear away the pots and beakers himself before turning to leave. The glance he gave Hildegard smouldered over her.

There could be no mistaking what he meant.

Her fingers tightened round her knife.

When he disappeared into one of the shacks he pulled a screen of reeds across the entrance.

Aelred touched her on the sleeve. 'This way, domina.' He

led her to a lean-to built of reeds like the other shelters. Covered in rough thatch tied down by lengths of twine it looked robust enough to keep off the rain should the lee of the cliff be insufficient but it was alarmingly close to the one Black Harry had entered.

Making the best of it, she lay down and covered herself with her cloak. Her eyes, wide open, were fixed on the doorway. The only sounds were of the restless horses hobbled near by and the lulling whisper of the waves.

At some point her eyes must have drooped shut because when she opened them it was daylight.

A fresh breeze blew in off the sea, rustling the thatch and carrying in the piercing cries of herring gulls and terns. A figure was standing in the doorway. It was Aelred.

'Master Harry said to make sure you have what you want. He's away this morning with business to attend.'

She struggled to sitting. 'Business?'

'I know nothing more, domina. Here, this is a good brew made by our apothecary who knows how to pick herbs. It'll wake you up.'

She took the beaker with thanks and after he left considered this last turn of events. Her reprieve last night was as unexpected as it was welcome. But what was this business Black Harry was engaged in? Was it to demand an answer to his ransom note?

Although Elowen was not in evidence, it seemed rational to assume that a gang leader with so many bolt-holes would have the child hidden in some remote place where she could be kept safe until the time came for her to be handed over. Despite his denial of any knowledge of her she did not believe him.

With no particular role she walked about the beach until somebody came to fetch her back. 'Not too far, domina, if you will be so good. Master Harry would not like you to go missing.'

She gazed longingly out to sea. She might swim to freedom if she only knew where to go. Deciding that vigilance was the only recourse she went back into the camp and helped where she could. Nobody tried to engage her in conversation. She felt they had been warned off speaking to her. Aelred was busy with the horses, repairing their rope bridles, polishing their coats until they shone. Black Harry's own courser was missing with one or two others. She wondered when he would return.

It was late in the day when everyone was busy and their surveillance was not as strict as before that, passing his hut, she decided to take a quick look inside. She had no idea why. She acted on impulse. Maybe it was to find some other side to him, something that would give a better measure of the man, but whatever impulse it was she was not expecting the surprise she got.

Standing in the scattered light that crept through the reeds her eyes slowly grew accustomed to the half-light. It was a place as neat and well ordered as she might have expected.

What she had not expected was to see a blue cloak hanging on a peg.

She gazed at it in horror. Surely it was the one Elowen had been wearing when she made her fateful landfall at the Haven?

She hurried over to it. Hardly daring to have the truth confirmed she stretched out her fingers and ran them over it. Unmistakably an expensive garment of good Italian velvet, lined with silk, from its colour and quality it could only belong to one person.

So he had been lying? He did know about the kidnap? She felt an odd feeling of disillusionment. He had kidnapped Elowen and taken her prisoner and now here was her cloak hanging on a peg in his chamber to confirm it.

But where was Elowen now?

She shuddered at the thought that she might have been murdered.

Why else had her cloak been discarded?

She took it down as if it could tell her what had happened to its owner and, holding it, paced the floor. The *business* he was involved in had to be connected to her disappearance. Praying that she was still alive, she considered where he might have gone. Was he checking on the child in her prison to make sure she was still under his control? Maybe he was seeing someone who could act as go-between with Sir William when he collected his ransom? The overriding question was whether the poor child was still alive. She had to be, pray God. Head spinning she tried to decide whether it was likely.

A sound made her jerk round. Footsteps were coming towards the hut. Without thinking she flattened herself behind the door and held her breath. Boots scraped on the rock floor as someone entered. They came to a sudden stop inside the doorway.

A pause followed in which she forced herself not to breathe. He was standing only inches away on the other side of the reed partition. Who was it?

She heard a movement followed by another listening silence.

Then a voice, deep and distinct, 'Hildegard, my lady, do please make yourself at home in my humble abode.'

With a chuckle of triumph Harry ripped back the screen. Before she could move he banged it shut behind her and tied a piece of twine through the hasp.

'If you wish to leave I demand payment!' His eyes flashed as he turned towards her.

Why had she not heard him return to camp? Why had he appeared with such stealth? She managed to say, 'I'd like to leave.'

'Where? My private chamber or my camp?'

'Both!'

'You can't leave my camp yet. You'll only lead your Sir William and his mercenaries into my headquarters.'

'I wouldn't tell him. You may as well let me go.'

'Do you regard me as a fool? Anyway, I like having you around.'

'For revenge?'

'Revenge?' He looked puzzled.

'You hate monastics. Your lad says you don't approve of priests and—'

'And you imagine I'd blame you for their iniquities and vent my rage on you?' He looked startled and took a couple of steps towards her. 'After these few days when I thought we were becoming friends, you think that of me? Did it mean nothing, those jokes we made, our sport over the Latin of that poor clerk who drew up the deeds—'

'How can we be friends when I'm your captive?'

'That's a reasonable point. Friends and lovers should be

equals. But you see we cannot be equal just yet until this problem is resolved.'

'What problem? When Sir William pays your exorbitant ransom request?'

'I've made no such request. Did he say I have?'

This must be another lie. She glared and demanded, 'Where is Elowen? Have you harmed her? Tell me the truth!'

'Come, I am not one to yield to shouted demands, as you must know. Come—' he said again with one hand held out as if inviting her to take it.

'I will not! You might yourself have noticed that I'm not one to be ordered about.'

'Then we are at stalemate.'

'Why won't you tell me if she's well or – have you – is she dead?'

'Why would she be dead?'

She held up the blue cloak. 'Why is her cloak here? What have you done with her, you monster? Tell me – or I'll—'

'What?'

'Where is she, Harry?' She blurted his name without thinking.

His eyes glittered. 'I've already told you I'm not involved—'

Grasping the cloak she thrust it violently into his hands. 'This proves you're involved up to your neck! Why did she leave it behind? Was it when she ran from you in terror or when you disposed of her body and she no longer needed it!?'

'I cannot conduct a conversation like this. There are too many assumptions about me, my motives, the facts. The less you know, the safer you'll be. I am not prepared to implicate you.'

'What? I am implicated! How can I not be implicated? She was to be in my charge and now, due to you and your men, the child, if she is still alive, must be terrified out of her wits! She is my concern! How dare you tell me otherwise!'

'Sit down. I'll say enough to set your mind at rest.' He gestured to the straw where he slept.

Eyeing it she said, 'I'd rather stand.'

He noticed her glance and his eyes blazed with anger. 'Sit down! Do you distrust everything I say? I'm tired. I've ridden a way today to try to resolve this matter and not without a skirmish or two with your allies.' He licked the back of his hand and for the first time she noticed blood. Now he growled, 'Sit when I ask you, I beg you to oblige me. I will not talk to someone standing over me like a jailer. I've had enough of them.'

Before she could decide how to reply he took her by both elbows and forced her across the chamber and by a neat trick with one foot behind one of hers caused her to fall back onto the straw.

He lay full length beside her. 'Better.' With one hand gripping her arm so she could not escape he looked down into her face as she tried to struggle up but he held her firmly enough to be ready to prevent it. She jerked her head to one side to avoid his scrutiny.

'Listen, Hildegard, she is alive. I have seen her. She is unharmed. In fact she was practising her reading when I left, which is not before time as her education has been shamefully neglected. That's all I'm going to tell you at this point. It is not as you imagine. Rest assured.'

'Why should I believe you?' She turned a sceptical glance on him and he stopped what he had just been about to say and stared at her. In his eyes she could see something kindle and his voice dropped to a huskiness she had not heard before. 'Trust me. I beg you. Tell me what I can do to make you believe me.'

She hesitated for a moment then decided on an answer. 'Take me to her.'

At first she thought he was going to snarl some negative response and his lies would be shown for what they were but it was not so. 'Hildegard . . .' He bent his head and she could feel his breath on her skin. 'You know I cannot do that. When all this is over you will understand. I crave your trust now, I beg you, my dear—' He broke off and in a thicker tone said, 'Don't force me to bring down calamity on all concerned. I will do anything for you after this. But this one thing I cannot do. Not yet. I beg you to find it in your heart to bestow on me this one benediction, your trust.'

A silence followed. Hildegard struggled inwardly with the many wayward emotions that wrought such confusion when he looked at her like this and finally opted for the most innocuous.

'I suppose you need to know whether Sir William is going to pay your ransom? Is that it?' She struggled to sit up. 'Despite your talk of equality and justice you're no different from anyone else in the secular world. Your lust for gold will lead you to hell.'

'Lust may well lead me there but it will not be for gold.' He gripped her ferociously by both arms and pinned her deeper into the soft bed of straw. 'It will be for you.'

Her expression must have been so eloquent he jerked back as if she had spoken.

'I beg forgiveness.' His fingers trailed down the edge of her head covering as if he was preparing to rip it off but had not finished weighing the consequences.

His fingers trembled. 'I did not come to you last night. I stayed awake until it was time to rise, debating the issue with myself. You were sleeping no more than six feet from me.'

He continued to run his fingers over her kerchief and said, 'I wish now I'd told my men to bring one of your monks with us instead – at least I would not have to put myself through this torture.'

Her feelings were awry. It showed on her face and he gave a rueful smile.

'I assume those brothers can also read and write? Perhaps we might have had some swordplay to while away the hours . . . instead of this dragging of my soul into the flames of hell . . .?'

'Maybe you should have done,' she said in a strained voice.

'They certainly know how to use their swords.' He gave her an amused glance. 'I should have mentioned I encountered them in the woods riding with Sir William's men. We had an exchange. Nothing serious. Our hearts weren't in it.'

'Is Brother Gregory alive?'

'They both were, very much so, more than I wished when they encountered us. The tall one who looks as if he might fall over in a strong wind gave me this.' He licked his wound again.

'I thought—' Relief flooded over her then she shivered. 'Can I trust you in this? Harry,' she used his name again, 'are you telling me the truth?'

He looked saddened. 'Why will you not believe me?'

'You know why,' she said in a subdued tone. 'I have only

your word for any of it. And I have no idea why you've brought me here. I've read your documents for you. You could let me go. The person you want for real help is Gregory, the one who gave you that,' she gestured towards his cut hand.

Under some impulse she did not understand she added, 'If only things were different . . .'

'If only they were,' he murmured as he brought his head down close enough to allow the silken fronds of his beard to caress her cheek.

# TWENTY-SIX

After she offered to clean and bind his wound he made an announcement that took her by surprise and deepened her confusion.

'I brought someone back you will know.'

She glanced up.

'No need to look alarmed. It's a fellow from sanctuary. Come outside before we create a scandal in here and see who it is.'

'You love mysteries, don't you?'

'Isn't life a mystery? Why are we both here, you a bride of Christ and me an enemy of the realm?'

He made an ironic bow and stepped outside and with a sweep of one arm gestured across the camp. 'Look, over there. Recognize him?'

His silvery blond hair was unmistakable.

She turned to Harry with an astonished expression, 'Why?'

'He is my go-between.'

'*He* is?'

He flashed a smile at her surprise.

'Between you and who else?'

'That you must not ask because I will refuse an answer and make you angry again. Come and greet him.'

Locryn must have already known she was a prisoner in the camp because he showed no surprise when she walked up accompanied by Harry.

'Most warm greetings, domina. I trust our host is treating you as he should?' His quick glance at Harry and back gave away his thoughts on the matter and Hildegard pretended her flushed face was nothing to do with Harry nor the unexpected intimacy that had passed between them.

She gave him a cool glance. 'The outdoor life is hard on cloistered monastics but my host is impeccable in his hospitality. Are you here to join us or merely visiting?' If he was leaving she might try to persuade him to smuggle her out with him somehow or other.

Her hopes were dashed at once when he said, 'I'm leaving any moment now. Lord Harry is having a fresh horse saddled up, and then it's farewell.'

She stepped closer. 'Are you able to take out a message for me?'

Harry moved closer to listen.

Casting a covert glance at Locryn she said, 'Will you tell Egbert and Gregory that I am well and hope to be with them as soon as ever?'

Harry nodded. 'That seems harmless enough. Tell them, Locryn. Let them know they can call off the search and she'll be back with them tomorrow, all things being well.'

Hildegard felt her heart jump. Did he mean it? When she turned for confirmation he was already walking away.

Locryn was about to take his leave but before he did so she gripped him by one arm in a desperate plea for news. 'What's happening, Locryn? Is it true Elowen is safe?'

'She's under Harry's watch now. When Sir William returns things will move fast, so be prepared.'

'Where is he?'

'Still in Hampton.'

'And Elowen?'

'I cannot tell you that.'

His horse was brought and as he climbed into the saddle and spurred the horse on she ran alongside asking, 'What do you mean "she is under Harry's watch now" – hasn't she always been so?'

But he was already riding through the barricade and did not turn his head.

*       *       *

With nothing but more confusion to occupy her mind she returned to her reed hut and lay down on the straw. Unused to being so helpless she tried to see her predicament as a challenge to be overcome by patience. If it were true that things would move quickly for whatever reason as Locryn suggested then she would be ready.

There was nothing she need do to prepare herself.

Her knife was still tucked inside her sleeve in its soft leather sheath. She knew she would never use it except in self-defence and prayed that whatever happened next she would act wisely. Lack of patience was a failing. Wait and be ready, she warned herself. Lying on a mound of sweet-smelling straw, despite everything, she felt herself drifting off into an uneasy slumber.

Something made her snap open her eyes. Sunlight was streaming in through the door of her hut. Blocking it, in shadow, was a face close to her own. Watching her sleep was Harry.

When he saw her wake up he said, 'It's time to make a decision, Hildegard.'

'What decision?' She was still half asleep.

'You can stay here until we leave then make your own way back to the abbey, or you can come with us and see and hear the truth for yourself.'

She sat up.

Blinking she shook sleep away and repeated his words. There was no doubt what she would do. 'I want to hear the truth.'

'Are you sure? It's not a fear of finding your way back through the woods by yourself that makes you say that?'

She gave him a haughty glance. 'I'm not given to feelings of fear.'

'Good. Then come with us. Do you get seasick?'

'Never.'

'Even better.' He offered a hand to help her rise but she disdained it.

With an abrupt and dismissive shrug he turned and stalked from the hut, 'Hurry!'

Registering that it was the usual peremptory command she followed anyway, keen to put an end to fathoming what he meant. He soon made it clear. The men were getting ready to leave. One group had loaded the packhorses but a second one was waiting on the beach. While the packhorses left, under the whip of a fellow who looked no less than a hundred years old, one of the familiar campfire faces of a much younger man visible beneath his hood, the rest roamed restlessly at the water's edge. They were fully armed, she noticed.

Harry strode among them issuing a few final commands, answering questions, flexing his muscles with evident glee at what lay ahead. The mood of his men was bubbling over with barely suppressed excitement. A brisk offshore wind ruffled the surf right up the beach and the men milled about with the aimlessness of imminent action. When a small cog under full sail hove into view she understood why their mood was so febrile.

A flat-bottomed boat was beached on the shelving foreshore. The sail dropped. With a few shouts the men waded into the surf and began to scramble onboard. Harry was taking up the rear as usual. In a rout he would be the main target for the arrows of the enemy. Now he made sure everybody was safely aboard, leaving no sign of the camp entrance. Waves rippled over the scuffle of the men's footprints, obliterating them.

'Hurry,' he commanded when Hildegard stood on the shore with waves lapping at her boots. 'Why are you lagging? Are you changing your mind?'

Gritting her teeth she lifted the hem of her habit and waded into the icy waves. Harry was almost waist-deep in the water when he turned to her and taking her by surprise hefted her bodily on board. She fell to her knees and crawled from the side so he could scramble up after her.

The cog lurched as a stronger wave scudded beneath it. The deck tilted and the withdrawing wave dragged the ship further out. Soon it was lurching under a drenching spray as the wind grabbed the sails and carried the ship under billowing canvas into deep water.

'Why such haste?' she gasped as Harry dropped down beside her on the canted deck.

'The tide. It'll take us where we can meet your great friend.'

'My what?'

'Your ally Sir William.'

'I thought we were—'

'You thought I was going to take you to see this captive in one of my hideouts? Now do you see why I don't tell you anything?' He flashed a smile. 'Your Sir William will admit the truth or die.'

'As far as I know he's in Hampton. This is the opposite direction.'

'We're going to intercept a ship,' he replied with an enigmatic chuckle. 'That's all you know and all you need to know!'

The strong tidal flow took them westwards, as a look at the sun indicated. They were headed back towards the Beaulieu river. The cliffs here were low and crumbly and fell into the foaming tide that had made a hundred inroads into the land itself. She saw how well chosen the camp had been, based within the shelter of that one small rock outcrop. It was invisible from the sea.

Tide and wind combined to carry them along so swiftly that soon they were approaching a long, flat treeless island, little more than a bank of sand and shingle built up over generations of tides and storms.

It was home to colonies of seabirds. Their raucous cries reached them even before they were properly within sight. It was a warning of the proximity of land but the ship sailed straight on.

Hildegard waited in alarm for the crunch of hard sand beneath the keel, the inevitable bang as the ship's seams burst asunder and the planking broke apart but before they were wrecked they were slipping calmly into flat water in the lee of the sandbank and emerging into what she now recognized as the estuary. Ahead was the Haven where everything had started.

They were not being taken to seek Elowen in some new prison.

This was a different mission.

The shipman steered the cog into the anchorage behind the sandbar, ordered the sail and the anchor to be dropped, lashed the tiller in place then sat back, his feet resting on the gunwale. He closed his eyes and tilted a hat over his face. Job done.

Now what? she asked herself. No point in wasting breath

begging an answer from Harry. The crew, the gang, his men, however they now saw themselves, were silent. Watchful. Coiled like a single spring. Tense with expectation.

Harry leaned over and murmured, 'If things get rough, Hildegard, go down behind the housing where we put the stores. It's empty now. There may be arrows and one or two men may even get aboard. I don't want you hurt,' he added, as if it was something he hadn't thought to say before.

The tension rose.

Suddenly, without warning, a large tan-sailed merchant cog ghosted from behind the island sandbank. It loomed above them, massive and threatening and driving relentlessly towards them.

To be fair it had entered the estuary as if in expectation of finding an empty berth until the tide changed to take it further into the river and when the tillerman saw the smaller ship full of armed men lining the side he tried to avoid ramming them broadside. Such was the merchant cog's sail power it bore down on them despite his efforts.

The smaller ship, leaping like a panther from within the arm of the spit, drove hard forward under the power of the men on the sweeps and with some skill flew alongside, skimming the gunwales with only inches between the two vessels while Harry's men took their chance to swarm over the side as the grappling hooks bit and locked.

Harry remained where he was but was soon engaged in some hand-to-hand fighting with a couple of men who had impetuously leaped on board from the other ship. Their own men – Hildegard couldn't help thinking of them like this in the thick of the fight that followed – were searching the other one from stem to stern.

One of them struggled up from below deck shouting, 'He's not here! Where is the devil?'

A few desultory swipes at the enemy continued but slowly everything came to a halt. 'Who are you after?' the shipman shouted across. 'We're a merchant cog, loaded with wool clip.'

'We want that bastard William of Holderness,' Harry shouted back.

'Oh him!' The shipman roared with laughter. 'You're too late! We had to put him ashore. Stank the decks with his vomiting!'

'Who are you?'

'We were taken on in Hampton. Nothing to do with him apart from our pay.' The shipman paused. 'And now I think we've earned it. What do you say, lads?'

Those on board offered a general chorus of 'ayes' and 'more than earned it'.

Harry's crew looked undecided until one of them came up belatedly from below. 'Definitely no sign of him, Harry. Just bales and that.'

They began to jump back onto their own ship. The two ship masters, bound by the fealty of the sea, reached across and slapped hands.

'Where are you heading?' Harry called.

'The other side. He wants us to deliver his clip to Bruges Haven. What's your argument with him?'

'He's kidnapped a young lass, holding her to ransom. We were going to kidnap him and give him a taste of his own medicine – though for sure nobody's likely to ransom him.'

The ship master and both crews roared.

'Forgive us for not being able to help you,' the ship master called back.

The grappling hooks, thrown across in the first moments before boarding, were now unhooked.

'Why are you seeking shelter here?' Harry asked as if on an afterthought.

'He wanted dropping off near Lepe so he could hire a couple of horses. We thought those clouds looked likely.' He gestured to the south-west. 'As we were close by we decided to give them a miss. It's going to be a corker this night.'

'You'll be fair tucked in here until it passes,' Harry told him.

He lifted one hand in farewell as the two ships slid apart.

They anchored in the Haven but could go no further because of the draught of even their own small ship. On deck, anchored at ease, Harry gathered his men, and Hildegard, not invited to take part, overheard only snatches of a discussion about William and what they expected him to do next. It was likely that after

hiring the horses he sought he would make his way back to his
guest lodging at the abbey.

'Where is this heiress then, master? Where's he keeping
her?'

William? Could it be true, or was it connected to some malign
plan of Harry's own devising?

The question of her whereabouts was repeated in different
ways by many of the men and one that astonished her. Then
she had another surprise.

Mentioned by one or two was the name Mistress Goda. What?
She listened more intently but they returned to the difficulty of
guessing Sir William's whereabouts and where he was keeping
the girl.

'Harry will find them, don't doubt it!' somebody pointed out.
'He even bested the hangman!'

The group broke up. The mariners were happy to settle on
board and get out their cards especially if, as the master of the
wool ship believed, a storm was in the offing. The landsmen
were more doubtful, mentioning the stillness of the air, but
Harry suggested they stay where they were until first light when
he intended to send a scout back to the abbey to find out what
was going on.

Hildegard was puzzled. Locryn had suggested Elowen was
in Harry's care now, so where was she and why was he
pretending she was William's prisoner?

While the crewmen hooked fish from the river and the
landsmen grilled them over a campfire on the bank, Harry came
to sit beside her.

'So now you know what our problem is. Does that prove I
have had nothing to do with her abduction?'

'But it makes no sense. What has William to do with it?
Where is he?'

'I gather he went into Hampton for two reasons. One was to
attend to the export of his wool clip. The other was to have a
ransom demand sent on to the girl's father at St Keverne.'

Speaking slowly she asked, 'You seem to be suggesting
that William ordered his own men to abduct her? His future
daughter-in-law? . . . I don't believe you!'

He gave her a quizzical glance. 'You had no idea?'

She bit her lip. 'Not really.'

'It astonished me when I heard it.'

'But how . . .?' she asked, still not convinced. 'Why – and who told you this?'

'An impeccable source. It also fits with his actions. My men consider it to be most devious.'

'But who suggested such a plan to him?'

He gave her a glance that showed he knew more than he was admitting.

'I don't understand,' she persisted.

'Think, if the Earl her father pays her ransom, as he surely will, Sir William can win the rest of her dowry when she's handed over to her "rescuer" and a hefty ransom on top of it.'

'And he already possesses the little casket of gold she was carrying with a good part of her dowry in it?'

Harry nodded his head in wonderment. 'That as well.'

'But if it's true,' she paused, 'it's nothing short of diabolical.' She recalled her own suspicions.

'If we are the felons destined for hell – not the shire knights, our masters – I ask, how deep in hell should they lie?'

Later they sat side by side on deck for some time, each with their own thoughts. With little need for secrecy Harry's men ashore built up the campfire and struck up a ballad or two. As predicted the wind began to get up and the first spots of rain fell. The men bedded down as best they could under tarpaulins against the impending storm. Hildegard, permitted a place on board in the fo'c'sle, hesitated before bidding Harry goodnight.

'If I may,' she began, 'I have a proposition.'

When he raised his eyebrows she gave a hurried smile. 'Not that.'

'Go on.'

'I heard you say someone would have to go back to the abbey to find out what William's next move is. I'd like to do that. I'm least likely to attract suspicion. He'll never suspect me of carrying messages for you.'

'You'll leave' – he put a hand on her arm – 'but will you return?'

\*      \*      \*

The wind howled all night, trees bent double, rain fell in torrents, but, after the rain stopped, dawn broke, milky and pale, as Hildegard prepared to leave.

Black Harry looked deeply into her eyes as if he might read the future there. His hands wrapped round hers were the only warmth in the cold dawn.

'Hildegard, you will return?'

'I will find out what I can from William himself. I'll pass on your message and give his reply to Locryn.'

'Very well. That means you will not return?' He frowned.

She said, 'I still don't know why you were seen riding from the mounds with someone in a blue cloak sitting astride your horse.'

'Is that all there is between us? I'll tell you, then. It was a ruse, a bid to play for time and a somewhat desperate ploy to force him to reveal her hiding place.'

'It makes no sense—'

'Leave it!'

He half turned but she put a hand on his arm to detain him. 'William must have wondered what was going on when he was informed – believing her to be his captive, as you're suggesting. And the cloak? How did you get hold of Elowen's cloak? Who was wearing it if it wasn't her?'

'I said leave it! There's no time for this now. The quicker you leave the quicker we can find out what he's up to!'

He walked off.

Hildegard frowned. She hated the way he answered only the questions he felt like answering. How could she trust a man like that? And what was in it for him anyway? This pack of lies? He wasn't involved out of the goodness of his heart, was he? Surely it couldn't matter to him whether they found her or not. There would be no reward. Was he an ally of someone at the abbey and now playing a double game? The monks' involvement would fit with the ransom note in its neat clerical hand and scent of incense. What about Brother Simon and Marland? Were they all in league and was it a conspiracy to extract the gold they needed to pay the pope?

To say she was dissatisfied with the answers he consented to give would be an understatement.

A glance towards the cog showed that it was already preparing to catch the tide.

She set off on the path to the abbey.

As she eventually hiked down into the sanctuarymen's little vill and passed in front of the line of shacks near the bridge Locryn came out to greet her.

'He has released you?'

'So it would seem.'

'Unharmed.'

Ignoring that she asked, 'Any news?'

'Only that Sir William rode back late last night. He's telling everybody he decided to leave his wool ship once she started safely on her voyage.'

'That's not the version we heard.'

'We? So Black Harry has recruited you as well?'

'No one recruits me. Certainly no one in the secular world will ever do so.'

'He knows how to bind people to him and make use of them. Be warned.'

'And there are those who call you a liar. I've been warned about that too! We have only our own common sense to guide us through the thicket of rumour and opinion. What I want to ask you, Locryn, is if you're willing to pass on a message to him?'

'I owe you payment.'

'For what?'

'For persuading your brother monk to comb through the evidence of my case. He thinks he sees a way to lift my punishment.'

'If anyone can, he can . . .' She hesitated. 'You owe me nothing for that. I hope you will not let him down if he begins to trust you?'

Locryn gave that scathing smile she had noticed before. He closed his eyes with a suffering kind of expression that could be interpreted many ways. 'Bring your message to me, domina, and if you cannot speak to me leave a sign under a stone on the quay, a sprig of broom and if necessary I will find you.'

He nodded and returned indoors.

*     *     *

As she crossed the bridge to the gatehouse the porter appeared. When he clapped eyes on her he threw both arms up in delight and astonishment.

'Arisen from the dead! Oh, my dear, such joy! We would be feasting this night if only it wasn't Lent! Dear lady . . .' He stood beaming at her with a gratitude she could not misinterpret. 'Are you unharmed, hungry, tired? Have you walked far? Look at your boots! The rain, oh, the rain last night! I pray you did not sleep in the open, my dear lady. Come in, come in!'

He sent one of his assistants running into the cloister to tell the brothers that their fellow Cistercian, the dear lady Hildegard, had returned unscathed.

'Unscathed, I hope and pray? Here,' he bobbed back inside the gatehouse and she heard the clink of a jug. When he returned he offered a beaker of warm wine filled to the brim. 'Sit awhile, or must you get back inside? They are all at prayer in the church. Except your two brothers . . . Run, boy, fetch them! What's that other slow coach doing? Where is he? Run now!'

Cheered by his warmth she sat down on the bench outside his door for a moment. 'I am well. Nothing alarming happened. Black Harry showed me the greatest courtesy. He simply wanted help with his Latin.'

He exclaimed with delight and clapped his hands.

Hildegard stood up. 'I'm told Sir William has returned?'

The porter's round face lost its joy for a moment. 'He has.'

'Then I must go to him. When Brothers Egbert and Gregory appear will you let them know where I am? I assume Sir William is not at prayer but in his lodging?'

'Aye, demanding this, that and the other for his personal comfort.'

'And the little heiress is still missing?'

'Aye. Even now we know not who is at the bottom of this terrible crime.'

'Mistress Goda must be in great distress?'

He frowned again. 'Poor woman. It is more than her life's worth to have her charge snatched from under her very nose. She's in a lather of anxiety. But what can we do? The St Keverne men and our lay-brothers have been out every day, searching – searching and never finding.'

'Soon perhaps we shall be able to put all that behind us.'

Leaving him to berate his assistants for their tardiness in finding the monks and bringing them out from prayer if that's where they were, she hurried over to the guest lodging. A servant on the door, seeing her, was pop-eyed and let her through at once. 'He's in the solar, domina.'

When she entered the hall the fire was out, the place somewhat neglected. William's muddy riding boots were lying randomly on the bare boards and his cloak in a similar state was thrown down where he had dropped it when he came in. She wondered what had happened to his followers and whether Brigge, his poor, bullied body servant, remained in the hospitium.

With no sign of William himself she climbed the wooden stairs to where she expected the solar to be located and began to walk along the gallery overlooking the hall. As she did so William's voice suddenly boomed from down below. He must have been in the guardroom when she entered. A door slammed. His loud voice was unmistakable but the voice of the man he was addressing was less distinct.

About to go down to greet him it was only when she heard her own name that she hesitated.

'That nun,' he was saying in his usual dogmatic manner, 'that Hildegard of Meaux, I pray she's done for! If I have anything to do with it she won't be the one taking this accursed wench to the north. We'll send her up under armed guard to the priory and make sure nobody else gets in on it with a different story.'

Grumbling he strode across the hall, kicking his discarded boots as he did so. 'Will someone attend me! Clear up this mess and bring that wine over here. Get the fire built up. I had a hard ride from some benighted port called Lepe. That horse was the best they could find, an old nag, ready for the knacker's yard.'

The servant muttered something inaudible and, peering over the gallery rail, Hildegard saw him pick up the boots and the cloak. Before he left he said something and William gave a sneering laugh.

'It was well worth it. A couple of nights in the stews of Hampton? It's set me up for a day or two more in this hellish place with all their praying. They're at it now! What do they get out of it? I tell you, there's nothing like the whores in a sea port. Take my advice, they're the only ones to go for.'

Looking down she saw him put his right hand over the bulge under his tunic and give it a shake. 'I was almost persuaded never to come back,' he continued. 'Only trouble is they're damned expensive and I'm nearly out of credit. Can't be having that, can we, fellow, what's your name. Where's my personal body servant? Brigge?' he bellowed.

'Sick, my lord. He's in the hospitium.'

'Sick? Sick from lack of work, lazy losel, we'll soon have him back where he belongs. Have you seen the fires he makes? Half the Forest in that hearth. Still it's not my wood he burns. I might stay here longer, you know that? Why should I pay when these sotwit monks are happy to do it for me? . . . Anyway,' he continued, 'we'll have to hunker down until that ship reaches St Keverne and the earl does the decent thing.'

He went to attend to something underneath the gallery and Hildegard lost sight of him. She prayed that he wouldn't climb the stairs otherwise she was lost.

A few moments later there was a sound on the lower treads. William's heavy footsteps began to creak upwards. Hastily pushing at a nearby door she found it locked. He was coming closer. What would he say if he found her spying, as he would see it, in his domain? With her heart in her mouth she prepared to face him.

A loud noise from below like the crashing of a door as someone entered the hall brought the steps on the stairs to a sudden halt.

William roared down, 'Who enters?' He must have glanced over the balustrade. 'Oh, it's you. What do you want?'

'An audience with you, my lord.' It was Egbert of all people. 'We heard the glad news of your return.'

'I expect it's all over the abbey by now.' Footsteps descended the stairs again. 'I finished my business in Hampton. My ship has set sail for Bruges with my wool clip. All's right with the world!'

'Except, surely for the matter concerning the lady Elowen?' It was Gregory. He went on in his dry, even tones, 'Her continued disappearance must be a cause of great distress to you, my lord?'

Of course, thought Hildegard, they could not know that William himself might have abducted her if what Black Harry had told her was true, outrageous though it was. William was making some sort of reply and Gregory was responding but Hildegard was more concerned to let them know she was trapped in the gallery. She peered cautiously over the rail.

Gregory was standing in the middle of the hall still exchanging words with William but Egbert must have glimpsed something out of the corner of his eye because he looked up then stared in amazement. Hildegard signalled that she was caught. To her relief he got the message.

'My lord,' he stepped briskly forward, 'I beg you come with us at once. Passing the stables on our way out of church we fell into conversation with the horse master. He was concerned about your destrier, a wonderful beast, what is his name? Something Greek or is it Roman, quite in keeping with the nobility of the animal.'

Gregory was staring at Egbert in astonishment and it was left to William to say, 'Cerberus? You mean that incompetent swine has harmed my Cerberus while fetching him back from Hythe?'

'I trust it isn't serious. He is most assiduous in his duties and will have done whatever needed to be done. But he craves the boon of your attendance to ensure everything is to your satisfaction. It may well be that the wonderful creature is merely pining for your presence, such is the sensitivity of so finely bred an animal.'

In fact the horse was known for its ill temper and the stable lads hung back whenever they had to go into its stall. William, however, gave a roar as if struck.

'If he has harmed Cerberus he shall pay!'

Grabbing his boots from out of his servant's hands and thrusting his feet into them he stamped from the hall with both monks taking their time about following in his wake. When Egbert looked up at the gallery Hildegard was speeding down towards them.

Gregory's astonishment changed to delight. 'So that's why you suddenly started talking gibberish, Egbert? I thought you were suddenly moonstruck!'

He reached out and pulled Hildegard into his arms. 'Are you all right?'

'Absolutely. I'll tell you everything later. I must speak to William. He doesn't know I was waiting for him. I hoped to find him in the solar but then he came back – I'll tell you later. But for Egbert's quick thinking I'd still be trapped up there!'

'We'll have to go on and square things with the stable master. We'll send William back then you can do what you have to do. We'll be close by, you can be sure of that.'

William returned to find Hildegard waiting in the porch. 'I thought you were a prisoner of Black Harry? How did you escape?' he greeted her, in marked difference to the porter.

'We came to an agreement,' she replied, truthfully.

'Oh, did you? I trust it was as pleasurable as my visit to Hampton.'

'I doubt that, my lord. But I have a personal message for you from Black Harry.'

'The devil? What does he want with me?' William's glance flickered from side to side like a man entering a trap.

'He begs you attend him in a place to suit yourself to discuss some deal or other he thinks might interest you.'

'Is there gold involved?'

'Much, so he claims.'

'Tell me more.'

'I cannot. I was not party to his private discussions with his lieutenants. He mentioned—' She pretended to think, even though she was very sure of what Black Harry had instructed her to say.

'Come on!' William urged. 'Use your brain, if you have one.'

Speaking slowly she said, 'I believe it's something to do with salt?' She gave him a quizzical glance. 'Could that be right?

I'm afraid, my lord, it makes no sense to me. I am only a messenger.'

'Salt? . . . The abbey has the monopoly on the production of salt down here. They even send some of it up to your abbot at Meaux. Thriving industry. You won't have noticed the salt pans. Tell him I am interested. Very interested indeed. And how are you going to inform this blackguard where to meet me? I take it he's not going to come knocking on the gatehouse door for an answer.'

'As an outlaw he has to use a go-between for safety. I am instructed to leave a message in a certain place.'

His eyes narrowed. 'Where?'

She bit her lip. 'He mentioned a particular stone that lifts easily on the quay. I may put your reply for "yes" under the stone in the form of a sprig of broom and at some time his messenger will find it and take your reply to him, wherever he is hiding—' She waved her arms in a vague fashion and continued to look baffled.

'The sotwit,' William murmured. 'Does he not have the nous to imagine I won't post a spy to watch who takes the message? Does he not imagine that he won't follow them to his very lair?' He chuckled. 'This is an unexpected amusement. I shall enjoy this.' He became brusque and, dismissing her, said, 'Add a note. Can he read? Tell him to meet me at the burned farm. There we'll parlay and he can explain to me about the profit in salt.'

'There is one thing more,' Hildegard said when she reached the door. 'It is such good news. I know you'll be delighted. He said he knows where the lady Elowen is being held prisoner and who her abductors are.'

William made a swift step like a man stumbling on an unexpected stair. He regained his balance and waved her away. After her retreating back he repeated. 'Tell him, at the burned farm – then we'll see who the man is round here.'

# TWENTY-SEVEN

Shortly after she left, while she happened to be standing in the shadow of Locryn's hovel as they brought each other up-to-date, she saw one of William's men riding out of the abbey.

He crossed the bridge at a leisurely canter, taking care not to draw too much attention to himself. As he drew level with Locryn the broiderer stepped boldly out in front of the horse flapping his arms to make it swerve and the rider, taken by surprise, clung on half out of the saddle.

The horse was dragged to a halt by Locryn catching hold of the loose reins. He adopted an evil smile as he pulled the rider to the ground.

The man was shocked to be dragged off for what seemed no good reason and began to protest.

'It's like this,' whispered Locryn in his ear as he forced him to his knees, 'I'm an inquisitive sort of fellow and I want to know where you're going. Maybe you can give me a lift?'

'I'm only going to the—'

Locryn gripped him round the throat when he clamped his lips shut. 'You know why I'm here in sanctuary? It's because I kill men. It's my delight. I'm especially delighted when they refuse to tell me where they're going when I ask them. I enjoy finding ways to force the truth out of them. What is it worth? A quiet word to me or some special pleasure before I take your life?'

'I'm off to the bergerie. Follow me. I don't care. It's nothing to me. Now give me my horse.'

'Only if you'll come with me.'

'And be murdered in the woods?'

'Either there or here. Neither if you're speaking the truth. What the hell's he sending you to the bergerie for?'

'It's his business.'

'Suits me,' replied Locryn. He drew a large blade from his belt.

'You wouldn't dare, not here—' He glanced about but apart from a nun who would be no help he could see no one except a huge fellow with fists like hams standing in a nearby doorway with a look of evil expectation on his ugly face.

Seeing him waver Locryn remarked, 'I've nothing to lose. That's why I'm here in sanctuary.' He slapped the flat of the blade against his palm a few times.

'I'll tell you,' stuttered the messenger, backing away. 'He's got somebody there. That's all I know.'

'Is it who we think it is?'

'Likely. He wants me to tell them to move her on. Somebody's discovered where she is again. Now can I go?'

'Where are they going to move her?'

'I don't know. Somebody else decides, not me. Let me get on.'

'I told you. I'm coming with you. Better still, I'll go on ahead. You can walk, can't you?' Locryn threw himself into the saddle before the messenger could move. 'Don't let Sir William catch sight of you on foot. Wasting shoe leather plus the price of good horseflesh. I'd get on quick sharp if I were you.'

With that he spurred the horse forward and galloped off.

William's man shrugged. 'I thought it would be a quiet rest, as guests at a royal abbey. Still, there it is.' He nodded to Hildegard and began to trudge on after his stolen horse and was soon lost among the trees.

Gregory and Egbert had followed Hildegard as she left Sir William's guest lodge and now they strolled up looking interested. 'What was all that about?', they greeted her.

She told them. Then she explained about Black Harry and what had happened the previous day.

'It's a story devious enough to suit the Devil himself,' observed Egbert.

Gregory was frowning. 'So has he got the heiress or not?'

'If we get along to the bergerie we might find out if it's Harry in charge or William.' Hildegard turned towards the bridge. 'Our horses?'

'We've already warned the stable master.'

They walked back, mounted the horses and followed in the same direction as Locryn.

When they approached Beaufre where the hounds had hit on a trail that led them over the river to Marland's far grange on the other bank they slowed and Egbert rode into the yard and called out.

The master emerged. 'What's to do? Not another alarm! That sanctuary fellow Locryn has just ridden past whipping along like the Devil's after him. Is something up?'

'May be. Do you have men to back us up?'

'Most are down at the abbey for the Lent prayers. I'll see who I can find. We'll catch you up. Where are you headed?'

'Bergerie.'

Egbert re-joined the other two. 'Let's go. We don't want to catch up with Locryn and warn him we're on his trail. Let's give him time to make himself known and see who comes out to parlay with him.'

'What will Chad be doing in all this?' Hildegard looked worried. With uncertainty hanging over them they hastened on.

At the junction in the road where it led down to Chad's bergerie Egbert decided to leave his horse and go on foot.

'You two come after me in a moment or two. I'll check the lie of the land and see what's what. I'll give a call—' He put two fingers in his mouth and made a call like an owl then grinned at Gregory. 'You know the drill. One for safety, two for action.'

He set off through the underwood in the direction of the sheep farm. He moved as stealthily as a cat.

They watched him melt into the trees.

Gregory sat his horse in silence while they waited but then in a scarcely audible voice said, 'We failed you during that skirmish with Black Harry's men when he abducted you. I will never forgive myself.'

'There's nothing to forgive. We could not foresee he would do that.'

'We should have foreseen it. I should have done so. I behaved like a reckless amateur.'

'Did you get a crack on the head?'

'It would have been a killer blow if Egbert hadn't thrown himself at the perpetrator in time.' He showed her his bandaged hand. 'I got this later.' He reached out to touch her sleeve. 'I owe Egbert my gratitude for many reasons, Hildi.' Tightening the reins of his horse, he spoke more briskly, 'We must not lose sight of him now. Let's move forward. I'll bring his horse.'

With the utmost caution they went on a short way until the buildings of the bergerie came into view through a small gap in the low-growing branches of a beech. A figure was up ahead looking like nothing more than a shift of light. It was Egbert. They had to guess his progress as he circled the buildings then watch to see where he would appear next.

Distantly they heard the hooting of an owl. Once it came. Then silence.

With one accord they dismounted and left their horses ready for a quick escape if necessary and began to follow on to the place where they had last seen him. All three met up silently with a view down to the farm.

'Is she really here? It seems unnaturally quiet,' Egbert whispered. 'Just that one fellow sitting outside the door. See him?'

They could hardly miss him. He had a sword lying across his knees. It looked nothing like a toy.

'Know who he is?'

Hildegard shook her head. 'What about you, Gregory?'

'No idea.'

'I thought you said he had a family of girls, this Chad, the shepherd? If I know anything about children they'll be running around outside. Where are they?'

Hildegard felt a cold hand squeeze her heart. 'Pray that they're safe. He has a wife, too, and her sister, and one or two others maybe who were here when we arrived before.'

'I'm going inside.' Gregory moved forward. Easily the taller of the two men he was eyeing the roof of a lean-to built against the main building. 'If I get onto that low roof I can get onto the main roof and climb in through one of the casements.'

Egbert followed his glance. 'I'll take care of the door-keeper.'

As Gregory skirted the building under cover of the trees he

found where there was an open space to traverse. He was across it in the blinking of an eye and hauled himself up onto the lean-to. From there he was able to jump across onto the roof ridge.

Without a sound he sank down into the thatch and, gripping onto the wooden spars that held it in place, waited for a reaction but again the silence continued. Working his way towards the overhang he was able to lean over and peer in through the window.

Evidently there was no one within and he began to edge his way to the next one.

This time he had more luck and when he lifted his head he raised one thumb. Hildegard watched in amazement as he slid over the edge of the thatch and managed to hook himself in where he vanished from sight.

There was no sound from inside. Hildegard's glance was fixed on the window opening. Nothing happened for some time.

She whispered, 'Do you think she's there?'

After a moment Egbert breathed, 'I'm going in.'

Unable to enter the building in the same way as his taller companion he ran across the open space between the trees and the building without a sound and pressing himself flat worked his way along the wall until he reached the main door.

The guard did not even look up until he felt an arm crucked round his neck and his sword disappear and by then it was too late. He gave a token struggle but Egbert said something and released him and he fled to the trees.

She saw Egbert press his shoulder to the door to make it swing open. In a trice he was inside. Again, the rest of the house remained silent.

Unable to bear the uncertainty but strongly aware that she must not jeopardize their plan, she sped lightly across to the building and followed in Egbert's steps to the entrance. She stood still long enough to be aware of an ominous silence within. Afraid to find out what on earth was happening, she peered through a crack in the door, saw no movement on the other side and, as Egbert had done, slipped over the threshold.

An untidy kitchen met her gaze, with chairs turned over, a milk jug spilled and other signs of disturbance but she was in time to witness Egbert stealthily climbing an open-tread staircase to the upper floor.

A movement sounded from above. She saw him increase his speed to take the stairs two at a time and she quickly ran after him. The thump of something falling over was followed by Gregory's unmistakable voice. He sounded reassuring. Eventually a voice answered. To her astonishment it was a man's deep growl, vaguely familiar.

Egbert was at the top by now where the upper floor divided into two, a door on each side. Voices came from the one at the front. She reached the top just as Egbert pushed his way inside. She followed.

Gregory was bending over the humped shape of a man sprawled on the floor. It was Chad, as Hildegard recognized at once, but he was bound and only now beginning to free himself from his bonds. That he had been gagged was obvious from the blotches on his face where a neckerchief had been tightly tied.

Of Lady Elowen there was no sign.

'Chad, what happened?' Hildegard went to unknot the twine that kept him tethered to the leg of a big double bed. Gregory was already freeing his wrists while Egbert, after a brief glance out of the window, worked at the ones clamping him round the body.

Whoever had tied him had wanted to make sure he did not escape in a hurry. With the three of them helping he was soon freed and rubbing the life back into his limbs.

'They've gone! Somebody disturbed them and they were off. Keeping her overnight in that empty barn out back. The audacity!'

'Who were they?'

'Never seen 'em before. Didn't say much. Burst in while we were eating.' Chad's big friendly face was creased with rage. 'My wife and daughters, my sister – have you seen them?'

'We've seen nobody.'

'I kept these brutes talking until they could get away. My girls know where to go, if only they made it in time—' He went to the window and looked out as Egbert had done as if he expected to see his little family running off through the trees.

He had no idea how long he'd been tied up because they had hit him on the back of the head and he had gone out like a light, he told them.

He felt he had been tied up for ages but it might only have been moments.

He plumped down on the bed with a dazed look and rubbed both hands over his face.

For some reason Egbert suddenly ran to the stairhead. They heard him thumping down to the kitchen and after a moment a shout came followed by a bang as something as solid as a body was thrown against the wall making it shake. Then came the sound of grappling and boots tramping up the stairs heralding Egbert's return with someone grasped firmly by the back of the neck.

'I thought I heard something,' he announced. 'It was this!' He threw his captive into the chamber where a man fell to his knees.

He lifted his head and gazed round. 'It's me! Lay off!'

Hildegard exclaimed when she saw Locryn. 'I wondered where you were. Did you see what happened?'

'I saw them leaving as I arrived but there was nothing I could do but follow and then they decided to double back.' He seemed half-incoherent with fright. 'You gave me a wallop there, brother, nearly knocked me brains out!'

'Double back? So where are they now?'

Still looking terrified, Locryn gave a helpless shrug and rose shakily to his feet.

'Who did they have with them?' Chad demanded in a voice much weaker than his usual one.

'It was a girl. They rode off in a hurry. Some others came creeping out and vanished into the woods. Two women, a lad and two children.'

'Did they get away safely?'

Locryn nodded. 'Yours, were they? Worry not. William's bully-boys were not interested in them. Your lot made off in a hurry towards the saltings as if they knew where they were going.'

'They do,' replied Chad with as much satisfaction as he could muster at present. 'They're going to hide out in the salt sheds.'

Gregory stepped forward throwing the last of the bonds to the floor. 'Tell me, Locryn, were they Sir William's men?'

He nodded as if everybody knew that. But he had told her she was in Harry's control now. Before she could pick him up on it Gregory asked, 'And when you say they doubled back?'

'They were in confusion. A signal or sign had reached them before I got here. It threw them into a panic. They were looking for somewhere safe to put the girl.'

'How did she seem?' asked Hildegard.

'Difficult to tell.'

'And no blue cloak,' she said half to herself.

'Rough fustian, nothing special.'

She had forgotten for a moment that Locryn was a broiderer and had an interest in fabrics.

'Hold your tongues for a moment!' Egbert, beside the window was peering down into the yard. 'Someone approaches. Let's give them a surprise.'

He went to the door and stood alongside it. The others moved out of the direct line of vision of anyone glancing in. They waited. Eventually the sound of men coming into the chamber below was heard, the scrape of metal-tipped riding boots, a chair scraping across the floor as it was righted, the rough, deep rumble of male voices.

Gregory mouthed, Five? Six? to Egbert and he nodded. Both men waited. Egbert still had the sword he'd taken from the guard.

Chad, ready for a fight as much as he could be in his present state, glanced at the two monks for his cue then banged on the floor and made a gagging sound. A pause in the noise below followed. Then a voice, 'Who's that?'

Chad looked puzzled. 'Who the hell does he think it is, the sotwit! They tied me up!' He groaned again, loudly and with determination.

Footsteps came to the bottom of the stairs. 'Chad? Is that you?'

Chad gaped at the monks and shook his head in puzzlement.

'Answer him,' whispered Gregory.

'How does he know my name?' he mouthed.

'Answer him,' Gregory repeated.

'Up here!' Chad yelled.

They all waited to see who would appear. As a youngish fellow in woodsman's gear shouldered his way into the chamber, Egbert stepped behind him and put a knife to his throat.

The man froze.

Looking straight at Chad he croaked, 'What the hell is this?'

Chad stepped forward gesturing to Egbert to release him. He put both arms round the fellow and hugged him. 'It's my dear son-in-law. Don't touch him. He means no harm. Who have you got down there, fella?' He nodded towards the chamber underneath.

'Some mates, that's all. Thought we'd ride out and see how things were doing. We're still on the hunt for that missing heiress but Master Guido told us to take some time off as we weren't getting anywhere. William's sick in his head, he says.'

He gave Egbert a wary glance and asked Chad, 'Who are your friends?'

Chad explained. Afterwards a greater air of affability pervaded the chamber. The other woodsmen were called up.

While they were discussing the situation Hildegard turned to Locryn. 'What makes you say these men who assaulted Chad had doubled back?'

'I was riding behind them at a distance, following like, and they stopped near a turn-off leading down to the river. They argued, the three of 'em, then decided to come back to the farmhouse. I heard one of 'em say, "to await further orders," and the other two finally agreed. I dropped back into the woods as quick as you can imagine and they passed by without seeing me, arguing again, but when I followed on I couldn't find them. They must have turned off somewhere on the way here. Maybe a short cut.' He glanced nervously outside. 'They might be outside now for all I know.'

'Was Elowen with them?'

'She was.'

'What was she doing?'

'Looking as meek and mild as a lass might, probably scared out of her wits. Her little pony was led on a rope,' he added, 'and her wrists were bound.'

She went over to Gregory and told him what Locryn had said and that if nobody had a better idea she was going to go outside, to see if she could draw the gang closer to the farm-house. They must be standing off out of caution now their guard had run off and would be more likely to approach, if they intended to return, when they saw only a harmless nun idling about.

'Are you sure you want to do that?' He looked concerned.

'Aware that you're close by,' she glanced at the two monks and at Chad and his son-in-law and his woodsmen mates, 'I couldn't be more safe.' She touched the knife in her sleeve for reassurance and prayed she wouldn't need to use it.

'It's good odds,' Locryn stated. 'Eight against three.'

Noting that he included himself, she smiled. Somehow she couldn't imagine him in a proper skirmish, although he seemed good at using his fists and had given William's messenger short shrift earlier but this next encounter would need more than threats.

Wondering for a moment how far along the path William's messenger had managed to walk and why the guards had moved Elowen so suddenly she went down to the yard and took up a visible position on the stone bench where the other guard had been sitting. She wondered if he had somehow met up with the fellows guarding Elowen and she waited with some impatience to see how it would turn out.

A scan of the woods showed no sign of anyone. Nothing much moved. She got up after a few moments, stretched, walked idly about, pretended to examine the little herb garden Chad's wife must have planted, and all the while managed to keep an eye on anything suspicious amongst the trees. She tried to make it look as if she was waiting for Chad's wife to return with no sign that she knew why she was absent.

If the gang were returning with Elowen they were being as circumspect as they had themselves been when they arrived.

When they did not show up – having been given ample time to ride up from where Locryn said he had seen them – she began to doubt that they were returning to the bergerie after all.

She remembered how Locryn was held to be an out-and-out-liar.

She remembered, too, how he was a go-between for Black Harry. It made her uneasy. There was much in this game she did not understand.

Then, while she was doing her best to play the decoy, she noticed a movement in the thicket. It was nothing much, no more than a silvering-over of the leaves by the light, a branch moving and abruptly stilled.

Shortly afterwards a bird sang but it sounded false. A similar one replied. Neither of them were ones she could name.

Another moment of suspense stretched her nerves to breaking point.

It was a relief when the attack burst upon them.

If Locryn had suggested three men he was wrong. At least fifteen burst from the cover of the trees and, swords and knives in evidence, began to run from all sides towards the farmhouse.

Instinctively Hildegard threw herself across the doorway to prevent them getting inside but some ruffian grabbed her and pushed her out of the way. She clung on, reaching for his eyes. With a roar of pain he battered her against the wall and as she slid down she kicked out with all her force at his knee joint and, cursing, he tumbled into the dirt.

Crawling towards her he tried to locate his sword where it had fallen but she grasped the hand that reached out for it and bit hard on his wrist with all her might. Blood sprang from her teeth marks and he roared again and dropped the sword.

Lifting his hand to swipe her across the head he was suddenly jerked off his feet and landed in a heap in the dirt.

She looked up at his assailant. It was Gregory. He had jumped the short distance from the upper window and grabbed Hildegard's attacker by the scruff of the neck to throw him to one side. Now he pulled Hildegard to her feet.

'I'm all right,' she gasped. 'Look out!'

The point of a sword came lunging towards him and he sidestepped with practised skill and, allowing the fellow to be propelled forward by his own momentum, he stuck out a foot to trip him then reached down to pluck his sword from his grasp.

'Give it to me!' Hildegard shouted.

He threw it to her and by that time the others were crowding outside to deal with their attackers.

Chad, massive and full of rage at having his wife and children frightened and his peaceful sheep farm attacked by strangers, waded like a bull into the melee, laying about him with a sword in one hand and a cudgel in the other. His son-in-law was by his side and the two were a fighting machine, laying waste to their enemies on both sides. The rest of the woodsmen swarmed out to defend the farm and close-quarter fighting became savage.

Egbert was dealing with a couple of swordsmen at once, sending one fleeing into the woods and the other throwing down his sword and pleading for mercy.

Hildegard made good use of the skills the monks had taught her and disposed of a man who at first jeered at being attacked by a nun but soon saw his way to a better opinion and, losing his sword and putting up both hands in surrender, backed away before sprinting off after his companions.

Out of the corner of her eyes she saw one of the enemy run up behind Gregory with the intention of ramming his sword into the monk's back but before she could deflect him, Locryn shot from nowhere in a flying leap, tackling the man to the ground. He drove his fist into the fellow's face until he lay still.

The rest of the gang began to scramble for safety into the woods. A few moments later the sound of horses and men crashing away through the undergrowth reached them.

'Quite a collection,' observed Gregory as, breath heaving, he threw the last captured sword onto the pile. 'We might set up as armourers when we return to Beaulieu.'

'I know one thing – they were not William's mercenaries,' Egbert announced. 'I've never seen them before in my life.'

'Are you sure?' Hildegard stared at him.

'I know who they were.' It was Locryn. He wiped blood off his mouth. 'They were followers of Black Harry.'

# TWENTY-EIGHT

G regory jerked his head in surprise. 'Harry? I've a score to settle with him!'

'So have I,' added Hildegard. 'He lied to me.'

Their horses had to be rounded up first. Roaming about the woods they had not, however, strayed far from the grange and together with Chad's own horses everyone was soon ready to set off in pursuit.

It was an easy task to catch up with one of the laggards and, when he saw he was surrounded, he fell to his knees, pleading, 'Go on then. I'm ready! Make it quick!'

Fully expecting to have his throat slit, he gave them a dangerous and undefeated glare when nobody attempted to dismount. 'What's stopping you?' he ground out. 'Get the job done!'

Gregory only then slid out of the saddle and strolled over. The man stared in defiance, unbowed by the prospect of his imminent fate. The monk stood over him. 'Are you one of Harry's men?'

'What if I am?'

'If you are,' went on Gregory in an affable sort of voice, 'then rather than slit your throat we'd like to talk to you.'

'Don't play with me,' growled the man. 'Get your fun some other way. Now do it!'

'I'm not out for fun right now,' Gregory replied, 'I'm simply interested in clearing up one or two mysteries, like, for instance, where is your erstwhile leader? Will you take us to him so we can parlay? We have a few questions only he can answer.'

'It's a trick. I'm not falling for that one.'

'No trick. How can it be a trick?'

'You'll be after the sheriff's bounty. I know your sort. I'm not going to betray Harry no matter what you do to me. Try me!' His face was gleaming with perspiration but otherwise he kept his fear under control by sheer force of will.

Gregory spoke again in a conciliatory tone. 'Listen, friend. I'm a monk. I don't slit men's throats. I like to talk. My brothers will tell you that. And at this moment I very much want to talk to Harry. I believe we may have something useful to say to each other. You can see we are few—' He spread his arms to include the others. 'We're hardly sufficient to cause harm to a leader like him.' He ignored the recent rout.

Hildegard stepped forward. 'Don't you remember me from the camp? I was with you for a day or two. You must have noticed me sitting next to Harry at his table working at his documents?'

'Was that you?' The man peered up into her face. 'One nun looks like another to me.'

'I took a message from Harry when I left the ship.'

After a moment a tentative grin began to split his face. 'It is you! Well, I'll be – what the hell are you doing here with William's crew?'

'They're not with William. Anything but. Harry sent me to make contact with William and—' she shrugged impatiently, 'you'll find out the rest later. But it's urgent. William's men must have Elowen. We must reach Harry.'

The man was still looking suspiciously at the others. 'If this is a ruse to get at him you'll be in hell before he is. But I'll trust you this once. Follow.'

He led them swiftly along a narrow deer track that wound deep into the wildwood where it had never been tamed by the foresters since William of Normandy's day. Briars and vines snagged at them as the single file of horses followed what had been their captive but felt now more like their captor. Deeper they went. Birdsong seemed to cease. The trees grew thick among brakes and briars.

Everyone looked uneasy. It could well be a trap the fellow was leading them into.

He came to a halt in the middle of a beech wood where a wide-open glade was densely bounded by ramparts of hawthorn. The intertwined branches surrounded the glade like a cage, the perfect place for an ambush. The monks had their hands on their swords, fingers twitching, not to be caught out twice, Chad and his son-in-law were pale, the foresters silent and alert. Hildegard's glance darted from one side of the clearing to the other.

The fellow gave a bird call like the one they had heard before.

She noticed Egbert give Gregory a glance.

After a pause the call was answered.

Into the ominous silence came the sound of arms, the clink of metal, but then, instead of the eruption of a band of armed men a voice, deep and unmistakably that of Black Harry, growled a welcome.

He called, 'Now I must ask you to throw down your weapons.' He was nowhere to be seen.

Casting a glance round the two monks replied almost in unison, 'Why should we do that?'

'Because I ask it,' came the voice, 'and because I do not allow arms within my camp.' He added, with a note of humour, 'I understand you yourselves do not allow arms within your camps – what you call your abbeys and your churches?'

'Good argument,' Gregory agreed.

He raised his eyebrows at Egbert who shrugged and muttered, 'He can't take our fists away.' They placed their swords neatly side by side against the trunk of a tree.

'Bring our visitors up, Baldwin.'

The voice came from somewhere above them. Lifting her head Hildegard peered into the treetops. And then she noticed the movement, a great rustling of branches, and Black Harry appeared above their heads, standing on a wooden platform like a pulpit.

'Now come up. I assume there's a reason for your visit?' He leaned over to get a good look at everyone. 'Greetings, domina. Did you meet Sir William?'

'I did.'

'Did you discuss salt?'

'I did. Word for word. He wishes to meet you at the burned farmhouse.'

He chuckled. 'Ascend if you have a head for heights, as I expect you have. Baldwin, good work, although not as good as I would have liked. I see you do not have the hostage. Come up with them.'

Black Harry's face with its great curling beard disappeared into the mesh of branches and a rope ladder slithered to the ground. One by one they climbed up into the tree canopy above the grove of ancient beeches. At the top they discovered a network of wooden walkways and ladders to different levels linking tree to tree, all invisible from the ground. Everyone was looking round in wonder and nobody could tear their glance away long enough to speak.

Harry seemed amused at their obvious amazement. He took his place on a kind of throne adapted by means of some expert wood craft at the centre of a network of branches where they could all be seated. Hildegard recalled their evening moots and guessed the habit continued even here. The place was so well-hidden it was no wonder the sheriff had been in such difficulties trying to recapture him, if he had ever seriously tried to do so.

'What else did William say to you, Hildegard?' Black Harry began, guiding her to a seat beside him with one hand on her back. Gregory looked askance.

'He was mightily interested in the idea of salt and the profit to be made from it.'

'I knew that would draw him. Then what?'

'He said he would parlay with you at the burned farmhouse. I don't doubt it's his plan to spring a trap in order to cash in on the bounty on your head. I told him I'd leave a sprig of broom under the stone for his go-between as you suggested to show you agree.'

He nodded with satisfaction. 'That will no doubt show up in someone's possession.'

Hildegard gave him a close look. 'And now may I ask why you claimed to have Elowen under your watch?'

'I knew William's mercenaries were holding the girl. But paid men can change their paymaster if they see an advantage.' His teeth flashed.

'But why attack the bergerie?'

'They were told to move her on but by the time my men turned up it seems you had already taken over.'

'Locryn stopped his messenger on the way to the bergerie and asked him where he was going.'

'Asked with due courtesy, I hope?'

She pursed her mouth. 'To some extent.'

Locryn kept his head down.

Hildegard continued in a puzzled tone, 'William's men left the bergerie before Locryn had time to get there – as if already warned to move her to a more secret place.'

Harry looked thoughtful but characteristically made no reply.

'May I ask more?' She had to ask twice to get his attention.

He glanced up. 'What?'

'You must have another link with the outside. May I ask who it is?' Expecting him to mention one of the Beaulieu monks, Brother Simon, perhaps, she waited for his answer but he was vague.

'I expected William to move her on if you told him what I bade you tell him. I knew it would almost certainly flush her out. That he moved with such speed, almost as soon as you gave him my message, is impressive.' He was frowning.

'Maybe he has second sight,' remarked Baldwin.

He dismissed this. 'There's only one way.' His eyes were cold. 'It seems we have a traitor in our midst.'

There was a chilling silence.

Glancing up to the heights of the great and ancient beech limbs above their heads he put two fingers in his mouth and gave a piercing whistle. A call came from somewhere above.

He bellowed, 'How's the water?'

A voice shouted back. 'Near all the way down, Harry.'

Black Harry smiled. 'That's how they did it. Whoever it was floated down on the ebb to warn the guards at the bergerie and if I'm not mistaken they'll be somewhere on the riverbank, waiting for a ride upriver again when the tide turns. It'll take them back to the abbey, or maybe elsewhere, who knows?'

Gregory leaned forward from his seat in a cruck of one of the branches. 'I'm Brother Gregory of Meaux. From what has been said I assume we are now in league with a brotherhood of outlaws?'

Harry chuckled. 'You read the situation right, Gregory. Does it bother you?'

'On the contrary. I find customs are not absolute. They pertain to the region in which they are practised. Both I and Brother

Egbert here are used to shifting standards. The way I read this
situation is that we have two shared aims, namely to find the
murderer of the young lay-brother, Godric, and to rescue this
little heiress, hopefully unharmed, and return her to the St
Keverne household?'

Black Harry pulled at his beard.

'If that is so,' Gregory continued, 'may I ask the basis of
your interest?'

Harry was succinct. 'Justice.'

He rose to his feet and roared, 'Men! Let's move!'

From out of the trees from all directions men began to swing
down from their perches – lookouts, cooks, ordinary men-at-
arms, every one – and a scramble to reach ground level followed.
Well-drilled, they scattered to their separate duties. Horses were
brought out from where they were hidden. Men retrieved their
swords from a secret cache. The first group began to file out
onto a barely discernible pathway.

Harry glanced at Baldwin. 'You stay here and when the others
make their way back from the bergerie and the beating these
lads gave them—' he eyed Gregory and company with respect,
'see to their wounds and get them fed. When you're ready,
come after us.'

'Their wounds are not great,' Gregory murmured apologetic-
ally. 'It was more that we took them by surprise and they did
not know who we were or why we were so ready to defend
ourselves.'

Black Harry's courser was brought out of a hidden compound
and the cavalcade moved off. No one asked where they were
going. Either they guessed what was about to happen or they
were drilled to follow him without question wherever he led.

When they reached the river a short time later, it was at a point
covered thickly with trees down to the water's edge. Right up to
the lip of the bank the mudflats were revealed in their glutinous
and treacherously yielding slime as the tide began to turn.

Black Harry included Hildegard, the two monks and Chad
and the foresters in his next suggestion. 'You folk will not
want to be present for a while. There's a private matter I have

to attend to. If you'll leave your horses here and walk some way upriver you'll come across some coracles on the bank. Wait beside them. We'll join you when we've found out where she is.'

It was an order. Despite his reasonable tone of voice there was no doubt that he would accept no argument.

His men were already beginning to spread out along the bank.

As soon as Harry stopped speaking, Chad hurried off, calling over his shoulder to Hildegard and the others, 'Come on, you heard! Do as he says! Hurry! It's for the best. Don't get involved. It's nothing to do with us!'

When Gregory heard Chad making off he called, 'What's the hurry?'

'We do as he says. Don't get involved,' Chad shouted back. He increased his pace, beating a path through the undergrowth as if the hounds of hell were after him.

Eventually they saw him reach some coracles pulled up on the bank. 'Here they are! This should be it! Wait here! Come on!'

He was out of breath, his face white, and it struck Hildegard that it was stark fear that was driving him to such haste.

'What's happening?' she asked in bewilderment.

'Nothing. It's Harry's business. Nothing to do with us. We're nothing to him. Nothing's happening. Don't look back!'

'What do you mean? I thought he was going to take us to where Elowen is held captive? Does he know where she is?'

'He will. Give him time. He'll do what he says. You can count on it. He'll find out where she is.'

'So what's wrong, Chad?'

Egbert stepped forward and gripped the big shepherd by the arm. 'What is it, fella? You can tell us.'

'You heard what he said. He's going to find the girl and hand her back to you. That's his plan. Justice, he told you.'

Egbert frowned. Slowly he put into words what Hildegard was beginning to fear. 'You're saying he'll find out where she is? But he wants no witnesses? Is that it?'

Chad backed off. 'I want nothing do with him. The sheriff can take him for all I care.'

'Come on, Chad.' It was his son-in-law. 'You might have got

him wrong. Not everything they say about him is true. And where is this double-dealing losel he's after, anyway? Was he there on the riverbank? Did you see anybody? I didn't.'

'He'll do what he has to do. It's his way. It's not mine and I'm not having anything to do with it.'

They argued for a moment or two longer but Chad was a bag of nerves and would not be pacified.

Suddenly a shriek like the sound of a hawk or some other bird of prey making a kill rent the air. It reverberated through the trees, rousing a flock of crows to caw and scatter.

From along the river path not much later Black Harry emerged with one of his lieutenants by his side. He looked no different to usual. 'She's at Otterwood. If you will kindly step into the coracles, the tide is sufficient to carry you to where you'll find a small wooden landing stage. Pull in there and wait for my men to come up . . . If you'll be so kind,' he added with mock-courtesy.

Hildegard gave him a sharp glance. He caught her eye and averted his head.

To the men he said, 'Can you scull upriver? Better take two of them. They'll hold four but not five.' Without another word he strode back with his man at his heels.

'Come on,' urged Chad. 'Let's just do it. Let's get away. We don't want violence. God help the poor soul.' Chad crossed himself several times. Tears stood in his eyes. 'Get in the boats, I beg you, and let's do as he says.'

Egbert went to one of the coracles. 'We'll get this thing over and done with. Time for judgement later on. It's clear he's discovered what he wanted to know.'

Gregory held Hildegard by the sleeve for a moment but did not speak until she turned to stare as Egbert pushed the coracle into the water. He said, 'Listen to him, Hildi. He's right. It's too late to do anything about it now. Let's pray we're wrong.'

With a leaden feeling she allowed herself to be ushered into a coracle. She could still hear that sound she had mistaken for a bird of prey. And so it was, though human. She shuddered and sat down in the frail craft. She felt numbed.

They allowed the current in midstream to carry them along and although the tide was shortly after the turn it was sufficient to drift them up with the help of paddles towards Otterwood and the final reckoning.

The rest of Harry's army crossed the river in a leisurely fashion. There was no need to hurry. Coracles, some dozen, dragged from out of the bushes, plied back and forth, taking men over to the side where they gathered to wait.

Harry was one of the last to cross and when he arrived he showed he was in no hurry by sitting down on a log and beginning a long yarn about nothing at all. It kept the men entertained until it was time to move on. Nobody had said when that would be and a few began to pass the time by throwing dice.

It eventually came onto rain but the trees, though leafless, grew in such profusion that they were not much bothered. 'It's that storm the mariners mentioned,' somebody warned. 'Last night was just a taster.'

The monastics put on their waterproof cloaks and stamped about.

Hildegard noticed Black Harry give instructions to one of his followers and the man disappeared into the woods in the direction of the grange. Was Harry waiting for Elowen to be conducted there by her captors? Had they decided to take the long way round by land and cross over by the abbey bridge? Why had they not crossed the river by boat as they themselves had done?

She watched and waited. 'I don't like not knowing what's being planned,' she murmured to the monks.

'We can only do as we are doing. He's obviously got some scheme in mind.'

A while later the man who had been sent off returned in similar haste. He gave a nod to Harry.

'All done?' she heard him murmur.

He rose to his feet. 'We go in good order up to Otterwood. I want half of you to surround the buildings just to be certain.' He set about organizing who was to go where and his captains quickly got the men on the move.

It was a steep climb through the woods but soon they reached the meadow where Hildegard remembered they had come across Marland chopping wood. That was another unsolved mystery, she thought now. He seemed to have been destroying a shelter but it might equally have been a coracle as Simon had told them. Who had crossed in it? That was a question Marland had neatly side-stepped.

Now, with no role in this next manoeuvre she followed in the wake of Harry and his men.

# TWENTY-NINE

As soon as they came within view of the outer buildings of the farmstead Harry gave an order, evidently understood at once, and his men deployed themselves round the perimeter. Making sure they were well out of sight, he pushed aside the flimsy palisade and followed by the others, walked up to the door. Banging on it with the hilt of his sword he had to rap twice until the racket brought somebody complaining to unlock it with a rattle of chains.

Marland poked his head out. 'Impatient fellow,' he greeted affably. 'I was in the middle of pouring milk for the cat. You expect me to starve the little fellow?'

'You old warlock,' replied Harry, equally affable as he stepped over the threshold. 'Shut the door. They should be here soon. We'll wait inside. Let him in but no more than a couple of his men. The rest are to be kept outside in the yard. Only let in those I tell you.'

'I hope nobody's going to break my chairs and this good table,' Marland muttered, tapping it with his knuckles.

'You can always make more.'

'Bones then? I can't make more of them.'

'We'll be careful.'

Marland went over to a bench near the window, picking up his cat as he went, and sat there, half-turned to watch outside. The others found places to sit, not knowing how long they were going to be there, while Harry himself paced back and forth, frowning a little but with nothing to show what had happened on the other side of the river to cause that harrowing scream.

Hildegard wondered at that. How could he look as he always did after that?

His black beard was worn like a mask concealing his expression, his feelings and intentions. Was there now the mutilated body of a man floating in the river? Worse, was he trapped on one of the mudflats in a rising tide? She shuddered.

If that shriek meant what it seemed to mean what were they themselves doing here as part of the nightmare? They were monastics. It was Lent. They should by all the laws of St Benedict be on their knees, praying for the salvation of a world gone bad. Now they seemed to be part of that world.

Gregory leaned over to attract her attention.

A sound had come from outside. It was distant. A faint scuffle of horses arriving unhurriedly along the upper track.

Marland shifted on his bench and turned his head. 'You cut it fine, Harry. He's here already.'

Harry looked puzzled. 'He must be better ordered than I've given him credit for.'

He moved to the door, sword dangling ready to be withdrawn from its scabbard, and when the knock came he called, 'Who's there?'

A voice on the other side said, 'We're men from St Keverne. Open up.'

Frowning Harry opened the door but prudently stepped behind it as the men entered. They glanced round, noticed Marland stroking his cat and the monastics sitting in a group and were about to greet them when Harry stepped from concealment.

'Who are you?'

'We've just told you.'

'What do you want?'

'Who wants to know?'

'Tell him,' Hildegard advised.

'We've already said who we are. Now we're searching all the buildings in the Forest in the hope of locating our lady Elowen as nobody else seems able to help us.' He added in an insulting tone, 'If you're from round here you might have heard a young heiress has gone missing?'

'Be seated, friends,' replied Harry, unperturbed by the man's sarcasm. 'We may shortly have the little lady you seek. It was careless of you to allow her to be abducted. Shame on your military prowess.'

'Aye,' agreed another St Keverne man, 'we rue paying heed to the order to allow the child off the ship first. We were all for going ahead to ensure her safety, as who worth their pay wouldn't be.'

Before they could air their grievances and apportion blame there was the sound of a large group of riders cutting their way through the undergrowth alongside the lane. They came to a loud and untidy halt. Voices were raised. An order given.

Harry smiled.

Before he reached the door it flew open and one of William's pages came in. He stood smartly aside to allow William himself, wearing hauberk, greaves, gauntlets and basinet, with a sword swinging by his side, to march into the chamber without invitation. When he saw his reception committee he stopped short. 'I thought it was just you and me, Harry?'

'I have no secrets from my friends,' Harry blandly replied. 'Was it about salt you wished to speak to me?'

William looked nonplussed for a moment, then as if imagining it was some formal game, nodded. 'As you say.'

'Call off your men,' Harry suggested with a glance through the open door. 'They make me nervous. You can understand why, no doubt?' He chuckled. Sounding friendly.

William told his page to tell the men to stand down. Then he found a seat for himself and spread his legs. 'So, salt?'

Black Harry pulled up a stool and sat facing him. 'It seems to me, William, we come from opposite ends of the earth. But we will meet, I'm sure of it. First there's something else to settle, if you will. It's been bothering me for some time. You see, this is my fief.' He waved an arm as if to claim the whole of the Great Close of Beaulieu. 'We have no reputation for kidnapping young women. It is not our game. You can guess what it is I'm going to clear up. It's this question of a young heiress. These St Keverne men, guests in our Forest, are naturally anxious about her safety.'

William sighed as if with tedium. He raised his eyebrows. 'This is my own business and nothing to do with anyone else.'

Before any of the St Keverne men could object Harry leaned

forward. 'My friend, I fear you do not understand me. Now, be a good fellow and tell us where she is?'

'We've brought her here, of course.' He looked puzzled. 'For some reason they fled the bergerie. I thought that's why you decided to change the location of our meeting?'

'Your contact was quick off the mark . . .'

William nodded. 'Yes. She came—' He was about to say more but bit off what it was with a darting glance at the others.

Harry noticed but pretended not to. 'You led us quite a dance, first here, then there. I applaud your knowledge of the terrain.'

'I've my falconer Bagsby to thank for that, the ghost rider! Ha!'

'He had the advantage of our friends from St Keverne, newly arrived from Cornwall. Or are they?' He glanced at the three men.

They looked mystified. 'We were warned by our mariners about what it was like here. That's why we brought a couple of hounds and our own falconer, expecting a little sport – but nothing like this.' Their spokesman scowled. 'If we knew the terrain we'd have found her by now but – expect help from anybody here? Don't make me laugh.'

'Ah!' exclaimed Harry but said no more.

Falconer. Bagsby. And the other one, Master Robin. Hildegard tensed with speculation and glanced covertly at Gregory and Egbert. The former was meditatively rubbing a forefinger over the slight bulge where the hilt of his sword was concealed. His eyes met hers.

Harry, meanwhile, displayed his dazzling white teeth in the black nest with evident good humour. 'We ourselves were led into what might have turned into an ambush that would have no doubt pleased the Sheriff of Hampton somewhat but for our superior local knowledge of the lie of the land.'

'I heard about that.' William, evidently unfazed, sprawled at his ease. 'That nun nearly caught you out at the grave mounds. They say she tracked you like a hound with those two monks she brought with her.'

'You mean the lady Hildegard and Brothers Gregory and Egbert?' Harry indicated them in the shadows.

William gave them a dismissive once-over as if he hadn't noticed them until now.

'You probably also heard that we got Locryn – that fellow over there,' Harry indicated him, 'to don a blue cloak. He bestrode my horse's saddle like a girl. The idea that we should pretend to have captured the little heiress came from someone you know.'

With no answer forthcoming Harry inserted his own word and to Hildegard said, 'Pray forgive me my rough language, domina. It is a name I do not apply to all women. I hate lies, as you well know.' He turned back to William. 'And you live on lies, my friend, as does your accomplice. She'll arrive shortly. And then we may discuss truth, and after that, the question of salt? Later I may show you the salt pans if you insist. As I'm sure you may.'

Hildegard shuddered at the implied threat and cast a glance at William but he did not understand what it meant and, lulled by Harry's affable manner, remained at ease.

The clatter of hooves in the yard announced a new arrival. 'Go and fetch her, somebody.'

Locryn stood up. 'I'll go.' With a determined tread he made for the yard and after a moment returned with a St Keverne servant.

Behind him came Mistress Goda. She wore a sprig of yellow broom in her bodice.

Hildegard watched as her flustered glance took in Black Harry, Sir William, and the rest of them.

'What is this?' she demanded in a strong voice. 'I was told I would find my beloved mistress here. Has she been found?' She glanced about everywhere as if expecting to find a full-grown girl miraculously appear before her eyes.

'Welcome,' Harry indicated a seat on the end of one of the benches and ignoring her flurry of questions waited until she was seated before announcing, 'I believe we now have the full set of participants in this little matter.'

'Where is she? What have you done with her?' Goda pointed an accusing finger at William. 'Have you harmed her, you blackguard? What have you done? Where is she? I demand to know!'

William laughed uneasily. 'I'm hardly likely to desecrate my own honey-pot, am I?'

Black Harry broke in. 'On behalf of these poor innocents hearing only half a story, I beseech you to tell us the truth. Mistress Goda, why have I invited you here?'

Her fingers played with the sprig of broom on her bodice. 'Because she is in my charge and has gone missing. And you say you know where she is as this sign testifies.'

'Be assured, I do know and she is unharmed. No thanks to you.'

'How was I to know he was such a black-hearted devil? He'd sell his own grandmother if there was profit in it!'

William half-rose from his seat. 'It was your idea, you imbecilic woman! Who was it sent me a message to suggest such a plan? Who warned me to have my men ready to take her off the ship the minute it arrived? Who told me this fellow, this outlaw, got wind of our plan and wanted to be in on it?'

'I said no such thing!' Her glance flew towards Black Harry. 'Believe me, Harry, I only—'

'Let him speak.'

'You implied it, woman! Don't deny it! Local help, you said!' William turned to Harry. 'She said you were interested in sharing the bounty we intended to extract from Earl Richard for hiding the wench where she wouldn't be found. I thought a three-way split was too fine and wasn't worth the effort for mere local knowledge, but she insisted, saying that we could do you down because you were a wanted man and would be willing to pay to keep your whereabouts quiet.'

'How did she know of his whereabouts?' Hildegard could not help asking. Everyone turned to stare and, undeterred, she asked, 'More to the point, how do you and Goda come to be allies?'

Black Harry got to his feet. 'This is how I understand it to have gone.' He made a mock-bow to Goda. 'My thanks for the detail you supplied, mistress. It was like this. It goes back to when the fishing fleet was last here. The talk was all about the betrothal of Elowen and William's son. Goda has a nephew, working on the boats, and that's how the idea must have been planted in her mind. It was relatively easy to set up, given the contact between St Keverne priory and Beaulieu. A meeting with Sir William was not necessary. When the fleet next sailed in, the shipman, unbeknown to himself, passed on what he thought was an innocent missive to arrange for Elowen's reception by Sir William. It included Mistress Goda's suggestion for a share of the spoils if he would kidnap her and hold her to ransom. Me, well, I might do anything to keep myself out of the hands of the justices.' His expression was masked behind his beard but his tone was heavy with sarcasm. 'Even to accepting a piffling share of the spoils because I know no better! But I have useful local knowledge and she begged me to keep an eye on her.'

'So where is the lady Elowen now? You all talk about her but where is she?' Hildegard demanded. 'Is she close by?'

Marland put down his cat. 'Worry not. She is comfortable. There are kittens to play with. She is quite at home.'

'Here?'

He looked confused then added, 'I confess, domina, I was concealing someone when you three from Meaux turned up so unexpectedly. I acted foolishly but the situation somehow touched my heart.'

'We suspected there was someone here after we saw you breaking up a coracle.'

'It was needed to cross the river but more than that, it was a shelter for nights in the woods. They would not enter the house.'

Harry broke in impatiently. 'This is by the by. The point is, Mistress Goda, you have betrayed your lord, you have deceived your partner in this enterprise, and you planned to defraud me to add to your trickery. That appearance at the grave mound seemed an unfeasible plan to me, unless this fellow,' he indicated William, 'is a total sotwit but I wanted to know what would happen if I went along with you.' He showed his teeth for a moment. 'You can be a very persuasive woman to a fellow living wild with only men for company.'

Goda looked furious.

'Can someone tell me where Elowen is now?' Hildegard raised her voice. She was still on her feet and she went over to Marland. 'Is she where I hope she is? You said she was here—?'

'So she is. Safe and snug in my attic.'

William rose to his feet. He was roaring with laughter. 'You're all mad! What a bunch of imbeciles! You deserve to be plucked bare and served on a platter! Have you not a brain amongst you? I don't know who this old fella has hidden in his attic but it's a sure fact it's not my son's betrothed! I have her! I've had her safe in my keeping all along! I'm going to wrest as much gold from this escapade as I can. No one can stop me! Just you try!'

He took two strides to the door and yelled for his men to come up.

From behind every tree and bush armed men began to emerge. They made straight for the farmstead with swords and cudgels at the ready. William stared at them. He stepped back in surprise.

Then another wave of armed men bundled in some disarray from the meadow, where they had been lounging about.

William saw them and gave a full-throated roar. 'I am besieged! To arms!'

Drawing his own sword he stepped outside.

The two monks followed with alacrity. Black Harry was not far behind. Chad and his brother-in-law drew shearing knives from their sheepskins and followed. Locryn picked up the fire irons in one hand and a knife appeared in the other and went out after them.

Of Marland nothing was to be seen. Both he and his cat had vanished.

Hildegard went to the door. For once this was men's business.

Before she could move, someone across the yard drew her attention. It was a girl with plaits looking somewhat dishevelled. She wore a brown fustian gown and came running out from behind William's horses to stand bewildered for a moment before making up her mind and running round the side of the house towards the orchard. Hildegard followed.

She was easy to catch. Hampered by long skirts she tripped just as Hildegard caught up with her.

'Let me get away!' she panted scrambling to her feet. 'It's my only chance!'

'It's all right. We're your friends. I'm Hildegard. We will not allow those men to hold you captive any longer!'

With a cry of relief and exhaustion the girl fell into Hildegard's arms and howled her eyes out.

Meanwhile the chaos of several rival gangs of men were locked in a brawl of extraordinary proportions. As the St Keverne men stood together, fielding blows from anyone who came near them, a group of conversi appeared, striding breathlessly up through the woods, took in the situation at once then brought their muscle-power to bear.

On the road at the top of the hill the sheriff appeared at the head of a small posse of horsemen, and roared down into the thick of it. Locryn, a silver streak, dealt many wounding blows before being felled by a brute who was handier with his fists than the erstwhile King of the Britons. Others were in contention with anyone who looked like an adversary.

Egbert and Gregory were already rounding up William's confused militia and urging them into a barn with the threat of decapitation backed up by the glitter of no-nonsense steel if they resisted and the woodsmen rammed down the wooden bars as soon as the mercenaries stumbled inside.

Meanwhile Black Harry was in hand-to-hand combat with Sir William. When those two remained their blows, sword on sword, became the only sound. Everyone gathered to watch.

Hildegard and the girl went unnoticed.

The sword fight ended suddenly when William was tricked by a feint under one arm that nearly hooked him off his feet. His sword fell from his grasp.

On his knees, he put up both hands in surrender. Both men were breathing heavily.

Black Harry held his sword at William's throat. 'Yield?'

'I yield.'

William's wrists were rapidly bound. Everyone else began brushing themselves down, mopping up blood, holding cracked heads, flexing sword arms and glancing round to see who of their comrades were still standing.

All this time Goda had been hovering near the house ready to hurry inside but now when she noticed Hildegard and the girl who accompanied her she ran forward with a great cry, both arms outstretched.

Everyone gathered for the long-hoped-for moment when the heiress would be reinstated to her rightful place. But consternation took over.

Goda was staring at the girl with tears streaming down her cheeks. 'All for nothing, lovey!' she cried. 'All for nothing! Oh, save me! We are ruined! Help us! Bless us both! Oh, Mary Mother of God! Have mercy on us! We have lost!'

With loud sobs she ran to the girl and slapped her hard across the face.

Without a word Hildegard ran into the house. Marland was still nowhere to be seen.

Racing two at a time up the stairs to the top, she was guided by the murmur of voices from a chamber under the eaves. When she flung herself inside the two poaching lads were playing with a bundle of striped kittens while Marland stood watching with a beaming smile on his face.

When he saw Hildegard he nodded. Startled, the two lads glanced up.

'It's all right,' she said. 'You can come down now. Black Harry has given Sir William a thrashing. We're your friends from Meaux, waiting to greet you.'

Marland beamed at a job well done for which no compliments were necessary. 'Meet Hildegard of Meaux, my dears. She is to escort you to the North – or, if you prefer, to escort you safely on board a ship back home to Cornwall.'

The two lads stood up. One of them was still holding a kitten.

It was the taller of the two who brought the kittens down to where the men were assembled while Marland mumbled something in Hildegard's ear. With the little creatures romping in their laps with their mother the two poaching lads sat close together in one chair and looked round with wide eyes.

The chamber was beginning to be crowded and Marland suggested they went outside into the yard.

Black Harry, the monks from Meaux, Chad of the bergerie, his brother-in-law and the woodsmen, the St Keverne men-at-arms and their captain, Locryn, sucking his bloodied knuckles, and Mistress Goda weeping, went outside to join a motley group of lay-brothers including Allard and Mark, arm in a sling, Sir William's servant Brigge, and men from the Beaufre, having just ridden over as their master said they would and at a loss to understand what had happened, there were also some monks from the abbey itself, hoping to fetch Marland back for the Lent service, Brother Simon, still tactfully holding his tongue, and the triumphant but slightly mystified men of Black Harry's gang, sanctuarymen all and definitely high on the sheriff's wanted list – all waiting for explanations. The sheriff himself was as eager as everyone else to hear what had happened.

Hildegard stood with her hands on the shoulders of both poaching lads. She glanced at Marland but he waved her forward and everyone fell silent.

'May I present Lady Elowen of St Keverne!' A gasp went round as one of the ragged poacher boys stepped forth. 'And her betrothed, Sir Tristan of Zennor.' The second lad beamed round, arms full of kittens.

The men of the St Keverne household gave three rousing cheers.

It was made more lusty by the cheers of everyone else when the truth sank in.

Goda was trying to fade into the background but Black Harry strode into the middle of the group, nodded to the sheriff as to an old friend, a greeting nonchalantly returned, and pointed to Goda.

'She,' Harry announced, 'tried to pass off a maid as the rightful heiress, kidnap her, then share the ransom between them.'

When the gasps of astonishment died down he smoothed his beard and said, 'Tell me, Goda, why did you think of such a diabolical plan in the first place?'

'I can tell you!' The heiress, confident and smiling, at least fifteen, and as pretty as you like despite her ragged poaching lad's garb, explained. 'My dear governess, mistress Goda, has been like a loving mother to me since my own mother died. She knew full well I would not be happy married to anyone but my dearly beloved sweetheart Tristan.'

The maid stepped forward. 'The plan was – my lady, if I may?'

Elowen waved a hand. 'Continue, Katie, my dear.'

'The plan was,' said the maid, cheek still red from Goda's slap, 'as a reward for my help I was to have a part share of the ransom and become a lady in the North where no one knew me. But Sir William will not want me for his son now. Even the dowry my lord promised me should I ever marry will be forfeit. All is lost and gone for nothing!' She forced a tear down her cheek.

William shrugged off his captors and, ignoring the bonds that restrained him, asked, 'Dowry?'

The maid gave him a steady look.

'Who says it's lost?' William went over to peer intently into her face. 'Would the Earl break his promise to you? . . . I say this in all honesty. I like the idea of a daughter-in-law with spirit. My men have been in awe of you from the start. Any one of the idle losels would marry you on the instant if I'd allow it. But my son has a prior claim!' His glance swept the faces of his astonished captors. 'This is the wife for my son!' He took her by the hand and held it high. 'Forget the ransom! You've got a dowry and I've still got the casket as my servant Brigge discovered!' He added hypocritically, 'Surely everybody agrees Katie should have a dowry after all she's been through?'

The maid dropped a curtsey. 'I'm sure my lord will agree.'

Black Harry turned to the sheriff, who read his mind and growled, 'I expect we can reach an accommodation.'

Harry smoothed his beard. 'I believe that's settled, then?'

The sheriff spread his arms and looked as if he wanted to make a speech but Hildegard stepped forward.

'There is harm done, however: the death of an innocent young lay-brother, Godric, murdered at the Great Barn.'

William scowled. 'That was one of my mercenaries stepping out of line.'

'Haul him forth!' ordered the sheriff with great authority.

'Can't.' William heaved a dramatic sigh. 'I would if I could – but he fell foul of the Black Death in Hampton.' He turned to the sheriff. 'But for your warning I might have succumbed myself if I'd followed him into that bawdy house you mentioned.'

Harry turned away with a nod to his men. Silently and one by one they took their leave, disappearing into the wildwood from whence they sprang.

Black Harry himself, one hand smoothing his beard again as if to establish a look of respectability to its wildness, crossed the yard to where Hildegard was standing and murmured something only she could hear. 'That's that then. Coming with us?'

'I can't.'

'I would beg you – if it was a begging matter. But it's free will or nothing. What do you say?'

'I cannot say. I'm not free like you.'

He gave her a long look. 'One kiss in parting?'

When she made no move he bent his head and the black silk of his beard engulfed her face as the sweet heat of his lips met hers in its secret thicket.

He stepped back. 'You know where to find me if you change your mind.' He bestowed on her one last smouldering glance before turning and plunging off into the woods.

Everyone watched in silence as the leader of the outlaws disappeared. The sheriff gave no order for his men to set off in pursuit. A collective sigh ran round the group at justice done.

While his men rounded up their horses, Sir William ushered the maid, Katie, towards the little jennet she had been riding throughout her captivity and helped her to mount. Hildegard found Gregory beside her. He was tight-lipped.

'And before he assaulted you without encountering any resistance what did he say to you?'

'Nothing much.' When he held her glance she added, 'He merely said goodbye.'

Marland was smiling broadly as he stepped forward to make an announcement. 'Now, my lord sheriff, friends from the North, our esteemed St Keverne brothers, everyone! I suggest it's back to Beaulieu Abbey to celebrate the Feast of Our Lady and give thanks to the angels for the forgiveness of sins and life everlasting!'

# AFTERWARDS

Hildegard and her monks militant eventually accompanied Katie, the lady Elowen's spirited maid, to the priory at Swyne where Hildegard recounted everything she knew to the Prioress, including the disarray in the allegiance of the monks at Beaulieu. It was no surprise that her holy mother, saddened by Godric's death but satisfied by God's judgement on his murderer, was made thoughtful, adding, 'The Schism is not yet ended.'

Later she summoned Hildegard back into her presence. 'Katie is causing quite a stir here. She's fifteen, she tells me, ready to be married, and that will be the best thing. I thought you'd like to know that Sir William's eldest son has broken his betrothal to a local heiress and fallen head over heels in love with her. I trust Lady Avice is ready for the storm about to break over her head!'

The real Lady Elowen returned to St Keverne with her household and her childhood sweetheart. Her father the earl forgave both, glanced with interest at the dagger young Tristan swore laid between them every night when they slept in the Forest, and was wealthy enough to write off the loss of the maid, her dowry and the casket with the words, 'Better have you safe and happy, my beloved daughter, than possess all the gold in heaven.'

Locryn, as Will Smailes, with Gregory's help was pronounced innocent of murder at a retrial and was readmitted to the Guild of Broiderers where he eventually became Master. His temptress was taken by her old husband to live on a remote manor where she dreamed of her many lovers as she embroidered the name Locryn onto her sleeve.

Brigge became a novice, apprenticed to the peaceful old master herberer in the curtilage, and found the godly existence he desired. Mark's arm healed and he eventually became grange master at St Leonard's and Allard got his wish to be master of the horse at the abbey, but not for a very long time which suited him well.

A year after the pope's threat the monks of Beaulieu were indeed excommunicated. King Richard appointed his step-brother to sort things out and a well-respected monk was elected as abbot. The Papal Schism played out its long game with Rome and Avignon sending discord throughout Europe. The Clementists soon ousted the new abbot at Beaulieu by acts of outrageous theft and violence in order to put in their own man, who survived many years beyond the regicide of the King himself.

Despite these ructions the lay-brothers continued to run the granges as usual for the benefit of the monks until eventually a Tudor king decided otherwise.

Sir William, black of heart as ever, suffered terrible physical agony as the plague, picked up in the stews of Hampton, rampaged through his body. The buboes, in what we might call his groin, swelled to an enormous size and became as hard as turnips. They would not burst until a healer from Beverley was called in. An agonizing cure involving acid and excoriation was used and to everyone's amazement the buboes burst one night and the fever abated.

It was a moot point whether Sir William was ever able to visit the stews again and his vow, uttered in the throes of his delirium, to give half his annual income to the poor came back to haunt him when his expected profit on the export from Hampton of his illegally untaxed wool clip disappeared.

As for Black Harry, although stories about his presence in the Royal Forest were heard for many years afterwards, he was never seen again.

# ACKNOWLEDGEMENTS

A huge and special thank you to the people I had the good fortune to meet at Beaulieu Abbey and in the New Forest who so enthusiastically answered all my questions about medieval matters in this fascinating and very special part of Hampshire before lockdown put an end to my research. They had so much to share about a place they clearly love that I have been set on a course to discover more about both King William's royal hunting ground and the abbey founded by King John in extirpation of his many sins.

Special thanks go to Dr Kath Walker, archivist at Christopher Tower Lyndhurst, and to Sylvia Crocker for tirelessly searching out so many vital sources for me. I'd also like to thank Susan Tomkins at the archive at Beaulieu Abbey and Lord and Lady Strathcarron for Otterwood, Mite the cat, and their knowledge of those tricky tides in the Beaulieu River.

Thanks also, of course, without stint to my editor Rachel Slatter, Natasha Bell, the design team and everyone at Severn House, soldiering on in such difficult times during this seemingly endless lockdown. As Hildegard might say: may all be well and all things be well.